—MAIDEN—
VOYAGER

MAIDEN VOYAGER

R. EDWARD MAIN

Five Star • Waterville, Maine

First Edition
First Printing: November 2005

Published in 2005 in conjunction with
Tekno Books and Ed Gorman.

Set in 11 pt. Plantin.

Printed in the United States on permanent paper.

Library of Congress Cataloging-in-Publication Data

Main, R. Edward (Ray Edward), 1937–
    Maiden voyager : a novel / by R. Edward Main.—1st ed.
      p. cm.
    "Published in 2005 in conjunction with Tekno Books and Ed Gorman."
    ISBN 1-59414-420-6 (hc : alk. paper)
    1. Teenage girls—Fiction. 2. Missing persons—Fiction. 3. Fathers and daughters—Fiction. 4. Space travel—Fiction. I. Title.
PS3613.A34938M35 2005
  813′.6—dc22
                                      2005019411

This novel is dedicated to my wife, Jackie, who not only shares my protagonist's name, but her readiness to jump into the sorts of situations where it is said that angels fear to tread. Her enthusiastic demands for more *Maiden Voyager* chapters provided me with a strong incentive to keep them coming.

—CHAPTER—
1

Jackie raced down the now empty hallway that led to the visitor's room of Mrs. Denning's Music and Drama Conservatory, the thudding of her feet softened by the antique twentieth-century hall runners. Portraits of distinguished past members stared down from heavy gilt frames, disapprovingly. A robomouse cleaner scuttled out of her way as she pounded past, almost tripping over the silly thing. The electronic hall monitor whined its stock reminder: "Running through the halls is not proper decorum for a Denning's girl." Its camera eye followed her, recording her image for later disciplinary action.

Normally, the seventeen-year-old would have considered it beneath her dignity to be caught running through these venerable halls of learning. Not today. Today, a lot more was at stake than dignity.

Breathing rapidly, she drew up at the heavy oak door that had guarded the privacy of the visitor's room for the better part of the past two centuries. She reached for the brass knob, worn into dullness by the many hands that had turned it over the years. Her own hand trembled so that she drew it back.

You must calm yourself Jackie, the disembodied voice of her computer advisor cautioned. *It's self-defeating to let your emotions run away with you.*

"Please, CAP," she said aloud, "this isn't the time to be

bugging me with platitudes." She didn't have to speak to communicate with CAP, but it took more concentration to mind-talk without speaking. And at the moment her mind was thoroughly occupied.

You told your teacher I would be acting as your advisor in this matter.

"And I want you to. But not now. Not till I find out what's happened to my father." Still, she hesitated, fearful of the message that waited for her inside. At least she knew her father was alive. She could always pick up feelings from him, even from another part of the galaxy. Like the time he slipped on an oil spill and fractured his wrist. A sharp, sudden sensation of pain had flashed through her mind. She spent a week worrying before he showed up at the Conservatory, a big smile on his face and his arm in a sling. Normally though, all she sensed from him was a warm, comforting feeling. He had laughed when she told him. Said it was all in her head. But she knew what she felt.

Yesterday, she had sensed something more disturbing than pain. A sudden panic followed by an aura of despair. And the impressions were fuzzier and less distinct than normal. CAP had tried to reassure her, claiming that PanGalactic would have informed her if anything serious had happened.

And now, someone from PanGalactic was on the other side of this door—here to see her. She felt like she was about to burst into a thousand pieces.

But as fearful as she was of discovering what had happened to her father, not knowing was worse. Taking a deep breath, she clasped the knob, turned it, and pushed open the door. A large man in one of the latest styled loose-draped business suits rose from a wingback chair that looked too fragile to support his bulk (one of Mrs. Denning's "moldy monstrosities" as her roommate, Cherral, called the antique reproductions). The man eyed her uncertainly.

"Miss Jackie Claver? I'm Bradly Goodman, Vice President of Personnel." He glanced behind her, frowning. "You should have a counselor with you."

She shook her head. "I'm equipped with a fully functional computerized internal advisory program."

"A computer advisor?" He raised a disapproving eyebrow. "I'd rather a human counselor be present."

"Please, just tell me why you're here."

His craggy face took on the expression of an ailing basset hound. "It's about your father. I'm afraid I bring bad news."

A sudden urge to giggle and cry at the same time made her realize how close she was to losing it. Legs suddenly weak, she collapsed into another of the antique chairs. Her throat constricted and a rushing sound filled her head. "Tell me," she managed to say.

"Your father's ship, the *Golden Arrow*, was lost in a Void crossing between Maddoc and Draco-3."

"How?" she heard herself ask.

"A Void crossing is always a chancy affair. Jack Claver was one of the best, but somehow he must have lost focus."

She stiffened in her chair. "My father would never have botched a crossing. Something must have happened to his ship." She stared up at him, searching for anything in his expression that might give her hope. "Has PanGalactic sent out search parties?"

He grimaced and shook his head. "No ship lost in the Void has ever been rescued. No one even tries anymore. It's pointless. Physicists have concluded that matter under the influence of the Void for more than a few minutes ceases to exist. When a ship fails to complete a Void crossing, its occupants are declared legally dead."

Her hands clenched tightly into fists. "You're telling me my father is dead?"

"I'm sorry, but that's the truth of it." He bowed his head, as if her father's corpse were laid out in state, right there in the room.

For a moment, she almost lost control. She wanted to scream a denial—that her father wasn't dead—that she still sensed his life force. But she clamped her lips together. An outburst would be pointless. She could see it in his eyes. There would be no attempt at a rescue. Not by PanGalactic. Anything that happened now would be up to her.

She needed a persona. It was a trick she had learned in drama class. Whenever something really upset her she'd pretend she was someone else—someone who could handle the problem. She took a deep breath, visualizing Dawn Pearson in her role as the cool, confident space lawyer in the tri-D series, "Moon of Sirus Four."

Casually, she crossed her legs, just as Dawn Pearson would have done. Her show of poise would undoubtedly have been more impressive had she been wearing something more sophisticated than her dark-blue student jumper. Still, when it came to acting, attitude counted for a lot more than costume.

"What financial arrangements have been made?" she asked, her voice like a wind off a glacier.

Goodman's head lifted. "Excuse me?" he asked, peering down at her as if he couldn't believe he had heard her correctly.

"My father's life is insured?"

He pursed his mouth, as if in reaction to a sour taste.

"An ample compensation has been established. PanGalactic provides survivor benefits on all its personnel. And the compensation for pilots is especially generous. But I thought we could take that up at a later date."

"I want to know now. What are the arrangements?"

His face flushed. "PanGalactic's corporate policy specifies an allowance of one hundred thousand credits a year until you reach twenty-one. At that time the full amount of the policy will be turned over to you—approximately two million credits. You'll be well provided for."

When she turned twenty-one. She couldn't wait that long. Not with what she had in mind. "What about PanGalactic's liability in this matter?"

He eyed her warily. "I'm not sure what you mean."

She leaned back in her chair and examined her fingernails. "Since it's your ship that cost me my father, it seems only fair that you compensate me for my loss."

His voice took on a patronizing quality. "I know you're upset, but I'm afraid you just don't understand how these things work. The pilot is responsible for the loss of his ship, not the company he works for."

"Really? And just how is responsibility determined? What if the ship suffered a mechanical breakdown? Since your people refuse to retrieve it, there's no way we can tell. But given my father's excellent record, a jury might just decide that a mechanical breakdown is more likely than pilot error. What do you think, CAP?" she asked aloud, so the man would know she was consulting her advisor.

Few suits of this type have been successfully pursued in the past. Besides, now is hardly the time to deal with such matters.

She stared blankly ahead and nodded, as if CAP had fully agreed with her. Then she refocused her gaze on the representative. "My advisor feels we have a solid basis for a major suit. But there's really no need for such a messy legal action. Give me the insurance money now and I'll sign away all rights to future claims."

I strongly oppose any waiving of any rights, CAP projected. *You are upset. You need time to consider.*

Jackie answered silently: *Can I legally sign the release?*

If I validate your signature. But given the circumstances it would not be appropriate for me to—

CAP, I need that money. Either you validate or I terminate you and get myself a human guardian I can bribe.

She held her thoughts to herself, trying not to let CAP know she was bluffing. She could, in fact, make good on her threat to replace him with a human guardian. With her father legally dead, she had that right. She might even be able to find one she could bribe into going along with her. But the process would require a lengthy court proceeding. If she missed this opportunity, there would be no telling how long it would take her to get anything out of PanGalactic. She counted on CAP recognizing that her present need for his counsel and assistance outweighed any nebulous future right to sue that might never earn her a credit. She sensed the odd grinding sensation that sometimes came when she placed strong, conflicting demands on his programming.

This is not advisable.

Will you validate or not?

CAP made a clicking sound of disapproval. *Very well, but I don't like it.*

She started breathing again and turned to Goodman. "My two million credits now and no future hassle. You'll be paying it to me anyway. I'll just be getting the money a few years early."

A nervous tic dimpled the side of Goodman's mouth. "I really don't know if the board will go along with this.

12

Perhaps a lesser amount . . ."

She made a point of looking at her watch. "My offer is good for the next fifteen minutes. After that, I instruct CAP to initiate the action."

Goodman blanched. "I'll see what I can do." He walked to the far end of the room and turned his back on her. She could hear him mumbling into his wristcom although she couldn't make out the words. Minutes later he turned back. "My people are faxing a release for you to sign. I am authorized to deposit two million credits into a private account in your name. I assume your advisor can validate through a thumb print?"

She nodded. She had done it before and knew the procedure. Computer advisors validated agreements by temporarily disrupting surface blood vessels in the epidermis of the thumb, forming a coded pattern a scanner can recognize.

"One other thing," she said. "My father keeps a condo in Coronado where he stays between flights. He told me he left a copy of his access card with you people. I'll be taking over the condo. I want the card."

This isn't like you, CAP protested as she headed to her room following Goodman's promise that the access card would be sent to her by courier on the following day. *The disappearance of your father's ship has unsettled you more than you realize. You appear to be in a state of denial. It would be wise to consult a therapist. There are several I can recommend.*

"I don't need therapy, CAP, I need to find my father. Since PanGalactic won't go after him, it's up to me."

But what can you do?

"Hire someone to take me into the Void. That's why I need the money. I don't know what it's going to cost, but it's bound to be expensive."

But you heard that Goodman fellow. No ship lost in the Void has ever been rescued.

"Void Pilot David Klein once pulled out his brother's ship. Dad told me about it."

That was no rescue. The ships just happened to make their jumps at the same time. Somehow David's brother Adam picked up on David's mind-set and his ship followed David's in to Galodea. It proves nothing.

"It proves it's possible to pull a ship out of the Void."

It was a freak occurrence. The Kleins were identical twins, sensitive to each other and both with ten-plus ratings. Somehow, they meshed minds and were drawn together.

She shrugged. "If twins can do it, why not a father and daughter? I've always been sensitive to my father's mental state. And I share his potential."

According to physiologists, matter quickly collapses on itself in the vicinity of the Void, losing all of its physical attributes. Successful Void crossings must be made in a matter of minutes. No one has ever been rescued once they become lost.

"According to Goodman, no one even tries."

There's no point. And how do you think your father would feel about you tearing off into the Void on such a futile and dangerous errand?

She grinned, remembering the lengths her father had gone to keep her away from any form of space travel. "He'd be against it," she admitted. "He was always way too protective with me. But I can't let that stop me now. He's still alive, CAP, I can sense it. And it's up to me to get him out."

She could feel CAP's building frustration as a tiny hotspot inside her skull.

But you have no experience with the Void.

She nodded a solemn acknowledgment. "That's why I

14

need to find someone who does."

There was little else she could do until they brought her the access card to her father's apartment, so she spent the rest of the day in her room, thinking about her father. He had always been so confident and proud of his occupation. "It was the early Void pilots who opened up the galaxy for exploration," he had often told her. "And in only half a century. If not for them sacrificing their lives to learn how to navigate the Void, we'd still be dragging our tails to the nearest stars at light speed."

She had managed to convince herself that Void crossings were no longer all that dangerous for highly capable pilots. And her father had always seemed so confident in his ability to make the crossings. Now, she could only wonder what he might be experiencing, trapped in the non-physical reality of Void space. She asked CAP, but for once even he, with his great reservoir of knowledge, could be of little help. *There's no way to know,* he told her.

None of the other girls at the Conservatory had a computer advisory implant. They were outrageously expensive. But after her mother died, her father had insisted. "A top Void pilot with a ten-plus rating can afford a few luxuries," he told her. "And with one of these gizmos watching over you I'll feel a lot better about leaving you alone so often."

She was only nine at the time and not all that sure she wanted a computer chip inserted into her skull. But she soon came to appreciate CAP's abilities. In addition to serving as her legal advisor, he could come up with a library's worth of information on any subject she cared to ask about. He monitored her physical well-being and could call in medics, police, or firemen, should she need them. But most of all, he acted as a companion—someone she could talk to when something important happened—good or bad. Someone she could ask for advice.

Of course he could be a pain at times, scolding her for staying up too late or not eating enough vegetables. And now, fussing about her mental state when she had a far more important matter to consider.

She tried reaching out to her father, hoping to pick up something more from him, but all she could sense was a sort of dull apathy, faint and indistinct. Not up to eating, she skipped the evening meal. She was lying on top of her Quaker-styled bed quilt, laying out plans in her mind for the next day, when the door opened and her roommate burst in to the room.

"Oh, Jackie," Cherral wailed. "I just heard. How awful you must feel."

Sighing, she rose to a sitting position and swung her legs over the edge of the bed. Apparently the school's unofficial intelligence system was working as well as ever. The gangly girl stood posed in the doorway, one hand extended to Jackie, eyes red and puffy. Cherral's typical response to any crisis was to burst into tears. But Jackie hadn't the time for bereavements just now. She still had things to plan. Patting the space beside her on the bed, she invited Cherral to join her.

"I'm still kind of numb over this," she said, placing an arm around Cherral's shoulders, struck with the oddity of comforting her friend when she was the one experiencing the loss. "I need time to myself, time to deal with this. Could you sleep-in with Lisa and Beth tonight?"

Cherral pushed back a ripple of blond, spiraling curls and threw her a worried glance. A trickle of moisture traced its way down her freckled cheeks. "Are you sure you want to be alone?"

Jackie nodded. "For now, I think it's best."

Cherral sniffed and nodded back. "Okay then, but you let me know when you're ready for company."

Later, Jackie lay on her back and stared at the ceiling. A cold emptiness filled her. There would be no later time for Cherral. Tomorrow Jackie would be leaving—walking away from everything that had meant so much to her for the past seven years. The Conservatory had been her sanctuary. Every friend she had in the world lived within its walls. And her acting. God, how she would miss it! But she couldn't stay here, subject to the school's strict rules, better suited to the beginning of the twentieth century, when it first opened, than now at the end of the twenty-first. Up to now, she had put up with living in the past, understanding her father's need to have her raised in a sheltered environment. But if she was to have any hope of rescuing him, she had to be off on her own. Struck by the enormity of the task that lay before her, she finally gave way to tears.

—CHAPTER—
2

The following morning she awoke feeling somewhat better, having put all her regrets behind her. But she ordered breakfast sent to her room rather than eat in the dining hall. The sidelong glances and expressions of pity would be too much to take.

Around nine, the micro-com built into the Queen Anne bureau by her bed beeped to inform her that the courier from PanGalactic had arrived with the access card to her father's residence. She found him in the visitor's room, a slim young man in the maroon livery of PanGalactic who could have moonlighted as a model for men's clothing. He stood in the middle of the room, as if distrustful of the antique furnishings.

"Miss Claver?" he asked, and drew a laser scanner from his coat pocket. "I'll need to confirm your identity." She nodded and a short burst of red light flashed in her face. He checked the reading on the scanner, then handed her the card. "PanGalactic sends its sympathy and best regards," he said, reciting the words woodenly.

She felt like telling him what PanGalactic could do with its best regards but held her tongue. It wasn't his fault that the people he worked for were such yucks. He may have sensed her mood, though, because he left without further comment.

Excited now about what she might find at her father's

place, she telephoned for an auto-cab. Minutes later, she stood at the curb with a small bag of her personal belongings. A driverless auto-cab with broad bands of yellow and black stripes pulled up in front of her. The silly things reminded her of giant bumblebees. She boarded this one and punched in the address of her father's Coronado high-rise. Today she felt back in control. She was a huntress, like in the role of Sandra Slick, interplanetary tracer of missing persons.

Just what do you expect to accomplish at your father's? CAP asked.

She smiled to herself. She knew how much it upset CAP not to know what she was up to. He had been quiet all morning, accepting her claim that she needed time to herself. What she really wanted was not to be deluged with questions she couldn't answer.

"I'm not sure," she admitted. "I guess I'll be looking for any clues as to someone who can help me."

You're looking for the wrong kind of help. What you need is emotional support.

"What I need," she said, "is for you to support me in what I'm doing."

The access card admitted her to the plush lobby of the highrise and up to her father's rooms on the twentieth floor. She had been there many times before, but always with her father. Modern and masculine, his quarters reminded her of the interior of a space liner. An expanse of gray tones in the walls and drapes softened the starkly contrasting black and white furnishings and accessories. The walls were hung with a collection of abstract vid-art displays, bold slashes of primary colors that constantly changed both in form and hue.

His rooms had always held an attraction for her, simply

because they were his. Now, however, standing alone in the apartment with all the windows covered up, she found it oppressive. "House computer," she said, "open the drapes."

They slid silently open, the interior lighting automatically dimming as sunlight flooded the room. Two hundred feet below, row upon row of rolling waves surged in to break and foam. For a moment she just stood there watching them, as she had done so many times before. But she quickly turned away. She had no time to spend admiring a stretch of beach. She needed help for her father and she needed it now.

"How do I get to his addresses and phone numbers?" she asked CAP.

Try the command: 'Access files,' he suggested.

"Access files," she ordered and the large vid-art abstract across from her father's black leather recliner dissolved into a list of files. Scanning down the list, she found file seventeen titled: " 'Names, Numbers, and Addresses.' "

"Access file seventeen," she said and a long list of alphabetical entries scrolled onto the screen. She felt a surge of relief. This might prove easier than she expected. "Print list," she said and a metal basket slid out from a slot beneath the screen. Sheets of paper, covered with names, addresses, and phone numbers, rapidly fed into the basket. She picked up the top sheet and frowned. Mostly women's names. She doubted that many of these would be spacer types, but she had to check.

She flopped down on a massive black recliner. "Access phone service," she ordered. "Contact Adams, Elsa F," she continued, reading off the first name on the list.

Three hours later, she sat, head in hands, mentally

exhausted, frustrated, and discouraged. Most of the females on the list had turned out to be, as she suspected, women her father had dated. Since her mother's death, he had been involved with many women for brief periods but no long-term commitments.

Only a dozen of the names had turned out to be Void pilots and half of them were currently in other parts of the galaxy and couldn't be contacted. Those she spoke with were sympathetic when she identified herself and told them why she was calling, but none could offer her a shred of hope. They basically repeated what she had been told by the PanGalactic representative. Lost in the Void meant lost for good.

"CAP," she said. "What am I going to do?"

Your bio data indicate a mental state incompatible with effective thinking and planning. My advice is to take a rest period to replenish your resources.

She sighed. Perhaps CAP was right. Her mind seemed to be running in circles. Wearily, she rose to her feet and headed for the bedroom—not the guestroom that she used during overnight stays, but the master bedroom. She wanted to surround herself with her father's personal things—to feel his presence in every way she could. A huge bed, large enough to sleep five, dominated the interior. She lifted a pillow from beneath its black and gray satin quilt, and held it to her, cherishing the faint scent of aftershave. An image of her father's boyish grin filled her mind. Tears streamed down her cheeks.

"How am I ever going to find him, CAP?" she moaned.

CAP's voice came soft and sympathetic. *You must realize there are things beyond your power to change. Accept your limitations and work within them.*

"You think too much like a machine," she said. Dropping the pillow she daubed at her eyes and face with a tissue taken from her jacket pocket—her last. She sniffed several times and looked around the room, hoping to find a new supply to draw from. Nothing.

She turned to her father's built-in wall-bureau. In the top-left drawer she found handkerchiefs and socks, neatly folded and stacked. She pulled out a white linen cloth and blew vigorously. About to close the half-opened drawer, she noticed a piece of paper sticking out from under one of the sock groupings. Curious, she drew the drawer open a little more. An untidy collection of paper scraps lay beneath the socks, held loosely together by a large paper clip. She examined the shakily scribbled lines on the top piece. "Crow owes Jack Claver two big ones. Safe passage, Jack." It was signed: "Hank Crow," and dated. Her father had loaned this person money as recently as last month. Two big ones. Two hundred credits? He must be a friend, even though his name didn't show up on the computer list. And maybe a spacer. "Safe passage" was a standard spacer greeting. She said it to her father whenever he called in to say goodbye before leaving on a trip. It was the last thing she had said to him.

That did it. She was fighting back tears again. She forced herself to ignore them and concentrate on the stack of IOUs. They dated over the last two years with amounts ranging from one hundred to five hundred credits, all signed by this Crow person. No address or telephone number. Most were written on soiled, torn pieces of paper. Several had once served as cocktail napkins. She turned one of these over. The printing on the other side read: "The Odyssey Club."

"CAP," she squealed, "this must be where my father met with Crow."

Perhaps he shared a few drinks with the man, CAP conceded.

"And perhaps—just maybe—this is someone who can help me."

She rushed back into the living room and ran down the list of files. "Access file fifteen," she ordered, keying her father's commercial telephone directory. "Enter: 'Odyssey Club.'" Words flashed on the screen, providing an address, a telephone number, and the following brief description of the establishment:

Thε Odyssεy Club

An upscale bar featuring exotic off-Earth drinks and entertainment. Open to the public, the Odyssey Club provides a primitive ambiance. Its decor is based on the communities of Denab-4, settled by immigrants of Polynesian descent, looking to recreate the lost island paradises of their ancestors.

She ordered the house computer to print out the address.

You aren't thinking of going there? CAP said, disapproval clear in his projection.

"Not yet," she answered, her voice edged with excitement. "First I have some heavy shopping to do."

She first stopped at the Plaza, a dress shop catering to "women who dress with flash," according to the advertisement in the classifieds. Sitting at the store's computer console, she called up some "adult" looking dresses, appropriate for bar wear, and had them superimposed over her body image. Thank heavens the small-chested, waif-eyed look was in. Dressed right, she was sure she could pass for twenty-one. She had played roles of adult women more than once.

She chose a tight-fitting black shift, slit on one side. A good thing since without the slit she wouldn't have been able to walk or sit. She bought a matching sequined jacket and a pair of spiked pneumatic heels, advertised as putting more bounce in your flounce. Finally, she purchased several pairs of slacks and some bulky drape shirts, casual dress to replace the blue Conservatory jumpers she would no longer be wearing. They were the one part of Conservatory life that she wouldn't be missing.

Through much of her buying spree CAP harangued her about her choice of clothes. *That slit dress isn't at all suitable for a girl your age,* he sputtered.

"Machines have no business handing out advice on fashion," she retorted, silencing him for a while. But she sensed his disapproval as a hot spot at the back of her head.

She traded her school jumper for a drape shirt and slacks, grabbed a sandwich to eat on the way, and took another bumblebee auto-cab back to the Conservatory for what would be her last time. She would be signing the paperwork that ended her status as a student and released the school from further responsibility for her welfare.

CAP tried to talk her out of it. *You're cutting yourself off from everything that ever mattered to you. Can't you at least give yourself time to think this over?*

"I don't have the luxury of time," she told him. "There's no telling how long Dad can hold out in the Void. If I'm going to find a way to help him, I have to be able to go wherever I need to."

She had another errand to perform at the Conservatory but did not disclose it to CAP.

They arrived there at twenty to four. She hurriedly

signed the release documents and had CAP validate them. Then, just before the Conservatory bell announced the end of the last class period for the day, she positioned herself outside Miss Rawlins' drama history class. She was looking for a girl named Debora. Not a friend, Debora had a vulgar way about her and was always trying to get away with something. But she did have a reputation for forging passable IDs.

The bell clanged, releasing a chattering stream of girls from the classroom. They poured out in a sea of dark blue jumpers, a uniform unchanged at the Conservatory for over a century. Jackie recognized Debora's shambling stride and moved up behind to touch her shoulder. Debora spun about, as if angered at the familiarity. She stopped when she saw Jackie.

"Oh, it's you," she said, eyeing Jackie's non-regulation clothes. "You leaving?"

Jackie detected a touch of envy in the girl's nasal whine. She motioned to her, affecting a conspiratorial air. "There are places I need to go. Places where under-agers aren't allowed."

Debora raised an eyebrow. "You want an age boost on your ID? You're the last person I'd have expected." She gave Jackie a calculating look. "I guess you can afford it, though. I hear you lucked into big money."

The words stung. Jackie felt like slapping the girl's flat, greedy face. But she forced a smile. "Everyone says you're the best. That's worth paying for."

Debora nodded smugly. Without further comment, she led Jackie up to her room. "You got your school card?"

Jackie handed her the plastic rectangle. Debora opened a bureau drawer and brought out a box-like device with two insertion slots. In the left-hand insert she placed Jackie's current card. Reaching back into her drawer, she withdrew a stack of blank plastic cards. She slid one from the stack and placed it in the right-hand insert.

"We'll duplicate everything except date of birth," Debora said. She adjusted a computerized device on the front of the box to set the new date, closed the box, and pushed a red button on its side. An odd buzzing sound issued from the box. Jackie caught a faint odor of melting plastic. When the buzzing stopped, Debora withdrew an apparent duplicate of Jackie's original card. She gave Jackie a knowing smirk and handed her the duplicate. The birth date read five years earlier than it had before.

Jackie paid Debora the fifty credits she demanded and headed downstairs. She considered stopping to say goodbye to her roommate, Cherral. But Cherral would want to know why Jackie was leaving, and there was no way Jackie could explain her reasons. She couldn't let anyone know what she was up to. And she didn't want to lie to her friend.

With her newly acquired goods she took another of the striped auto-cabs back to her father's condo. On the way, CAP besieged her with questions as to what she intended to do with the falsified identification card.

"I've got to find this man Crow," Jackie told him, "and the only place I know to look is a bar."

None of the others you contacted could help you. What makes you think this man will?

"Dad loaned him money. He may feel grateful. He may need more money. Either way, he's the only lead I have."

It's illegal for a minor to frequent a bar.

"Only a misdemeanor. I won't be drinking anything alcoholic. And if there's trouble, you can protect me by signaling the police. I have to do this, CAP, and I really need your help. But if you try and stop me, I'll have to dump you."

Once again, CAP gave in.

Jackie spent the rest of the afternoon experimenting with lipsticks and layers of fleshtone and eye shadow. With her theatrical experience, it was easy enough to give her face a more mature appearance. She added highlights to her hair and swept it up in a Grecian Goddess style, popular now on the tri-D. Standing in front of the full-length bathroom mirror, she admired her handiwork.

"I might wobble a bit on the bounce heels," she told CAP, "but at least I should be able to enter a bar without looking as if I belonged in an ice-cream parlor. What do you think?"

You'll be lucky if you don't get picked up for prostitution, the computer grumped. *Have you any idea how much trouble a young girl can get into, dressed like this?*

"Don't be silly. The Odyssey doesn't have that kind of reputation."

It may by the time you're done with it. And even if you find this Crow person, what can you expect to gain from him? You need a Void pilot. The sort of man who goes about constantly borrowing credits would hardly be drawing down a Void pilot's salary.

"Anyone who knew my father is a potential source of information. If this man can't help me, he may know of others who can."

She hoped CAP was just overreacting to her new outfit. She wanted to look adult but not promiscuous. And while she led a protected life at the Conservatory, she thought she had a good feel for the latest styles and fashions from watching tri-D programs.

She snatched up her new sequin jacket and flounced unsteadily out of the condo. An auto-cab dropped her off in front of the Odyssey, a respectable looking bistro in San

Diego's affluent uptown district. The interior decor presented a convincing imitation of a tropical setting on the planet Denab-4, complete with recordings of drums and native chants in the background.

At six, only a few of the fronded booths were occupied. The barstools, fashioned to resemble stumps of jilla trees, stood empty. The bar itself consisted of a giant aquarium filled with tiny water life forms that pulsed brightly with electrical charges. The man behind it had the bulk of a fullback. He gave her a noncommittal look as she balanced-walked over to him, imitating the leggy stroll of the models she had watched in the last Miss Universe contest. So far so good.

"I'm looking for a man," she said, imitating the husky voice of Joyce Lavender in a bar scene from one of her latest tri-Ds. "His name is Hank Crow. Has he been around?"

"Crow?" The man's mouth twisted into a sneer. "Hardly a night goes by when that bum isn't in here mooching drinks." He eyed her sharply. "What business have you with Crow?"

"I—I may have a job for him."

He looked as if he were having serious doubts about her sanity. "Void hopping? That guy hasn't been up any higher than a bar stool in years."

"He's a Void pilot?" She sucked in her breath, waiting for the man's reply.

"Used to be. But like I said, he hasn't jumped Void for quite a while." He eyed her again, a sudden hint of suspicion lighting his eyes. "You twenty-one, kid? No one under-age allowed here."

She sighed and made a show of digging out the fake ID, trying to give the impression she did this sort of thing all the time.

He held it up to the light and frowned but returned it without comment. "Take my advice, kid," he said, "don't bother with Crow. You'll waste your money."

"It's mine to waste," she snapped. Then, not wanting to put the man off, she softened her voice. "Please let me know when he gets here."

She managed to order a non-alcoholic Virgin Princess without blushing and carried it over to a booth with a view of the entrance. She sipped at it slowly, trying to keep her hand from shaking with excitement. A Void pilot. This Crow person had possibilities.

For almost an hour she stared at the front door, anxiously watching for the entrance of the lead actor in this drama. Twice, newcomers arrived in civilian dress. Both times she looked over to catch the bartender's eye, and both times he shook his head.

Traffic picked up a little around seven. She had just ordered her third Virgin from a bored waitress in a sarong resplendent with orange and purple flowers when half a dozen young men in space uniforms entered the bar, talking and laughing in high spirits. They sat at a nearby table. She tried to make out the insignia on their lapels. None carried the proud omega symbol of the Void pilot.

An athletic looking blond youth with piercing blue eyes met her gaze and smiled. Moving deliberately, he rose to his feet and sauntered over to her, drink in hand. His eyes seemed a little too bright, the pupils too large. His full lips twisted sardonically as he let his gaze ease up and down her body. She felt her face flush.

"Can't see any point in a pretty little thing like you drinking all by yourself," he said. "Why not join me and my mates?" He raised an eyebrow and nodded in the direction of his table.

She stared down at her drink, trying to imagine what sophisticated reply a tri-D star might use as a put-off, but she couldn't think. The spacer's unexpected interest had unnerved her. "Sorry," she finally muttered. "I—I'm waiting for a friend."

He leaned over her, insinuating himself into her personal space. "If that friend doesn't show up real soon, I know how you can make yourself a whole batch of new ones." He winked, snapped a mock-salute, and turned back to join his table.

Now what am I going to do? she projected to CAP. *That guy will be back again if Crow doesn't show up soon.*

Seeing as you have no business being here in the first place, the obvious thing is to leave.

CAP's smug, I-told-you-so tone infuriated her. She couldn't leave now. Crow was a Void pilot. She had to meet him. She considered waiting outside, but that might draw even more unwanted attention from passers-by. Besides, she needed to have the bartender point Crow out to her.

On the other hand, the spacer's attentions had shaken her. Though living in an age that viewed sex as a casual form of entertainment, she had been raised in an almost Victorian environment. The Conservatory frowned on most boy-girl contacts, the one exception being the quarterly dances where a socially acceptable class of young males was brought in as invited guests. Jackie had not been impressed with them. All they seemed able to talk about was last-year's vacation at Saturn's orbiting pleasure dome or next year's hunting safari on Gratis-four. Their concept of romantic involvement was limited to juvenile groping when none of the chaperons happened to be at hand.

One of the worst offenders was known by the girls at Denning's as PP and P—pudgy, pompous, and persistent.

He made the mistake of coming up behind Jackie and pinching her bottom. All of Mrs. Denning's girls received training in self-defense, and Jackie, responding reflexively, put hers to use. PP and P ended up on his portly butt in the middle of the floor, a dazed expression on his face. Jackie's counselor lectured her on the inappropriateness of her behavior. But contrary to her words, the woman's features registered nothing but approval.

A thick voice rumbled from outside the bar's entrance, the words sounding as if forced through a mouthful of gravel. "Just till my next paycheck. I'll pay you back then, I promise."

The door to the bar opened and another group of spacers entered the room. A tall, gawky individual with thick black hair and a lined, coppery face had his arm slung over the shoulder of one of the younger men. The older man's uniform looked shabby and wrinkled, but over the breast pocket it carried the omega insignia.

Jackie caught the attention of the bartender. He nodded and rolled his eyes, as if to say, "What did you expect?"

The younger spacer shook off Crow's arm. "You're into me enough as it is," he growled. "Find someone else to bankroll you."

Crow held up his hands and turned his eyes heavenward, as if taking his case to the gods. "As soon as I get some work I'll pay back every token—I swear it." He looked hopefully from one to the other. "I know one of you boys will at least buy old Crow a drink."

This was her best hope for finding her father? CAP was right. She ought to get out of here before she made a complete fool of herself.

But even as the thought passed her mind, she knew she couldn't back down. This derelict represented the only lead she had. Summoning up her determination, she rose to her feet.

"Mr. Crow," she said in a voice strident enough to override the muffled rhythm of a Denab fertility chant, "it would be my great pleasure to buy you a drink."

—CHAPTER—
3

Crow stood in the bar's entrance, staring at Jackie, openmouthed, his expression of surprise slowly transforming into a broad, toothy grin. Still grinning, he lurched toward her.

"Young lady," he said, making an ineffective bow, "your generous offer has saved me from a night of bleak sobriety."

He bent his lanky frame into the booth beside her, then turned toward the bar. "A shot of Rilean in this direction," he called to the bartender, ordering an expensive, off-world narcoholic brew. "Make it a double." The stocky server frowned disapprovingly, looking as if he'd much rather toss Crow out the door than wait on him.

Jackie settled back in her seat. "You're a Void pilot?"

"I am that, Miss, although I've not had the fortune to answer the call of hyperspace in recent days." He looked her over with yellowish, bloodshot eyes, undoubtedly trying to decide why she was interested in him and how many drinks she was good for. "And what would be the name of my benefactress?"

Jackie considered her options. If he was a friend of her father's, as she suspected, her best bet would be a direct appeal. "I'm Jack Claver's daughter," she said. "I want you to help me find him."

He stared back expressionless for several seconds. Then his wiry eyebrows knit in a frown. His fist came down hard on the table, making Jackie's glass jump. She pulled back as he rose unsteadily to his feet.

"You can keep your damn drink! I'm not about to help some bimbo go after my buddy, Jack—not for all the liquor in San Diego."

As he started to move away Jackie jumped up and grabbed at his arm, desperate not to lose him. "Please—wait—you don't understand. Jack Claver *is* my father. And he needs your help."

Suddenly, the blond spacer was back at Jackie's side. "This guy giving you trouble?" He squinted at Crow through eyes drawn into slits.

"Damn kiddie cruiser," Crow snarled at the young spacer. "I'll give you trouble." He yanked his arm from Jackie's grasp and brought it around in a roundhouse swing that the spacer easily ducked.

"No!" Jackie screamed as the younger man caught Crow in the stomach with a stiff left jab that doubled him over just in time to meet the man's right cross with his chin. Crow fell heavily, his head thudding against the wood flooring.

Without thinking, Jackie grasped the spacer's wrist. In a seamless series of moves she twisted herself under his arm and yanked it over her shoulder. Her would-be rescuer somersaulted heels-over-head to land on his back.

Shocked by her action, she raised her hands to her mouth. The spacer's friends laughed uproariously at his unexpected flying lesson, but the object of their merriment glared up at her.

"You little whore," he rasped, "I'll teach you to pull tricks on me."

Jackie shrank back as he rose to his feet. But as he started toward her, a large, meaty hand grasped his shoulder from behind. The spacer spun around to find the bartender standing there, menacing him with one of the carved hunting clubs that decorated the walls of the interior.

"That's enough," the big man growled. "I'm not about to have a brawl in here. Get back to your friends or get out."

The spacer muttered something under his breath but gave way before the burly drink server. The bartender watched him go, then thrust his heavy-browed face down to peer at Crow who now sat rubbing his chin.

Scowling, the bartender turned to Jackie. "This bum isn't fit to be in a place like this. I want him out—now. Either you take him with you or I call the police."

"I'll take him," Jackie said. "I don't want any trouble."

The bartender looked from Jackie to Crow and grimaced. "Stick around with this one and you'll have more trouble than you can handle." But he helped her get Crow on his feet and outside into the street.

I've already signaled the police, CAP informed her. *They should be here shortly.*

There's no need, she mentally chided her advisor. Supporting Crow with one arm, she located a transport call box, mounted waist-high by the curb. With her free hand she pressed the button to hail an auto-cab.

Crow pulled away from her. His face looked ashen. He took a small bottle of pills from his coat pocket, removed one, and placed it in his mouth.

"Are you okay?" Jackie asked.

"Yeah, I'm fine," he muttered.

"The police will be here shortly. We should get away before they arrive. If you'll come with me to Jack's place, I can prove that I'm his daughter. If I can't convince you, I'll give you this." She held up a 100 credit note.

Crow's eyes widened but he shook his head stubbornly. "No way you could be her. She's just a little kid in some girl's school. Jack told me all about her."

"And how long ago was that?"

Crow ran a hand through coarse black hair that showed no sign of graying. "It's been a while. Maybe a couple of years."

"Believe me, Mr. Crow, a lot can change in that much time."

One of the striped auto-cabs pulled up to the curb. She entered, slid over to the far side, and punched in the Coronado address as a destination. Then she turned back to Crow. "You coming or not?" she demanded with far more assurance than she felt.

He twisted his head from one side to the other, looking down the street in both directions. Reaching a decision, he folded himself into the seat beside her.

Just what do you intend doing with this seedy specimen? CAP asked.

I told you, she returned silently, *I need his help.*

The cab dropped them in front of her father's apartment building. A strong breeze blew off the bay, whipping her slitted dress against her legs. Crow looked about him, stretching his neck like some great water bird, scanning the horizon.

"Ever been here?" Jackie asked.

He shook his head. "Jack told me he lived in Coronado, but we always met at the Odyssey."

Really, CAP said, *you shouldn't be bringing someone like this to your father's residence.*

She ignored CAP and strode determinedly toward the imposing entrance to the building. She glanced back at Crow.

The lanky spacer followed uncertainly, eyes fixed ahead.

Inside, they received some hard looks from an elderly white-haired couple who exited the elevator just as they entered it. Thankfully, the two seniors kept their opinions to themselves. Once inside the apartment, Jackie ordered the curtains open and excused herself, pointing out the location of the liquor cabinet. She returned with most of the makeup wiped from her face, wearing her Conservatory jumper and carrying a picture taken from her father's bureau—a hologram of herself and her father standing together in front of the Conservatory. She handed it to Crow and flopped down on the couch beside him.

"This was taken a year and a half ago. See any resemblance?"

Crow set down the drink he had poured himself and glanced from the picture to Jackie and back to the picture, looking perplexed. Jackie held her head in profile for him to compare against the photo. Slowly, recognition lit his eyes. He set down the photo and downed the remaining contents of his glass. The deep lines of his craggy face drew into a frown, but he looked more disturbed than angry.

"What's a young girl like you going into bars for?" he said, as if chastising a misbehaving daughter. "Jack will go ballistic."

"My father isn't here to go ballistic," she said quietly. "His ship was lost in the Void. Haven't you heard?"

"Jack's ship? Lost?" His head jerked from one position to another as if he were looking about the room for someone to deny her statement. "That can't be. Jack is one of the best—a ten-plus rating. No way would he lose focus."

"PanGalactic says he did. His ship never showed—not at any of the stations." Jackie felt her eyes start to well with moisture. Holding back on her feelings, she took on the crisp efficiency of her Sandra Slick characterization. "I'm going to find him, Mr. Crow, and I want you to help me."

Crow stared at her, mouth half open, eyes glazed with confusion, as if dumfounded by what she had told him. "But if Jack is really lost in the Void, then it's over—there's nothing anyone can do."

Nothing anyone can do. She was so tired of hearing that. She felt ready to scream. But she needed to stay reasonable—be convincing. "What about Void pilot David Klein? He brought out his brother."

Crow snorted. "That was a singularity—a one-timer. Two ten-plus twins who just happened to jump Void at the same time. But no one has ever brought a ship back from the Void once it's been lost there."

She felt herself start to tremble. She was breaking out of character but she couldn't help it. Another minute and she'd be bawling like a baby. "Look, Mr. Crow," she pleaded, "we have to try to bring Dad out—it's his only chance." She paused. "I can pay you. I have money. Lots of it."

Crow reached out and touched her arm, his face furrowed with regret. "Jack was good to me. I'd do anything I could to help get him back—no pay needed. But even if it was possible to pull Jack's ship out of the Void, it would take a ten-plus rating to do it. I never ranked higher than a six at best. Only made easy jumps in hoppers. There's no way I could handle a space liner filled with passengers."

She shook her head. "That's not what I need you for."

His eyes clouded with confusion. "What then?"

"I take it you can fly a two-passenger craft?"

Crow nodded, hesitantly. "That's about my limit."

"Then take me into the Void."

Crow shook his head sorrowfully. "Like I just told you, Miss, even if by some miracle I could locate your father, there's no way I could pull out his ship."

Jackie leaned toward him, staring straight into his eyes. "You won't have to. You see, Mr. Crow, like my father, I'm rated a ten-plus."

Crow's head jerked back like someone had shoved a hot poker in his face. "You? A ten-plus? No way. With that kind of rating every major spacer company would be after you to sign with them."

"Dad made them bury the results. And he made me promise never to take up training as a spacer. He had a pre-monition that something awful would happen to me if I ever entered the Void. At least that's what he told me. He wouldn't even let me make a jump as a passenger."

Crow nodded. "He couldn't let you board a Void liner without giving away your potential. All passengers have to submit mental strength certificates. High-rated passengers are put in freeze-sleep during the jump. Can't have them in-terfering with the pilot's projections."

"I went along with him because he felt so strongly about it. But I would have liked to have had the experience of vis-iting another world."

Crow's features formed into sympathetic lines. "So in-stead of Space Academy, you got sent to a girl's school."

Jackie shrugged. "He knew I loved acting. I guess he figured it would keep me out of trouble. And I really didn't mind—up to now. But losing him has changed everything. I know I can bring him out of the Void. I'm as sensitive to him as those twin pilots were to each other. Will you help me?"

Crow's face looked pained. "I've been grounded for two years now with a bum ticker. They don't take chances on someone losing it in the middle of a jump." He stared down at his feet, looking completely miserable. "I'm sorry, kid, but there's no way I can fly you into the Void."

—CHAPTER—
4

Crow grounded! Jackie couldn't believe it. She had come so close to getting what she needed—finally found a Void pilot willing to help her. And the man couldn't even take up a hopper.

"Why didn't you get a transplant?" she demanded.

He drew back as if she had threatened his manhood. "A heart transplant? Not this boy. I don't like the idea of anyone taking a knife to my innards." His lips twisted in a show of distaste. "Anyway, my insurance had lapsed. I couldn't afford it."

"I can afford it. How long would it be before you could reapply for a license?"

"A month at the very least," he said, not looking thrilled at the prospect.

Jackie turned away, fighting down an urge to scream out her frustration and helplessness. She couldn't wait that long. Any day now, her father's emanations might stop. What could they do? She had money. There must be some way to make things work for them. But how?

Then it hit her. If a schoolgirl could manufacture fake IDs, there must be people who could rig bogus licenses for Void pilots. It would be highly illegal, but with her father's life at stake, she couldn't afford to be squeamish about bending rules. Unfortunately, CAP would never let her get away with it. Before she could bring it up to Crow, she had to turn him off.

"Excuse me a minute," she said. "I have to speak with my computer advisor."

Crow's eyes widened. "Jack told me he'd gotten his daughter one of those implant things. Not something I'd want in my head." He shuddered and finished off the rest of his drink.

"CAP," she said aloud, "I have decided to take on a human guardian. I want you to turn yourself off."

Taking a human guardian is your right. But if I turn myself off now you will be left without advisement. I shall continue to function until a human substitute is appointed.

CAP was going to be stubborn. Jackie didn't like what she was about to do, but she had no choice. She took a deep breath and rose to her feet. "You are endangering my welfare," she said. "I order you to terminate." These two key phrases would override any other consideration in CAP's programming and demand an immediate shutdown. Something clicked inside her head and she sensed a sudden cessation of CAP's presence. For a moment she just stood there feeling incomplete. CAP had been with her so long that she now felt as if a part of her own personality had been removed. Tears came to her eyes. Although CAP was basically just a computer, he had always seemed like something more to her—a friend. She couldn't help but believe he had been hurt by her rejection.

Crow stared at her, looking confused. "I couldn't let my advisor hear about this," she told him. "He would have called in the authorities." She sighed and pushed back a strand of hair. "Now, how do you suppose we might go about finding someone with a talent for forging Void pilot licenses?"

At Jackie's insistence, Crow shared her father's apartment

with her while he searched for a contact. Now that she had found someone to help her, she intended to keep a close watch over him. She moved back into her old room and gave Crow the master suite.

Living with Crow proved to be no hardship. Their bedrooms and bathrooms were well separated and he never intruded on her privacy. While there he mostly slept. Each evening, he would haunt the watering holes where some of the higher-class cons were known to hang out. He'd buy rounds of drinks—making friends—asking questions—looking for anyone who might have a lead on a first-rate forger. Jackie gave him whatever money he needed to finance his excursions.

Her biggest problem was keeping her sanity while she waited for Crow to score. Usually, by the time he returned from bar hopping, it was well past midnight. She'd run to the door, hoping this would be the night for good news, only to be disappointed.

During the days she found ways to occupy herself. One of her first chores was to get her mental rating officially registered. A rental agency would require that information. Her ten-plus score caused quite a stir at the testing bureau and she received calls from several space agencies interested in recruiting her. But she refused to talk with their representatives, claiming to be still in mourning over the loss of her father.

Another task that took up her time was learning how to set her mind for guiding a ship through the matterless space that made up the Void. Crow explained the procedure.

"The trick," he told her, "is in learning to split your concentration. You focus part of your mental energy on forming a link with your hopper. The rest of it you extend out into the Void—imaging your destination. You have to be clear on that, otherwise there's no telling where you could end up. When you sense you're in contact with where you want to go, you just sort of reel yourself in. That's for a normal jump. In your case, you have a third thing you'll be doing—trying to mesh minds with your father. That's the tough part, doing all three at once. And you have to be fast. The whole operation has to take place in under two minutes. Any longer and you're apt to get sucked in for good."

"How do I do that?" she asked, uncertain of what he telling her. "How do I go about splitting my mind?"

Crow paused in thought. "What we need is a way to give you some practice. At the Academy they use biofeedback equipment. You can get a rough feel for what's involved by forming your alpha patterns into separate sets of waves. I know a guy who sells the devices. I'll pick one up for you today, before I hit the bars."

Jackie sighed and shook her head. "The whole thing sounds so weird."

He nodded, sympathetically. "It's hard to explain it to someone who's never been on a jump. But mind splitting is a natural reaction to the Void. Otherwise, no one would ever have discovered how to do it. The first spacers who crossed the Void had no real understanding of what they were doing. You, at least, know what you're up against. And with a ten-plus rating, you've got all the mental horses you need. You just have to learn to control them. Once we hit the Void and you feel the whole galaxy inside your head, you'll see what I'm saying."

She sincerely hoped he knew what he was talking about.

Crow got her the biofeedback equipment and hooked her up so she could see her brain waves, displayed as a series of curves on the screen of the console. She soon learned how to change the size and shape of the pattern by sheer concentration. Forming it into two sets of overlapping curves proved more difficult. Just about the time the trace would start to split, it would shift and waver, drawing back into a single set of curves. She practiced the splitting action again and again, but could only hold up for a half-hour at a time before the mental effort exhausted her. After three days of such practice, she could keep the waves split into two over-lapping patterns for several minutes. Another two days and she could split them three ways for a minute or two. But it usually took her several tries to make the three-way split. This worried her since time would be a critical factor.

"The effects of the Void are progressive," Crow ex-plained. "You don't want to fool around in there any longer than you have to. Start your split the second you enter and haul ass out as soon as you connect with your dad. You'll only have a couple of minutes to play around with. If you haven't contacted Jack by then, jump clear. We can always come back for another try. But hang in too long, and it's all over."

In addition to worrying about forming mental links within the Void, Jackie was bothered by Crow's constant drinking. So much alcohol, she felt, couldn't be good for a man with a bad heart.

"You might at least try to cut back," she told him one night when he staggered in heavily loaded.

Crow held up a wobbly finger. "The people I deal with don't trust anyone more sober than they are. What I'm doing out there is building trust."

All Jackie could do was shake her head and hope for the best.

When not practicing with the feedback equipment, Jackie occupied herself with reading everything she could find in her father's computerized library about the Void and the faraway systems it led to. With CAP out of commission, she had to gather such information on her own. She hunted down scores of articles written about Void-linked worlds and the exotic forms of animal and plant life that inhabited them. Generally speaking, extraterrestrial animals were not an impressive bunch. None of those so far discovered had an intelligence rating much higher than that of a bright toad. Apparently large brains were not that common a feature throughout the galaxy.

A week went by, each day followed by a restless night spent wondering if she would ever again see her father. Each morning she reached out to him, just to be sure she could still sense his presence. She couldn't help but wonder how long it would be before she tried and found nothing there.

On the eighth night, she dozed off on the living room couch while waiting for Crow to return, pretty much exhausted from lack of sleep. She woke to a hand shaking her by the shoulder.

"Wake up, sugar," Crow said, his voice hoarse with excitement. His breath reeked of stale rum.

"Not so close." She wrinkled her nose and sat up to rub her eyes. "You smell like you brought half the bar back with you. What happened?"

Crow took a step back. "I've got great news. Met a guy with a friend of a friend who he says can get me most any kind of document I want."

Jackie sat up, suddenly alert. "When do you meet this friend of a friend?"

"Tomorrow. He wants a thousand credits. Void licenses are tough because of all the different sorts of data and certifications you have to dig up to put on the registration chip."

"You think he'll come through?"

"Oh yeah. The guy showed me some of his friend's work. Impressive stuff. He's built himself a reputation that he won't want to spoil with unhappy customers."

Jackie felt a sudden uneasiness. How good a judge of character could Crow be, halfway plastered from drinking? She didn't want to see him end up in an alley with a lump on his head and his money stolen. Or worse.

"These people aren't model citizens," she said. "You have to be careful."

Crow's head bobbed up and down in agreement. "I've bought me some insurance, just in case." He reached deep inside the open front of his gray uniform jacket and withdrew a long metallic object that looked something like a cross between a pistol and a soldering gun.

"A stunner?" Her body stiffened and she drew back from the sight of the weapon. Seeing it made her realize, for the first time, just how deep a mess they were getting themselves into.

"Purely defensive," Crow assured her. "It won't do any permanent damage, but it's guaranteed to make a wet noodle out of anyone for a good half-hour." He nodded his head over the stunner as if agreeing with himself.

Jackie sighed. "All right then, but please be careful. You're my only hope. I don't know what I'd do if anything happened to you."

He bent over and gave her a peck on the forehead. "Don't worry, sugar, Crow knows how to take care of himself."

The next evening Jackie waited impatiently for Crow to return with the forged license. She tried watching one of her father's tri-Ds on terraforming the planet Kilderal but quickly became restless, fidgeting nervously in her chair and changing positions every few seconds. Three times she ordered the player to fast-forward past descriptions of plant and animal life that normally would have held her interest.

She finally told the player to secure itself and took up with her biofeedback equipment. Her concentration wavered so badly she could barely separate the waves into two patterns and was completely unable to get a three-way split. She yanked the electrodes from her fingers and flung them to the floor. She was working herself into a state of nerves. Thoughts about things that might go wrong kept at her. What if Crow couldn't get the license after all? What if it didn't fool the authorities? What if no one would rent them a hopper? And most of all, what if she couldn't contact her father once they were in the Void?

She needed a way to calm herself. She tried to think of tri-D characters with a temperament for taking periods of waiting in stride, but none came to mind. She couldn't even call on CAP for reassurance. She missed his companionship even more than his advice.

By midnight her head hurt, her limbs ached, and she felt a hollow ache in the space behind her eyes. She lay slumped on her father's couch, all lights extinguished, drapes open, staring down at the tumbling waves, ghostly in the moonlight. Once again, she tried to imagine what her father might be experiencing. What was it like to be stranded in nothingness? No one knew. No one who had been lost in the Void had ever returned to tell about it. Still, at the edge of her consciousness she could sense her father's presence. Just the fact he existed—nothing more.

Jackie thrust her head up at the thin rattle of the front door's lock mechanism. The door swung open and Crow burst into the room, holding up a small plastic card for her inspection. He circled about, dancing an impromptu jig and waving the card about enthusiastically. "This little baby is going to get you and me up, up, and away, and that's a fact!"

She ran over and hugged him, ignoring the alcoholic stench. His long, gangly arms encircled her awkwardly, hands patting her back. Her days of study and practice had not been wasted. She would have her chance with the Void, however slim that might be.

—CHAPTER—
5

Jackie wasn't sure how she got any sleep that night. As soon as the sun came up she jumped out of bed, threw on a robe, and headed straight for Crow's bedroom. She pounded on his door several times but received no response. Finally, she flung it open and barged in. Crow lay on his back, his unshaven chin trembling in cadence with a whistling snore.

"Come on Crow," she said, yanking at his arm like a lioness worrying the limb of a downed prey. "You told me last night we could take off for the shuttle base first thing in the morning."

Crow retrieved his arm, opened an eye, groaned, and squinted, like some bedraggled Cyclops, at the light streaming through his east-facing window. "No need to rush," he muttered. "A man can't think this early with his head full of spider webs." He turned his back on the window and buried his face in his pillow.

"A pitcher of ice water will be improving your thinking," she said, affecting her best Irish accent. "And you'll be getting one for sure if you aren't up and going by the time I get back from my shower."

Crow only groaned in reply. But by the time Jackie had washed and dressed and stopped to listen at his door, she could hear water running. A short time later, he stumbled into the kitchen, bleary-eyed but properly attired in the new spacer's uniform she had bought him. His old one would not have impressed the sort of rental agencies that handled Void-hoppers.

Despite the new uniform, Crow looked haggard. He turned down the bacon and egg breakfast Jackie offered in favor of several cups of black coffee. They spent the rest of the morning on the house computer, setting up reservations. By noon they had boarded the fast-flyer commuter jet at San Diego's Lindbergh Field that would whisk them out to Mojave International. From there, they would ride a shuttle up to the orbiting space station where they would pick up their rental craft.

Jackie pressed her face against the window as the fast-flyer reduced speed and altitude in preparation for a landing. In the distance she could see the huge concrete structure of the booster ring that launched the shuttles. It stood out clearly in the dry desert air, rising up in massive isolation like a giant doughnut. Beyond it stretched the great, flat field where the shuttles landed on their return from space. Between the booster ring and the landing field, a broad road ran eastward, connecting to the airfield where their jet would soon be landing.

Jackie turned from the window. "How long will we be in free fall?" She was showing her ignorance but didn't care. This was to be her first trip into space and she had pelted Crow with questions for most of their flight. But he didn't seem to mind. He grinned at her like an approving uncle.

"From the time we stop accelerating until we dock at the station should only be a few hours. Better take your nausea inhibitors now. They take a while to kick in. We want to give a good impression and it won't help to have you green-faced and retching."

"At least the station has gravity. I saw that on one of my father's tri-Ds."

"Only the outer rim is maintained at Earth normal. But that's where we'll go to pick up the hopper, right after we disembark."

"You're sure they'll have it for us?"

"Relax. They aren't about to forfeit. Not after we paid a full five hundred thousand in advance." He pulled out his forged license with the flourish of a magician making an object appear. "All I have to do is wave this baby under their noses and we're as good as Void-bound."

She smiled weakly, wishing Crow didn't act quite so sure of himself. It worried her that he might become careless and overlook something important.

In size, Mojave International Airport was not impressive, smaller than those of many big cities, although it served the populations of both North and South America. But travel off-planet was expensive and only a wealthy few could afford it. The European Commonwealth and China had their own shuttle bases. But whether passengers caught their shuttles here or elsewhere, they rode them to the same destination, Space Station One-Eleven, the hub for all flights leaving Planet Earth. Similar space platforms orbited each of the Void-linked planets where humans had settled.

While modest in size, Mojave International boasted a unique appearance. Its interior, windowless to keep out the scorching desert sun, was blackened and strung with tiny glittering lights to replicate the view of the cosmos from high above the Earth's atmosphere. Two giant globes hung from its high-domed ceiling, the larger displaying the blue and white swirl pattern of a cloud-sheltered Earth, the smaller, the crater-strewn surface of its moon.

This, she thought, was how things would appear from Space Station One-Eleven. She hurried after the long-paced Crow, striving to keep an eye on him while she took in her surroundings. A portly man stepped in front of her and she collided with his ample stomach. Fighting back an urge to giggle, she apologized and ran off, following the bobbing head of her longer-legged companion as he strode through the crowded lobby, heading for the customs desk.

The customs man passed through their sparse collection of luggage without comment. Jackie guessed that most Void passengers traveled light. Clothes and other needs could be purchased at one's destination for far less than shipping costs.

They rode from the airport to the shuttle base in an air-conditioned limo, the standard mode of transportation for Mojave International's wealthy clientele. There, at the entrance to a building that housed waiting rooms, a uniformed attendant directed them to one reserved for passengers taking the four P.M. flight. Each shuttle carried up to eighty passengers. Several dozen passengers, already there, relaxed in plush, heavily padded lounge chairs.

Soon, others began to arrive. A young woman came around with complimentary drinks. Jackie took an iced tea but Crow grimaced at the collection of soft drinks the woman carried and asked for something stronger. She went back to her serving area and returned with a brandy.

Jackie pursed her lips in disapproval. "This isn't the best time to be boozing. We want to make a good impression with these rental people."

Crow gave her a wave of dismissal. "That's hours away. Besides, I function better with a few belts under my belt."

By three-thirty the room had filled to capacity. A bell sounded and the attendant herded them outside the building where an electric-powered train of cars awaited to carry them across the inner concrete surface of the ring to the shuttle. They stood under a long green and white striped canopy while they waited to board, but even with its shade, the hot, dry desert air felt like an oven.

The cars, thank heavens, were air-conditioned. Jackie actually shivered during the short drive out to the middle of the great concrete ring, but whether due to the cold or excitement, she wasn't sure. The shuttle sat upright, a long, silvery projectile with a tapered nose, capable of cutting through the atmosphere at speeds of Mach twenty-five according to Crow. He pointed out the closed slits in its side where retractable fins would extend during landing maneuvers.

But now it was preparing for lift-off. The tips of Jackie's fingers tingled with anticipation. Riding a shuttle into space had always seemed such an adventure. More so, perhaps, because her father had forbade it to her. She supposed she should be nervous about their upcoming flight into the Void—foolhardy from any conventional point of view. And yet, she couldn't help but feel optimistic. Those twin brothers had touched minds in the Void and drawn together. She felt certain she could do the same with her father. She did, after all, share his ten-plus mind-strength. And their minds were compatible. She could sense his life force. All the necessary elements were there. She only needed to bring them together—like a director orchestrating a play. The most important thing would be timing. She had to make contact in less than two minutes. But like Crow said, even if she muffed it on their first pass, they could always try again.

The train pulled to a stop at the base of the shuttle and they filed back out into the heat, under another canopy. Ahead of them towered the portable elevator that would lift them to their respective passenger areas. They rode up in groups of ten, each group transported to an open hatch at the level where they would be seated.

Jackie and Crow were among the last to be taken up. She grasped the rail tightly and looked all about her as the elevator climbed upward toward the highest hatch, the only one still open. The afternoon sun glistened brightly on the hull of the shuttlecraft, making her squint. As they approached the top of their climb she tried to get a view of what lay beyond the great concrete ring that surrounded them. But even at their present height, she could barely see over it.

Crow had told her that at lift-off the entire area inside the ring would be bathed in a hellish blast of rocket fire, the ship's drive coordinating with stationary boosters in the base of the acceleration pad. They would be literally blasted off the face of the Earth.

Not the most comfortable of thoughts. She reminded herself that shuttles made these flights dozens of times each day and that more people were killed each year by lightning than by shuttle mishaps. But the sudden dryness in her mouth was caused by something more than the shimmering desert heat.

She and Crow passed through the open hatch into a circular cabin, lined with heavily padded acceleration recliners. They sat side by side. A young-looking male crewmember passed among the passengers, securing them in their seats with a complex harness of webbing.

The cabin lacked windows or viewing screens so Jackie experienced the drama of their flight through sound, vibration, and pressure. A voice broadcasting a countdown. A low dull rumble slowly growing in volume and depth till it seemed it might shake loose the very molecules of the ship.

A great force weighing down on her, thrusting her deep into the confines of her padding.

As the noise and pressure mounted, she rolled her eyes toward Crow, trying to see from his expression whether this represented a catastrophe in the making or just a normal part of their lift-off. He seemed relaxed so she guessed the shuttle wasn't as likely to fall apart as it felt.

Crow had told her it would take no more than ten minutes of acceleration to reach escape velocity. It seemed much longer, but the roaring of thrusters finally slacked. At the same time, the heaviness lifted from her body and she felt a rising sensation of weightlessness. Her stomach turned, but she managed to hold on to its contents. She noticed several passengers mouthing suction tubes attached to their chairs and was thankful for the pills she had taken. Free-fall was no place for upchucking.

Regulations required that passengers stayed strapped to their seats for the rest of the two-hour flight. No floating above decks or bouncing off walls as she had pictured in anticipating this part of their journey. She tried to doze, but couldn't stop thinking about what lay ahead: renting the hopper, flying it to the Void, making the jump, reaching out to her father. Scenes kept repeating themselves over and over in her mind with variations, each one featuring another way something could go wrong. She heard the soft whistling of Crow's snore and turned to glare at him. He could at least act a little worried.

She experienced their docking as a series of metallic clangs and a whoosh of air as crewmembers released hatches to connect the shuttlecraft to station air locks. They drew in cables with handholds and assisted the passengers in removing their restraints. Jackie watched the other passengers float free from their seats to grasp the handholds and proceed, hand over hand, to the station air lock. When her turn came she followed suit, moving in the slow motion of weightlessness. From the air lock, attendants herded them into a large, circular elevator, its sides studded with more handholds.

"Use them to orient your bodies to the floor," one of the attendants told them. "When gravity increases you don't want to be standing on your head."

Jackie grabbed onto a handhold and, after a few tries, managed to swing herself into what she understood to be an upright position although it felt no more upright than any of the other positions she might assume. The rest of the passengers went through similar contortions. One older woman had difficulty in getting her feet pointed toward the floor and had to be assisted by the attendant. The door finally closed and the elevator picked up speed.

The station, Crow had told her, was shaped like a wheel. Their ship had docked at the inner hub and they now traveled through one of the spokes running out to the rim. She felt an increasing pull toward the floor as they progressed. By the time they reached the rim, her full body weight had returned.

They walked down the slowly curving corridor along the outer edge of Space Station One-Eleven, Jackie's body feeling overly heavy to her after the hours of weightlessness in the shuttle. Here, she found a greater mix of nationalities than she had seen at Mojave International, including passengers on the European and Chinese shuttles. Their only common feature seemed to be an aura of wealth and confidence.

Several uniformed spacers passed them. Jackie glanced up at Crow. Despite his new uniform, his appearance did little to inspire confidence, his eyes too glazed—his walk too loose-limbed and jerky. Jackie could only hope that hopper pilots were, in general, a different breed from those who crewed the great space liners, and that Crow's oddities would not cause concern.

A rainbow of lighted tiles set into the decking led customers to the various transportation services. Yellow and orange lights veered off for local travel within the solar system. A violet line took a turn toward the passenger areas for boarding Void liners. Jackie and Crow followed the brightly glowing blue line down a corridor of doors printed with the names and logos of rental agencies. Crow came to an abrupt halt before a door with the title: "Interplanetary Rentals," tastefully inscribed on a brass plate. Before entering he pulled a flask from a hip pocket and took a long pull.

"Crow," Jackie muttered, giving him a reproachful frown.

"One for luck, little lady. Just enough to keep the brain percolating."

She grimaced. "I've seen you 'percolate' before. You need to watch yourself here. Don't do anything to make them question your ability to handle the rental."

He gave her a thumbs-up and opened the door with a flourish. Inside, a short balding agent with watery blue eyes sat behind the plastiform counter. Crow gave him their reservation number and the man repeated it to his computer.

"Oh, yes, Mr. Crow. We received your payment in advance. I see you are taking a two-week rental. And your destination is Caliban?" He paused. "Are you sure you want to go by hopper? Caliban is on the passenger route and passage on a commercial liner would be far cheaper. I can change the reservation for you."

Crow waved a hand. "Caliban is just our first stop. My niece here only has a couple of weeks before starting college. I promised her we'd hit at least six different station worlds in that time, didn't I, sweetheart?" He turned and winked.

Jackie lowered her eyes and smiled sweetly, having all she could do to keep from trembling. *Don't overdo the act,* she pleaded silently.

The agent frowned. "You'll be hard put to cover that many stations in two weeks."

"No problem," Crow assured him. "I've been a licensed Void pilot for over twenty years. Six stations in two weeks I can do in my sleep."

Reassured, the agent looked back at the computer, then stiffened. "Your niece is a ten-plus?" He broke off to stare at Jackie. "Are you in training?"

It was really none of his business but she didn't want to act in any way that might make him suspicious. Not with so much at stake. "My parents were against it," she said.

His look of contempt made her cheeks flush. He obviously thought little of those so gifted who wasted their talents. Probably would have given ten years of his own life to be guiding passenger liners through the Void instead of handing out rentals.

"Your hopper is ready," he said primly. "All I need do is confirm the status of your license."

Crow dug determinedly through several pockets while Jackie tried to maintain a confident smile. Eventually he found his wallet and drew out the forged license. The man took it and ran it through a small, portable device. He eyed the printout and frowned. Again, he ran the card through. He turned and faced them, his face radiating mistrust.

"You say you've been licensed for the last twenty years?" he said, speaking each word as if he wanted to be absolutely sure they understood his precise meaning. "This card indicates that you only became a pilot two years ago."

Jackie felt herself tense. Crow hadn't checked on how long he supposedly had the license? If only he hadn't bragged about his years of experience. She stood motionless, waiting to see what her companion would do.

He drew himself up to his full height and eyed the clerk with haughty disapproval. "There must be some error. Perhaps your machine malfunctioned."

The agent's lips twisted into a sneer. "Why don't I just call in our security people to check things out?" It looked to Jackie as if he enjoyed their discomfort—pleased with himself for having caught them in a lie.

Jackie grasped Crow by his sleeve. "The man is only trying to do his job. Perhaps we can give him something for his trouble."

The agent snorted. "All you *can* give me is trouble. I'd be out of circulation for the next twenty years if I got caught taking a bribe."

Crow reached inside his jacket and pulled out the stunner he had carried for protection while bar hopping. Jackie stared at the weapon, horrified. But he pushed her aside and waved it in the agent's face. "Don't even think about energizing an alarm or your dependents will be collecting your next paycheck," he said as the man started to edge away. "We want our hopper and we want it now."

The man's eyes widened but his mouth tightened stubbornly. "You don't scare me," he said, unconvincingly. "All you can do with that is knock me out. And with me out, you don't get your hopper."

The rubbery lines of Crow's features stretched in a snarl. "Listen, baldy," he growled, "the stunner's just the first course on the menu. You give us trouble and I'll have you hurting in places you don't even know you have."

Jackie took on an expression of wide-eyed fright. "Oh please Crow, not like you did to that other one." She turned to the agent. "Just last week he got into a fight with a spacer. First he stunned the poor man, and then, when he had him helpless, he—" Her voice broke and she flung her hands to her face. "It was just too horrible."

The agent's eyes had attained the size of saucers. "Okay, okay," he said, "no need to threaten. I'll get you your access card." He reached into a container on his desk and pulled out a small white plastic rectangle. "It's for the hopper you rented," he said, his voice almost a squeak. "It's all set for Caliban."

Crow deftly plucked the card from the agent's fingers and examined it. "*The Wayfarer*, nice name for a hopper."

The man nodded silently, his features taut with fear.

Crow leaned toward him. "Call in and tell them to ready it for departure. But don't say anything that might upset me. You don't want me to be upset, believe me."

The agent gave his head a rapid up and down shake. He contacted the departure crew and, in a shaky voice, instructed them to ready the hopper. Jackie held her breath, expecting the agent to yell a warning into the communicator at any second. But he finished the call, switched off, and backed away.

"Everything's set," he said, his eyes shifting from one of them to the other.

"Fine. Now get down behind the counter," Crow ordered.

Trembling, the man sank to his knees and lowered himself onto his stomach. Crow extended the stunner over the counter and fired. Jackie let out a yelp as the man's body jerked and went limp. "Did you have to do that?" she demanded.

Crow pocketed the stunner, grabbed her hand, and pulled her toward the exit. "Couldn't let him call for help," he said. "Besides, a stunner doesn't hurt all that much. He'll be a little stiff when he wakes up is all. Now hurry. We need to get out of here before the security camera alerts someone."

Jackie looked back over her shoulder. "There was a security camera?"

"Don't worry. Even if someone was watching they probably didn't get a clear view of what happened. I kept the stunner shielded and the agent simply dropped out of sight behind the counter. But we still need to hurry. After they don't see him for a while, they may become suspicious."

They proceeded down the corridor, following the continuation of the lighted blue line toward the boarding area. Certain that security guards would come up on them at any minute, Jackie had all she could do to keep from breaking into a run.

"How did you get that stunner past the security checks?" she asked.

He gave her a wolfish grin. "Pilots are allowed to carry protective weapons. There's a device in the license that overrides alarms."

Crow suddenly stopped in his tracks. His face had paled and his lips were pressed together as if he were in pain.

Jackie felt a sinking feeling in her stomach. "What's the matter?" she demanded.

He passed a hand over his forehead. "Just a little shaky from all the excitement. I'll be all right in a second or two." He fumbled in his jacket pocket and removed the bottle of pills she had seen him take before. Beads of perspiration stood out on his forehead as he unscrewed the lid and popped one of the small white specks into his mouth.

"What are those?" she asked.

"Nitro. It's okay. I've got this under control." His

face gradually lost its pallor as they continued down the passageway.

At the boarding air locks for the rentals a worker examined Crow's access card and nodded. "*The Wayfarer* is set to go, sir. Safe passage to you both."

Safe passage. The familiar benediction of parting she had offered to her father on so many occasions gave her scant comfort now. The undertaking that had seemed so bold and exciting in the planning stages had turned into a nightmare. As soon as that agent recovered, security forces would be after them. Fleetingly, she wondered what her father would have to say about his daughter misappropriating a Void hopper. She suspected he would not be amused.

—CHAPTER—
6

The interior of the hopper was more confined than Jackie had expected. And cluttered. Lines of parallel cables ran along the sides and overhead of its crowded six- by eight-foot cabin, ending in banks of switches, gauges, and indicator lights of green, amber, and red. Two heavily padded black recliners, bolted to the deck on swivel platforms, took up the bulk of the space.

There were no viewing ports but a series of flat-screened monitors, mounted in front of the seats, gave a panoramic view of the star-dusted blackness surrounding them—so many more stars than she had ever seen from Earth. At the moment, however, she had other concerns.

"This is it?" she asked, as she grasped a handhold welded to the side of the cabin and swung herself over into the innermost reclining seat. "This is all the room we'll have?"

"Void hoppers don't waste space on incidentals," Crow said as he settled his lanky frame up into the seat beside her. "But there is another compartment. It's through the hatch behind our seats."

Jackie's only knowledge of Void ships had come from pictures of luxury liners such as her father had piloted. The cramped quarters of the tiny hopper made her claustrophobic. But she ignored the feeling and at Crow's direction wrapped a belt of webbing around her chest to hold her in place. She had more important issues to worry about than personal space.

"What will happen when they find the agent?" she asked, trying to keep the anxiety out of her voice. "Will they come after us?"

"No need to. Earth base will have communicated to Caliban by now about the theft. These rentals broadcast their IDs, and Caliban will have patrol ships ready to pick us up as soon as we break out of the Void. That means there will be no coming back for a second or third try like we planned. We'll only have one pass, so let's make it a good one."

Wonderful. Only one pass. She'd have to get everything right the first time. Her other major worry was Crow himself. Between his drinking and his periodic chest pains, she'd had doubts as to how well he would hold up in space. But she began to relax as she watched him perform pre-flight procedures—calmly and smoothly with a confidence that can only be gained from long years of practice. He jabbed at a vertical row of buttons and a bank of lights on the main panel glowed green. He manipulated a series of levers and knobs. More lights came on and a generator whined, quickly rising in pitch.

A faint rumbling came from deep within the hopper. Her fingers dug into the soft, gelatinous arms of her recliner. Briefly, she thought about trying to re-energize CAP. At this point the computer could do nothing to stop her and it would be comforting to have CAP's presence. But CAP would demand to know what was going on. Explaining her situation and justifying her actions was more than she wanted to cope with at the moment. She wasn't even sure she could bring him back. Terminating a computer advisor for cause could sometimes damage its programming.

A series of clanking sounds startled her. They were followed by a sensation of weight loss and short bursts of movement. She turned to Crow for reassurance.

"Just releasing us from the station and getting into position with the auxiliaries," he said. He leaned forward and engaged a lever. The low rumbling sound grew in volume. But no mighty force pushed her down in her seat. Instead, she sensed a gentle return of weight and direction. Her seat, along with the control panel and monitors, rotated to an upright position.

"Is everything okay?" she asked.

Crow nodded. "On course, and functioning smoothly. Time for our naps."

Jackie stiffened. "You don't mean for us to travel in freeze-sleep?"

"Oh, yeah. Once I input our destination codes the rest is automatic. We'll stay frozen for the five days it takes to get to the Void. The computer will wake us a few hours before we get there. We'll pop in just long enough for you to contact your old man so you can pull him along with us into the Caliban sector."

"But—but I thought they just used freeze sleep during the jump and only for passengers who might interfere with the pilot."

"On the big liners, sure. They can carry passengers in comfort. But hoppers aren't livable over long periods." He grinned reassuringly. "Come on, kid, it's not all that bad. Time passes like nothing. You'll wake up refreshed and raring to go."

"What if the ship's computer forgets to wake us?"

"It won't." He gave her a wicked grin. "And if it does, you'll never know." Her face must have reacted to his jest because his expression softened. "Hey, I'm only joking.

With all the risks we're taking, being left on ice is the least of our worries."

It didn't feel that way to Jackie, but she saw no way around it. To help her father she had to go willingly into freeze-sleep. What was the quote from that old Dickens novel? ". . . a far, far better rest I go to than I have ever known." She held back a shudder.

Crow undid his webbing and, grasping the handholds, swung himself down from his seat. The hatch in the bulkhead that had been behind them now lay beneath them. Crow unlatched it and climbed down a ladder into the cramped space beyond. Jackie followed reluctantly, lowering herself through the opening as if a pit of snakes awaited her there.

Two freeze-sleep modules of glass and steel sat stacked like bunk beds on one side of the cubicle, taking up a minimum of space. They reminded her of sterile coffins. A small toilet and sink took up the remainder of the cubicle. Crow pointed to the freeze-sleep modules. "You want the upper or the lower?"

Jackie rolled her eyes. This was a lot more intimate than sharing her father's apartment. "Lower," she said and bent over to look through the curved glass lid of the bottom unit. The inside, covered in some kind of metallic cloth, didn't look all that comfortable.

"You'll have to strip before you get in."

She jerked her head around to stare at Crow. She could actually feel the heat from her cheeks. She suspected they were red as beets.

Crow shrugged apologetically. "The super-cooled gasses have to make maximum contact with your skin. There's a light, open-weave covering at the foot of the module you can pull over yourself." He paused. "You want me to wait in the cabin while you get yourself settled?"

"Please," she said, strongly emphasizing the word.

She waited impatiently while he scrambled on up through the hatch, then undressed quickly, laying her clothes in a neat pile underneath the module. Following the instructions printed on its side, she pushed the button to open its cover. Wrinkling her nose at the sharp, chemical odor of the freezing compounds, she climbed into what would be her container for the next five days. Carefully, she worked the thin cloth covering up to her neck. She felt like a dead body laid out on a slab. They could at least, she thought, have provided a heavier covering than this piece of glorified cheesecloth.

"I'm ready," she called to Crow, her voice sounding strained in her ears.

He pulled himself down through the hatch and hovered over her, inspecting her container. "All we need now is to slip the injection cuff over your arm, close the capsule, and set the timer. Next thing you know you'll be waking up to meet the Void."

She could have reached out and kicked him for being so enthusiastic about all this, but her skimpy covering hardly allowed for it. Besides, she needed his reassurance. "Will I feel very cold?" she asked in a small voice as Crow adjusted the white Velcro band of the injection cuff around her biceps, taking care not to dislodge her meager covering.

"You'll never feel a thing. You'll be out of it before the module even starts to cool down. And by the time it wakes you, you'll be warm as toast. I guarantee it."

He closed the glass cover. Through it she could see him holding up his hand—wiggling his fingers in an abbreviated wave. You're trusting your life to this man, she thought as he reached over to energize the controls. Too late now to worry. She tensed as she felt a sharp prick in her arm beneath the cuff. A calm warmth washed over her. Crow's face blurred behind the glass. "CAP," she murmured, "you can come back now if you want to. I'm too sleepy to talk but I'll tell you all about it as soon as I wake up." She thought she heard CAP say something, but the words were too fuzzy to make out.

"Rise and shine," someone said.

She thought at first CAP was speaking inside her head. Then she opened her eyes. The curved glass cover on her module lay open and Crow's grinning face hung over it.

"I feel woozy," she said, "and light. Why do I feel so light?"

"We've cut way back on our acceleration. Only a tenth of a g."

Her mouth tasted like an old sock. "I thought you said I'd wake up raring to go."

"You will be, as soon as you're up and about."

Jackie suddenly remembered the scantiness of her covering. "Leave me alone for a few minutes."

He peered down at her. "You look a little pale still. Are you sure you can make it up on your own?"

"I'll be fine. Now go!"

Crow snapped a mock salute and headed for the ladder, moving in a sort of bouncy slow motion. The attachments had already been removed from her arm so all she had to do was maneuver herself out of the module—an easy task as little as she now weighed. She felt dizzy at first, but found she could get by if she moved slowly and carefully. She dressed, used the suction toilet, then stood at the tiny sink to wash her face and clear her mind. She started when a familiar voice spoke inside her head.

Would you care to tell me what's going on? Your body functions for the last five days have bordered on comatose. I've tried to alert a medical team but received no response. Where in heaven's name are we?

CAP's protective haranguing gave her a warm feeling in the pit of her stomach. "I'm sorry, CAP," she said, "I shouldn't have called you back until after I woke up. But I'm glad to know you were watching over me."

For all the good it did. I see you're still hanging out with this derelict person. What sort of place is this? Were you in an accident? Is this a hospital? All your physical indicators seem normal now except for muscle tone. Not surprising, considering how long you've gone without moving.

"No hospital, CAP," she said. "And I'm sorry I had to deactivate you. But you wouldn't have approved. Right now we're on a hopper near the boundary of the Void. We're going in after my father. I've been practicing for this, splitting my mind with biofeedback."

CAP's transmissions actually sputtered. *You'll only trap yourself in the Void along with him. Won't you please reconsider?*

"I don't need your advice on this," she said testily. "If you want to help me you can think up some legal maneuvers for my defense when we get to Caliban."

Defense for what? CAP's tone was ominous.

"Assaulting an agent and stealing a Void hopper. Now don't bother me for a while. I need to talk with Crow about our jump." It was probably her imagination, but she could have sworn she felt a mild shock in the place in her skull where CAP's chip was planted. At least he quieted down.

Jackie dressed herself and, at a tenth of her normal body weight, climbed easily up the ladder and into the crowded cockpit. Crow sat strapped into his recliner, facing the control board, studying a readout.

"How close are we to the entry point?" she asked as she drew herself into her own recliner and attached the webbing. The monitors showed nothing but the same thickly clustered star patterns she had seen at the space station.

"No more than two hours I'd guess. Just enough time to down some energy food and get ourselves mentally set for the jump." He handed her a packet of something enclosed in a wrapper. Suddenly ravenous, she opened it and wolfed down the fruity flavored grain bar in a few bites.

"It's fortified with enough good stuff to raise a dead horse," Crow said. "And the small tube by the head of your recliner holds a hot tea mix, also fortified. Careful—it's pretty warm."

Jackie placed the end of the slim, transparent tubing into her mouth and sucked on it, savoring the liquid's mildly spicy flavor on her tongue. Crow pulled his flask from his jacket pocket and sucked down a swallow. He then took out his bottle of Nitro and popped one of the little white pills under his tongue.

"Are you okay?" Jackie asked.

"Just a precaution. As you will soon see, crossing the Void is a mind-bending experience. My mind can take it. I just want to be sure my body can too."

About this hopper theft, CAP ventured, *what were the circumstances? Were you actually involved in it directly or did this Crow person commit the act on his own?*

"Oh for goodness sakes, CAP. We can talk about it after the jump."

"You talking to your computer?" Crow asked.

"I called it back on, now that it can't do anything to keep us from the Void."

Crow barked a laugh. "There's nothing in this universe that can stop us now."

"How will I know when we break through?"

"Oh, you'll know all right." He laughed again. "You'll know."

And she did. After two hours of growing anticipation, straining her eyes to see something that couldn't be detected by even the most sophisticated electronic equipment, she felt a sudden sensation of resistance and release, as if they had popped through the surface of a giant soap bubble. Her surroundings took on an insubstantial, ghostly quality and she had the odd feeling that she was pulling into herself.

"You're on!" Crow barked, breaking her out of her preoccupation with these strange sensations. She shut her eyes to concentrate. Even while a part of her seemed to pull into itself, the rest of her expanded—reaching out into distances she sensed to be cosmic. The part pulling in she mentally linked to the hopper. The expanding component she divided, one part reaching out to Caliban, the other to her father. The three-way split she had practiced. It seemed to be working. A rush of excitement filled her. She had never felt so free—so complete.

The sensation of a burning chest pain distracted her. At first she thought it came from her own body, but she soon realized she was getting it from Crow. He had told her that Void pilots often sense things from others during their jumps. She opened her eyes and saw him slumped back in his recliner, clawing at his uniform. "My pills," he mumbled, his voice so low she almost couldn't hear him. "Need my pills."

Frantically, Jackie pulled at her straps to get her webbing loose. Freed from her seat, she bent over him. His face had paled and his hands felt clammy to her touch as she pushed them away and undid his harness. She reached into his coat pocket where she had seen him place his pill bottle, withdrew it, unscrewed the top, and took one of the tiny pellets between thumb and finger. His mouth hung slackly open and she pushed her fingers past his lips, carefully placing the pill under his tongue.

"Don't worry about me," he lisped between gasps for breath. "Contact Jack. You haven't much time."

His face contorted in pain and he slumped forward.

"Crow!" she yelled as if she could make him hold on through the strength of her voice. Suddenly dizzy, she clung to the back of his recliner.

No, she thought. Can't fall apart now. Have to reach out. She pulled herself back into her seat and again, closed her eyes. Relief coursed through her as she felt a familiar pattern of thoughts, mingling with her own. Father! She tried to draw him to her but sensed a resistance. Something interfered. The shrinking sensation she had experienced all along now increased. She was closing up on herself, like a day-blooming flower, folding its petals in the face of darkness.

—CHAPTER—
7

A numbing chill enveloped Jackie. Water! She was immersed in it! Instinctively, she held back an urge to inhale and opened her eyes. Everything was dark and blurry but she could sense light, somewhere above her. She clawed her way upward—holding back breath—closing off her passages to the liquid world that surrounded her. How long had she gone without air? The pain in her chest seemed unbearable. She felt ready to burst. Her world spun dizzily as she fought to stay conscious.

Just when she felt certain that she couldn't hold on for another second without exploding, her face broke the surface and she sucked in great lungfulls of air, coughing and sputtering with each gasping breath.

Treading water, she shook the wet hair from her eyes. She had no idea where she could be. One moment she had been a pure mental essence, aware only of her selfness. She had reached out, not knowing even what she was reaching for. There had been a sensation of direction. The next thing she knew, she was floundering naked in this lake. A forested shoreline rose in the distance, its closest point several hundred yards away. She struck out for it, still coughing and hacking to clear her chest.

Each time she coughed she swallowed more water. She couldn't get a steady rhythm going. Her arm muscles strained with each movement. Just a few more, she kept telling herself, only a few more strokes. But she was tiring fast. She tried floating on her back, but still the coughing persisted. She had to keep going.

When her feet finally touched ground, she cried out with relief. But as she staggered into the shallows, the return of body weight proved too much. She fell to her knees. She crawled onto dry land and flopped facedown, grateful for the feel of the sandy grit under her chin and stomach. Gradually, the pounding of her heart and her rasping coughs eased. She rolled onto her back and squinted into the sky.

It had a purplish cast, as did the several puffy cloud formations that drifted high above her. The sun looked slightly larger than that she was used to and seemed a deeper shade of yellow. No matter. She welcomed its warmth on her body. A puff of cloud passed before the sun and she shivered, not so much from the cold as from a sudden sense of vulnerability. She was naked and without resources. And she hadn't the slightest idea of where she might be.

Good Lord, she thought, how did I ever get here? She remembered Crow dying, and the feeling of shrinking in on herself. Tears filled her eyes. Their plan had almost worked. She had felt her father's presence—tried to draw him to her. But there had been resistance.

And what had happened after that? She had become lost in nothingness, without physical sensations. Then, she had reached out and found herself here, fighting for breath, beating her way up through cold, dark waters. It made no sense. If she had somehow escaped from the Void she should be in her hopper, somewhere near the system of Caliban, not on an unknown planet in the middle of a lake.

Perplexed, she sat up and let her gaze sweep the surrounding forests. A balmy breeze caressed her naked skin. Could this be Caliban? She didn't think so. Caliban was a light gravity planet, no bigger than Mars. Here, her weight felt about the same as on Earth.

It occurred to her to ask CAP. CAP had a comprehensive database covering all the known planets in the galaxy. He could surely advise her. "CAP," she said but no response followed. Only a feeling of emptiness where his presence should be. The open silence of lake and sky heightened her feeling of aloneness. For the first time in her life, she suddenly realized, she was completely on her own. No Conservatory, no Crow, and no CAP. She could still sense her father when she reached out to him, but all she could discern was that he lived.

Stiffly, she rose to her feet, squeezed the water from her hair, and brushed at the damp grains of sand that clung to her skin. Once more, she scanned the entire shoreline, just to assure herself that there were no signs of habitation. Then, turning her back on the bright waters of the lake, she headed up the beach towards the forest. She had to explore her surroundings—find someone to help her. Besides, she thought, looking down at the whiter portions of her body, if I don't get some shade pretty soon, certain parts of me are going to get seriously sunburned.

She picked her way carefully among the thick, twining root systems of the wide-branching trees. With their broad, glossy leaves they reminded her of figs. There was relatively little undergrowth beneath their canopy. Fallen leaves carpeted most of the ground, giving it a springy cushioning feel. Still, she watched where she placed her feet. Not used to going barefoot, she had no wish to step on a sharp twig or rock. Or even worse, something alive.

The trees grew only thirty feet or so in height, spreading their branches to twice that distance. Vines with large, exotic blooms twined their way up many of their smooth grayish trunks. Like a tropical forest, she thought, but without all the tangle—almost as if designed for easy, shoeless walking.

The plants appeared more Earth-like than she would have expected. Perhaps some rich landowners had terraformed a portion of the planet. If so, they might live somewhere near. A happy thought.

Much of the sparse undergrowth had a lacy fern-like appearance. She toyed with the idea of tying some of the longer fronds together in a makeshift skirt, but the vines were too thick to use as string and there was little else to serve the purpose. She began to appreciate the difficulties that stone-age peoples must have experienced finding ways to clothe themselves.

A strange whoop-whoop sound from off to her right made her jump. She looked about, trying to locate its source, but saw nothing. A few minutes later, something like a foot-long dragonfly buzzed her head. Startled, she squealed and ducked behind a tree, her heart pounding wildly.

Holding her hand to her chest, she started forward more cautiously. Just then, something small and quick moving slithered from beneath her foot and scrambled off into the brush. She shrieked and yanked back the foot, setting it down with great care. Shivering, she hugged herself tightly.

I've got to calm down, she told herself. There's bound to be all sorts of animal life about. I can't throw a fit every time something moves. Too bad I never picked up on any of the "Jungle Queen" tri-Ds. That's a role I could use about now. Maybe I'd feel more confident if I had some sort of protection.

She found a fallen branch and broke off a length of it. It was too slender to be much of a weapon but at least she could bat away any smaller creatures that came too close. Anyway, holding the stick made her feel better. She carried it like a spear and tried to conjure up a jungle queen image but without much success. Her situation had become far too realistic for play-acting.

After what her legs told her must have been several miles of hiking, she came across a shallow creek, several feet wide, that trickled its way back down toward the lake. She was about to hop over it when some indentations in the soft mud along its bank caught her attention. She blinked and looked more closely. Footprints! Human footprints! The prints were shorter and considerably broader than her own feet, but the toe and heel marks looked decidedly human.

Children, she thought. Children would be more likely to run around barefoot. And going barefoot might make your feet spread. Just the opposite of binding them up like the Chinese did. That could explain why the prints looked so broad.

Her skin tingled with excitement. They had to be human footprints. No other life forms on the Void-linked planets could make tracks like these. To find help she had only to follow them. How embarrassing, though—to have to walk up to strangers naked and introduce yourself. She could only hope she would find something to cover herself with along the way.

Not far from the stream she ran across a well-traveled path leading back into the interior of the forest. She could see more of the same sort of footprints in the red clay soil. She quickened her pace. Her state of undress aside, she needed to contact the makers of these footprints.

A brief session of rapid walking brought her to the base of a cliff that rose some thirty feet above the path. Trickles of water seeped down a rock face softened by mosses, pooling to form the beginnings of a stream, probably the one she had crossed on her trek up from the lake.

The path she followed split here to run in both directions along the base of the cliff. The branch to her left seemed more heavily marked with footprints, so she chose that direction. A half-mile further along, she could see up ahead where the trees drew back from the cliff face, forming a clearing. Still embarrassed about her nudity, she slipped off the trail back into the forest a ways to look the situation over before barging into the open.

Moving from tree to tree and bush to bush, she worked her way up to where she could crouch behind one of the fern-like growths that edged the clearing. She caught a whiff of smoke and saw the charred remains of a fire in a pit edged with rocks. Behind it, rose the cliff. Along its base a large animal hide had been hung on a frame made of branches. It partially covered an opening into the face of the rock. The accommodations seemed primitive for a people who had terraformed a planet. But perhaps they were camping.

Taking a deep breath, she left the trees and cautiously approached the animal hide. Crossing over large, flat boulders, she noticed several shallow depressions. She had seen similar indentations in boulders in the foothills east of San Diego. Her father had told her that Indian women made them by grinding corn or grain into meal.

As she drew closer to the framed hide she saw, as she had suspected, that it covered an entrance to a cave. She paused there and listened. No sounds from within.

"Hey!" she called, "anybody home?"

No response.

She lifted the hide covering and peered inside, wrinkling her nose at a musky animal stench. It was too dark to see clearly. She pulled the hide off the frame to let more light in. The cave appeared large enough to hold several dozen people. The floor was strewn with piles of small pelts that might be used as bedding. In these ragged strips of fur she saw a solution to a most pressing problem. She stepped inside, laid down her spear-stick, and gathered up several of the pelts. By knotting them together and hanging them about her hips, she fashioned a rough sort of short, furry skirt.

She now directed her attention to a stack of broad strips of animal hide, piled together in one cleared corner. Picking up one of the strips, she rubbed it between thumb and finger. The skin felt reasonably soft and pliable. She gathered several of them and tied them together, adjusting them around her neck and breasts in a makeshift halter. A few adjustments and her covering fit fairly well.

Feeling a little less vulnerable, she poked around to see what else the place might offer. Traces of food lay about the floor. She found sprinklings of grain, some withered remains that might once have been apple cores, a few nutshells, and a quantity of small animal bones. Strings of cooked meat still clung to some of the bones.

She peered into a crudely woven basket of reeds and found it held a quantity of whole nuts, fruit, grain, and tubers. The sight of them reminded her how hungry she was. If humans had gathered these they should be safe to eat. She picked up a small, purplish fruit and took an experimental bite. She found it tasty if a bit tart.

In a cleared area of the cave she found a pile of small rounded rocks and pieces of a rough mineral she recognized as flint. Nearby lay a cutting blade chipped from a dark glassy material. Obsidian, she thought.

She picked up the blade to examine it. But an odd hooting sound from outside the cave drew her attention.

Quickly, she moved to the cave's entrance, snatching up her spear-stick in one hand, and holding the blade in her other. There she paused. She had been so anxious to make contact with other humans, she had more or less assumed they would welcome her. But she had also assumed them to be a technically advanced people. The inhabitants of this cave lived under the most primitive conditions. If their customs were as rough-edged as their lifestyle, they might resent a stranger coming in and making free with their belongings.

Too late, she thought, to worry about that now. Better to meet them outside the cave than to have them come upon me inside it. If nothing else, I can always run. She forced a smile of welcome on her lips and stepped out into the bright sunlight, squinting and blinking. There, at the entrance to the clearing, stood a half-dozen strange looking creatures, staring back at her. Erect and unmoving as if poised for flight, they looked something like a cross between apes and bears, with long, silky, apricot-colored hair. They were no more than five feet in height, a good half foot shorter than herself. But clearly adults. Even with the hair covering their bodies, she could see they had well-developed breasts.

The creatures seemed even more shocked by her appearance than she was by theirs. Shrieking in chorus, they turned and plunged back into the woods. Not humans then. But what were they? No such bizarre combination of animal features existed on any of the known worlds. If they did she would have certainly come across them in her studies. And they were intelligent, at least at a stone-age level of technology. She needed to find a way to communicate with these timid creatures—to learn something about this impossible world where she had landed. Perhaps there were other, more advanced beings here. But how was she to communicate with these silly things if they wouldn't come near her?

No point in running after them, she thought. It would only frighten them all the more. If this was their home they were bound to return to it sooner or later. She scanned the edge of the forest. They could even be watching her now from behind the trees and bushes. Maybe if they saw her acting peaceably they wouldn't be so frightened. They were bound to be curious about her.

She decided to start a fire. That would, at least, show them they had something in common. She gathered sticks from the edge of the forest and dried leaves from beneath the trees, keeping alert for any signs of the creatures' return. She placed her gatherings in the fire circle and returned to the cave to retrieve some of the pieces of flint she had seen. Back out at the fire circle, she practiced drawing sparks with them. It wasn't easy, but she was beginning to get the knack of it when she thought she saw movement in the trees out of the corner of her eye.

I was right, she thought, they are curious and looking me over. The question now is whether or not to let them know I've seen them. She didn't want to scare them off again. If she pretended not to notice them, they might come closer.

The quiet of the moment was shattered by an angry roar. Jackie leapt to her feet. One of the creatures had stepped into the clearing. This brute, however, stood well over six feet tall and was darker than the others, a sort of reddish-brown. It was clearly male and clearly upset. To make its point it howled again, displaying an impressive set of fangs. Then, glaring fiercely, it lumbered toward her, across the clearing.

All thoughts of establishing contact were immediately abandoned. Grabbing up her stick and blade, she darted down the rocky slope in the opposite direction from the beast and plunged into the forest.

—CHAPTER—
8

Jackie ran like she had never run in her life. Fear gave her a strength and energy beyond the ordinary. She bounded through the trees with amazing swiftness. She was an Olympic runner, leaving her beastly competitor trailing far behind, howling out its rage and frustration.

The toughness of her feet surprised her. She had seldom gone without shoes. And while the ground was carpeted in leaves, there were stones and twigs underfoot. But she skimmed over them lightly in her flight, scarcely seeming to touch the ground. She had heard that the effects of an adrenaline rush could be startling. Now, she believed it.

Glancing back over her shoulder, she saw the beast had fallen further behind. Either it couldn't keep up the pace or it didn't see her as worth the effort. Panting for breath, she slowed to a less demanding trot that she could keep up without over-extending herself.

What were these creatures she had stumbled on? The male appeared to be of the same specie as the females although considerably larger and more powerful. But they shouldn't exist. No intelligent, tool-using life forms had been reported on any of the station planets. A pang struck her as she realized what this meant. She could be on an unexplored world—lacking in any form of advanced technology.

She tightened her lips. She shouldn't leap to conclusions. At the start of space explorations on Earth, parts of Africa and South America still had tribes living under stone-age conditions. Perhaps one of the Void-linked planets had intelligent life forms that remained unrecognized. But the odds didn't favor it. She had to face the fact that she might be marooned here for the rest of her life. She slowed to a walk. She had to put such thoughts from her mind. She couldn't afford to wallow in misery—had to concentrate on surviving. Before, she had tried to visualize herself as a huntress. Now, despite her spear and knife, she was most definitely the prey.

Up ahead, she heard the sound of moving water. Her random path of flight had led her to another small stream. As she was about to leap over it, she had a thought. If the creature was still following her, she could throw it off her trail by wading in the water. The stream would hide her tracks and scent. At least that was how it worked in the tri-Ds.

She stopped and glanced back the way she had come. The beast wasn't in sight. She decided to head up-stream, away from the lake. Its sandy beaches were too open and exposed. She stepped gingerly into the water and gasped at the cold bite of the current as it swirled about her calves.

But Jackie quickly adapted. She actually found the coolness refreshing and soothing to her feet. Thirsty from her run, she bent down, cupped her hands, and drank of the sweet, clear liquid. But as she trudged on through the swirl, she found it hard not to lose her footing on the rocks. After a few hundred yards of bruising her limbs and dousing her body from slips and falls, she finally left the stream to continue along its bank.

Before long, she saw outcroppings of rock up ahead. The stream had led her back to a continuation of the cliff wall that housed the creatures. Fearing there might be some of them about, she hid behind a patch of heavy brush. But she saw no caves in the rock face—no fire pits or other signs of habitation. Even so, she decided it wasn't a good place to be. The creatures might commonly use the trail that ran along the cliff face.

Feeling greatly put upon, she turned back into the forest. Left with nowhere to go, she suddenly felt the effects of the day's activities. Her shoulders and leg muscles ached and her body stung with the many scratches she had taken while escaping and hiding in the brush. She felt hungry too, but almost too tired to care. As soon as she was well out of sight of the cliff face, she let herself drop to the ground. Must be late afternoon, she decided. Shadows were lengthening and the daylight softening. It had been a tough day for her—mentally and physically. She had found her way in and out of the Void, half drowned in a lake, hiked naked all over the countryside, and been chased by something fierce and hairy that she couldn't even give a name to. It was enough for anybody. She would rest now and put her mind to planning her next move.

Now she regretted having left all the flints behind in her mad rush to escape. A crackling fire would be welcome. Except it might not be a good an idea to advertise her location to that big hairy thing. A moot point since she had nothing to make a fire with anyway.

Looking about, she found an area of denser growth. Careful to leave no bent or broken branches as a sign of her passing, she crawled among the fern-like shrubbery and covered herself with a mulch of leaves, for warmth as well as concealment. At least the crackling brown leaves had a pleasant smell.

With no immediate threat, her thoughts returned to her long-term prospects. A lump formed in her throat. She was as badly lost now as she had been as a bodiless entity in the Void. She had no one to turn to—not Crow, not CAP, and not her father. She had failed her father. She had been so sure she could retrieve him from the Void—so certain she had the power. And all she had accomplished was to sacrifice Crow's life. Aware of his weak heart and drinking habits, she had recruited him anyway. Because of her, he had died. And all for nothing. Tears rolled down her cheeks. She tried to imagine herself back under the clean smelling sheets and soft quilt of her bed at the Conservatory, but the reality of her situation was too much with her. Only when her thoughts had exhausted all the depressing probabilities of her future did she finally drift off into a dreamless slumber.

She woke and looked about her, puzzled by the sounds of birds twittering and scratching about in the brush. Gradually, she began to remember the events that led to her being here, covered with leaves. Anxiously, she looked about for any sign of the hairy beast that had chased her. It was nowhere in sight. And the only sounds were of the birds that had wakened her. Again, it occurred to her that a planet's animal life and vegetation couldn't be so Earth-like without terraforming. Humans had to be shaping the biology of this planet. Could they be doing it secretly, without the knowledge of the authorities?

She would have to put the question aside for now. Yesterday had been spent with no more to eat than a sampling of fruit. She was decidedly hungry—famished, in fact, now that she thought about it. And with no way to feed herself. Her only thought had been to get as far away as possible from her hairy pursuer. Now, she realized, she had no place to get away to. She had little knowledge of her surroundings or of the plant and animal life that existed here. If she were to survive, she'd have to find a way to feed herself.

How, she wondered, do primitives find food in the wild? She tried to remember what she had heard or read about tribal peoples—African Bushmen, Australian Aborigines, and natives living along the Amazon River. But she could think of nothing that might help her in her present situation. Those peoples had spent lifetimes learning how to survive in their natural environments and had the resources of their tribes to support them. She was a city girl and alone.

Even so, as the product of a civilized society, she had knowledge of a good many things. There must be experiences she could call on to help her forage for food. One suddenly came to her. Fishing. Her father had taken her out after tuna once, off the coast of Baja. They had rented a powerboat. She could still savor the taste of those fresh tuna steaks when they had grilled them that evening. No ocean here, but the streams might have fish in their waters. No line or tackle either. But she did have her spear-stick. Didn't natives spear fish? She felt sure they did.

She grabbed up her spear-stick and the obsidian knife and trotted back toward the stream she had followed on the previous day. She hadn't noticed anything fish-like in its waters, but then, she hadn't been looking. Now, she walked along the bank, peering down into the swirling flow, searching for the telltale movement of living shadows.

Unable to see that well from the bank, she entered the streambed, starting nervously at any hint of motion beneath the surface. Again and again, she lunged with her spear-stick, only to find herself attacking a floating twig or leaf. She did see some creatures the size of sardines, but they were too small and fast for her to spear them. Besides, the light refraction through the water made everything appear in a different place from where it actually was.

Suddenly, something slippery brushed against her leg.

She shrieked and leapt up onto the mossy bank. Trembling, she stared back down into the stream, looking to see what had slithered up against her. But whatever it was had vanished for the moment, probably lurking nearby, she thought, just waiting for a chance to nip at her.

She shuddered. She was letting her imagination get the best of her. Firming her resolve, she forced herself back into the water. But try as she might, she couldn't spear anything. She just wasn't cut out to be a huntress. And even if she caught something, she'd have no way to cook it. The very thought of eating raw fish made her stomach turn. She doubted she'd be able to keep it down.

She had to face it, if she didn't want to starve she'd have to filch food from the hairy beasts, at least until she found the places where they went to gather their fruits, nuts, and grains. She had to return to the caves. It really isn't all that dangerous, she told herself. The females are more afraid of me than I am of them. And the big male I can easily outrun. As long as she didn't let him trap her she should be safe enough. What she needed to do was sneak back through the woods and find a spot where she could check out things without being seen. Then, if the big male beast wasn't around, she could dart in, grab some food and flints, and get back out before the females set up a howl.

Finding her way back was no problem. She only needed to follow the cliff line. But she stayed off the trail and kept within the woods, not wanting to accidentally run across the big hairy male on the way. As she drew close to the clearing, she dropped back deeper into the forest and moved with greater caution, gliding silently from tree to brush, working her way closer.

She finally reached a sheltered position where she could look out on the cave entrance, the grinding rocks, and the fire pit. She crouched there, muscles tense with remembered fear as she scanned the area, straining ears and eyes for sounds or movement. Feathered creatures with unfamiliar shapes and plumage flitted about the trees, and insects hummed about her, but she saw or heard nothing to indicate that the hairy ones were about. Of course they might be inside the cave. The hide covering had been replaced on the frame over the entrance, so the only way she could tell would be to sneak up and peak in.

Gathering her courage, she slid out from the brush and, in a low crouch, edged her way toward the cave entrance. In passing the fire pit she looked to see if the pieces of flint she had dropped in her flight were still there. They were gone. Obviously too valuable to leave lying around.

Still crouched low, she sidled up to the entrance and listened intently. Only silence within. Slowly, she lifted the corner of the hide covering, just enough so she could see inside. It was hard to make out details within the darkened interior, but she saw nothing of the creatures. She raised the hide higher to get a better view. Again, the musky odor of animal sweat assaulted her, but nothing more. Breathing a thankful sigh, she slipped inside.

Immediately, she went to where she had found the flints and snatched up several chunks of the rough-surfaced mineral. She then turned to the woven reed container that held a supply of food. She had intended to grab the basket and make her getaway without further delay. But a plump, yellowish fruit looked too inviting to put off. She raised it to her lips, biting deeply into its juicy flesh. It tasted heavenly—sweet and succulent if a trifle mushy. Grinning with satisfaction, she added her knife and the flints to the contents of the basket, stuck her spear-stick under her arm, and prepared to leave.

A shadow fell across the mouth of the cave. Jackie spun around. The basket fell from her arms, its contents rolling across the packed earth floor of the cave. The great, hairy male crouched at the entrance, its long arms spread across the opening.

—CHAPTER—
9

Jackie snatched her spear-stick from under her arm and made jabbing motions at the hairy creature as it lurched toward her, fangs bared, arms outspread, like a wrestler seeking a hold. A low, rumbling growl rose from deep within its chest. She had nowhere to retreat to—no room to edge around the grasping, claw-tipped hands.

As it came at her she thrust her spear-stick at his chest. But the powerful beast yanked it away from her and tossed it behind him. She tried to duck under its arm and scoot past it, but claws caught her hair and jerked her backwards. She hit and kicked wildly to free herself, but the creature pulled her to it. With an angry roar it bared its great fangs— inches from her throat.

Feeling its hot breath, Jackie closed her eyes and threw out one last mental cry for help, even though she knew it would be useless.

CAP! Help me CAP!

Who CAP?

The question entered her mind, free of words or images. She opened her eyes, just wide enough to squint at the creature that held her. Then she opened them wider, to stare in growing amazement. Its own beastly red-rimmed eyes gazed back at her with an expression that greatly resembled curiosity. Could this animal have spoken to her mentally?

Trembling in its grasp, she tried to answer back in kind.

CAP is a friend.

Where it? The beast turned its shaggy head to peer about the cave.

I don't know, she projected with overtones of sadness.

Who you?

With the realization that the creature wasn't going to kill her outright, her thoughts poured out in a torrent. *Me? I'm Jackie. I'm sorry about taking your things, but I was naked you see, and hungry, and I didn't know how to find clothes or food or anything . . .* She trailed off, unsure of the effect of her words.

You come hunt me?

Hunt you? Gosh no. I came to get help. I'm lost.

Where territory? it asked, suspicion clear in his mind.

Territory? I have no territory. I'm not from anywhere near here. I don't know how I got here. I don't even know where here is.

Here is here, the creature replied, matter-of-factly and released her hair.

Her body sagged with relief. This was no wild beast but a rational being. That showed promise. *As I say, I really don't know how I got here. But I can tell you what I'm trying to do.*

It wrapped a hairy hand about her wrist and drew her out of the cave. By the fire pit it released her from its powerful grasp and squatted down on the hard-packed earth. *Tell,* it ordered.

Jackie sat facing it and projected mental images, first of herself entering the Mojave International shuttle with Crow and the other passengers, then of the shuttle blasting off from Earth. But before she could continue, a wall of rejection cut her off.

No! the creature yelled. It leapt to its feet, towering over her, its fangs exposed, one great clawed hand drawn back as if to strike. *No more!*

She pulled back, shocked by its reaction. *I'm sorry,* she projected. *I didn't mean to upset you. I won't show you any more.*

Slowly, the wildness left its eyes. It grunted once, then settled back down beside her. Her breathing slowed to normal as she realized that the crisis had passed. She clasped her hands together in her lap to keep them from trembling. The creature had reacted so strongly against the notion of space travel. She would have to be more careful about what she showed him.

Now that it had calmed down, the hairy beast projected an impression of puzzlement—as if there were something about her that bothered it. Maybe it's seen other humans, Jackie mused. She felt tempted to ask him outright. But given its reaction to space travel she decided to hold back on her questioning until she learned a little more about its temperament. Besides, at the moment she had more pressing matters.

"What do you call yourself?" she asked, speaking aloud to see if the mental component of her message was still conveyed.

It apparently was. *Fanth,* came his projected reply.

"Well, Fanth, as much as I'm enjoying our little chat, my stomach is starting to rumble. I'm very hungry. Do you suppose I could have something to eat before we continue?" She formed a mental picture of herself stuffing handfuls of fruits and nuts into her mouth.

Fanth gave a growl of concurrence and led her back to the cave. He pointed at the basket she had dropped. Jackie quickly retrieved three of the yellow, plum-sized fruits and hungrily gobbled them down while Fanth looked on.

"What do you call your people?" she asked, wiping the

sweet, sticky juice from her mouth with her hand.

Hairy Hunters.

She smiled. "A descriptive title. How many of you are there?"

Me and five females.

"In your group. I understand. But aren't there other Hairy Hunter groups?"

Only us in this territory.

"Who lives in the territories around you?"

Other beings: Climbers, Swimmers, Flyers.

Flyers? Could he be talking about life forms with an advanced technology? "Tell me more about these Flyers. How do they fly?"

They Flyers so they fly. Do you ask if real?

His response confused her. "What do you mean by real?"

You real—I real.

Jackie sighed. "I guess the only way to find out about these others is to see them for myself."

Flyers not friendly. They attack—they kill.

Jackie frowned. This was not encouraging. But maybe Fanth was overstating the case. He hadn't appeared all that friendly at first himself. But since they were on the subject of other creatures, she decided to ask about humans.

"Fanth," she said, peering up at him, "have you ever seen or heard of others who look like me?"

He stared at her, and for a moment she thought he was going to say yes. But he finally shook his shaggy head and sent out a mental message of negation.

Her hopes deflated like a ruptured balloon. She was isolated, not only cut off from her father, but from all of humanity. "How am I ever going to get out of this place?" she wailed.

Stay with Fanth—be his female.

She drew back, startled by his suggestion. "Fanth has enough females already," she said flatly.

Females not real, Fanth projected with sulky overtones, like a child deprived of a desired treat.

She had no idea what he meant by this. "Real or not," she said, projecting an impression of firmness, "you'll have to make do with what you have. I can't stay here. I have to find someone who can help me leave this world."

Fanth suddenly looked toward the entrance to the cave. Jackie turned to see several of the apricot-colored females peering in at them. Apparently they felt braver now that Fanth was there to deal with the stranger. Still, they stayed back, sniffing the air with wiggling noses.

Jackie tried to reassure them mentally but found them difficult to read. Their projections were weak and simplistic, as if their minds were too feeble to convey thoughts with any degree of complexity. Perhaps, she thought, that was what Fanth meant in saying they weren't real. Strange though, that the females of this species should be so mentally inferior to the males.

While Jackie had no intention of remaining with Fanth, she did want to stick around long enough to pick up some lessons in survival. Over the next few days she accompanied him and his females on their forays to gather food. She learned where to find fruit and nut trees, how to dig up edible roots and tubers, and how to hunt the small, tree-dwelling animals that resembled fat-nosed tailless possums and bring them down with sling-thrown stones. Fanth even taught her how to take light refraction into account when spearing fish. He allowed her to keep the obsidian blade and made her a sturdier spear-stick, attaching a sharp flake of obsidian as a point. But still, he continued to argue against her leaving.

Other territories have different plants and animals, he warned her. *Dangerous beings too.*

"I'll just have to learn to deal with them," she replied. She suspected he might simply be trying to discourage her from leaving. "Why don't you come with me?" she suggested. "It would be a big help having you as a guide." Fanth merely grunted in response, leaving her with the feeling that he wasn't about to abandon his territory for any such ill-fated adventure.

She had actually grown fond of the big male. He had been patient in instructing her in gathering food and hunting and had made no further suggestions about her becoming one of his females. He seemed fascinated with her. Again and again, she caught him watching her, projecting conflicting emotions—as if there were something about her that both bothered him and drew him to her.

The females, in contrast, showed little interest in her. Her initial impression that they were brainless ninnies hadn't changed. She had given up trying to communicate with them. Their only interests seemed to be gathering food and vying for Fanth's sexual favors when they bedded down in the cave. Jackie had quickly decided that the fire pit was a better place for her to spend the night. The weather was mild and there were plenty of pelts to wrap around her for warmth. And by sleeping outside she avoided the objectionable odors that permeated the cave and the grunts and squirming of copulation that went on late into the night.

Besides, she liked to gaze up at the thickly strewn pinpoints of light that filled the night sky with a brightness more intense than anything she'd ever seen on Earth. We must be closer to the center of the galaxy here, she thought, to have such a density of stars about us. The planet's two satellites were small, pale things, half the size of Earth's moon. They traveled at different speeds as they arched across the sky. The slower one, called "Hunter," by Fanth, had a rich amber color. The faster, which he called "Flyer," was slightly smaller and more silvery. Silver and Gold, she thought. Un-reachable riches. She might well spend the rest of her life on this isolated world, cut off from the wealth of human civilization that lay beyond its skies. The thought of it constantly oppressed her.

After a week with the Hairy Hunters she felt ready to set off on her own. She might have no real hope of getting off this planet or helping her father, but she had to try. She especially wanted to meet some of the flying ones Fanth had spoken of. According to him, each type of creature had areas or territories that they controlled.

"You might at least guide me into the Flyers' territory," she urged.

I bring you to edge of Flyers' lands. No more. Here I strong—fight off those who hunt me. There I weaker.

She found his response puzzling. She could understand that he might not want to leave his own territory. But equating that with losing his strength seemed odd to her. Perhaps it was just that he felt more confident in his own territory than in one strange to him. Or he might simply be making up reasons for not bringing her to the Flyers. She looked up at him, wondering what intentions might be hiding below the threshold of his projections.

"All right then," she said. "You bring me to the edge of their territory and I'll make it from there on my own. But one way or another, I'm leaving tomorrow." She was anxious to get going after all the time she had wasted, and worried that he might come up with other excuses to delay her. But he only grunted his agreement. Tomorrow they would leave. She only wished she had a clearer picture as to what lay ahead.

—CHAPTER—
10

Early the next morning, Jackie and Fanth left the cave area and headed west, toward the territory of the Flyers. They traveled at an easy pace, stopping often to gather fruits or hunt the small, possum-like creatures that Fanth brought down with well-placed rocks. That evening they camped by a stream that cascaded wildly down a rocky slope. More than ten feet across, it was the largest and swiftest body of running water that she had seen in Fanth's territory.

Fanth roasted the possum-creatures over a crackling fire. From the way he fussed over his catch, holding them up for her to see how plump they were, and bringing her choice portions of their roasted flesh, Jackie suspected him of trying to impress her as a provider, hoping to change her mind about leaving. She did appreciate Fanth's help and felt bad about having to leave him behind. He'd been her only companion since her loss of Crow and CAP in the Void. And he was highly skillful. He was quite good at hunting and clever at making things from wood, stone, or animal bones and skins. At times he even displayed a sense of humor. He nearly laughed his head off when Jackie bit into a particularly sour fruit and went through a pantomime of being poisoned.

But there was something that deeply troubled him. Whenever she asked about his past and how he was raised he became agitated and seemed unable to give her any kind of satisfactory answer. *Can't remember,* he would say and refuse to talk about it further.

On the morning of their third day of travel they came to the edge of Fanth's forest. Beyond it, lay open plains, carpeted with high waving grasses. Off in the distance a solitary mound of rock rose up above the plains like a fortress. Fanth stopped to sniff the air and pointed a clawed finger in the direction of the towering rock formation.

Flyers there, he announced, projecting alertness and caution.

Jackie gazed at the distant flat-topped formation. "That looks awfully steep, and nearly a hundred feet high. How am I supposed to climb it?"

No way to climb.

"Then how do I get to the Flyers?"

They see you on plains, they attack.

"But I need to talk with them. There are things I want to ask. You told me that they mind-talk. If I project my thoughts they'll know I'm friendly."

Fanth's frustration ran clear in his own thought projection. *Flyers not care about friendly. You come back with Fanth.*

She went over to the big creature, threw her arms around his neck and gave him a loving hug. "I know that you want me to stay. But there's someone I need to find. And I need help to find him—help you can't give me. Maybe the Flyers can."

She gave him one more hug. "Goodbye you big old teddy-bear." She sniffed once, regretting the lack of tissues in a stone-age culture. "Take good care of your females," she called back over her shoulder as she strode out of the forest and onto the grassy plains. Fanth didn't answer and by the time she glanced back for one last look, he had disappeared into the trees. Just as well, she thought. Leaving him is hard enough without drawing it out. I should be thankful he didn't put up a bigger fuss. He must have sensed how determined I was.

The sun warmed her skin as she trudged toward the distant towering mound of rock through waist-high grasses, using her spear as a walking stick. By now she had stopped worrying about sunburns. She seemed to adapt to conditions more easily here than she ever did on Earth. The chill of night and the heat of day didn't bother her, at least not as much as she would have expected. Even running around in her bare feet had given her little trouble. And she felt stronger and more energetic than she had ever felt in her life.

Must be something about living out in nature, she mused. I never realized how easy it is to adapt to the great outdoors when you live in it like a native. Maybe something in the genes.

Before long, however, her sense of well-being was replaced by a vague wariness. Several times she felt as if she were being watched. Each time she stopped and looked about her, searching for any sort of living thing within her field of view, she saw nothing but grass, sky, and sun.

Just nerves, she decided. I shouldn't let Fanth's paranoid warnings upset me. To him, any stranger is an enemy. He even thought I was there to harm him. Still, she continued to keep a watchful eye about her and gripped her spear more firmly as she continued.

When the sun hung overhead in the cloudless violet sky she stopped for a rest, plopping down in the middle of the great, grassy plain. She pulled out the hide water pouch Fanth had given her at the start of their journey and took a brief swallow, aware of her need to conserve the precious liquid. The pouch was tightly sewn and waterproofed on the inside seams with a resinous substance, more evidence of Fanth's skills.

She lay back, buried in the sweet-smelling grasses, and gazed off toward the great flat-topped mound of rock. Such an unusual formation, she thought, jutting up like that from the middle of the plain. Why would anyone live in such a place? For protection? There didn't seem to be anything here to protect themselves from. Fanth hadn't mentioned anything dangerous except the Flyers themselves. It seemed an odd place for landing aircraft. But who knew what sorts of devices these creatures might use?

She wondered if they had seen her yet. That could explain her feeling of being watched. The great rock mound still seemed so far away. Looking back, she could see that she hadn't left much of a trail. The tough grasses flattened in passing had already sprung back upright. Nothing to draw the Flyers' attention.

While still at a distance, she might be close enough to call to them mentally. She had no idea if she could project her thoughts that far, but it was certainly worth a try. Without getting up, she closed her eyes and concentrated on broadcasting them far out beyond her, as if shouting to someone in the distance.

Please hear me, she projected, *I am a friend. I need your help.*

A distant surge of feeling drifted back to her. The projections were faint but the emotions generating them were strong—a roiling anger mixed with fright and suspicion. *Enemy!* it warned. *Enemy in our territory!* Jackie sat up and looked anxiously toward the great mound, shading her eyes. Two small specks now hung above the towering plateau. They quickly dropped out of sight against the dark cliff face. For several minutes she searched the empty sky, trying to detect them. Then she spotted them again, closer now.

At this distance she found it difficult to judge their size. But they seemed small for aircraft.

As the Flyers drew closer, any hope that they might be a race of advanced beings that had mastered motorized flight quickly faded. These were winged creatures, giant birds or bird-like humanoids. She began to pick up their hostile thoughts again, more clearly than before. Their communications were clipped, and heavy with emotional embellishments. One recognizable message kept repeating itself, tossed back and forth between them. *Kill intruders!*

Again, Jackie tried to project her desire for friendship. But the impact of her thoughts only seemed to increase their fury. Fanth hadn't exaggerated. These creatures were anything but friendly. Once more, she regretted not having CAP to call on, even though the computer could have done little more than offer her advice and comfort.

As the Flyers drew closer Jackie saw that their white feathered bodies were indeed as large as humans with a wingspan two to three times their height. They came on swiftly. In these open fields there would be no point in her running, no chance of escape. She could only stand and face them. Realizing this, a strange calm fell on her. She was a warrior princess facing her foes. If all she could do was die defending herself, she would do it with dignity. She grasped the shaft of her spear firmly in both hands and braced her legs beneath her.

The Flyers swooped in swiftly, aiming to pass her on both sides at once. Black eyes glared from sharp, beak-like faces. Their sinewy arms, separate from their wings, cradled long, three-pronged tridents. Twisting to the left, she jabbed at a Flyer with her spear. Pain clawed her back as the other one raked her in passing.

She yelped, seeing the flaw in her defense. Whichever

side she went for, the Flyer on the opposite side would attack. She had to even the odds. And quickly.

As they made a second pass, she hurled her spear at the
Flyer on her right and flung herself to the ground to avoid
the other. Her spear streaked past its target—a close miss.
The Flyers passed over her and circled back.

Her weapon lay out of reach, too far away to recover before they were on her. Ignoring the warm trickle of blood
down her shoulder, she rose to a crouch and pulled out her
obsidian blade. She had little faith she could throw it with
any accuracy, but it was all that was left to her.

They came in low on either side, tridents stretched out
to meet her. She drew back her hand.

Suddenly, a great, dark form sprang from the grasses,
grasping one of the Flyers in its arms. Beast and Flyer
plunged heavily to the ground.

"Fanth!" she yelled, hardly able to believe it.

The other Flyer, veered in flight and turned about
sharply. Seeing that, she stepped forward and hurled her
blade with all her strength. It sped toward the Flyer, spin-
ning end over end, light flickering from its chipped surface,
to strike him hilt-first, alongside the head.

The Flyer screeched and dropped his trident. Jackie
pounced on the weapon and swung it up into a defensive
position. The Flyer beat its wings strongly, rising beyond
her reach.

I tell Master! Its mental message fairly shrieked, sharp-
edged with feelings of hatred. *Master destroy intruders!* It
spiraled upward in a wide curve, banked sharply, and
headed off in a westerly direction.

Jackie turned to where Fanth lay unmoving beneath the
Flyer.

"Fanth!" she cried, and ran to him.

Wings stirred and the Flyer's body rolled aside. Slowly, Fanth rose, his dark reddish-brown coat smeared with gore.

"You're hurt!"

He spread his arms and looked down at his blood-matted front. *Blood not mine,* he projected, his mouth a grinning display of crimson-stained fangs. He shook himself like a big shaggy dog. *Where other?*

Jackie let out a sigh of relief. "It flew away after I bounced my knife off its head. I guess it didn't like the change of odds." She cocked her head and placed her hands on her hips. "And just where did you come from?"

Fanth brushed at his soiled fur ineffectively. *When you go, I follow.*

"You followed me?" No wonder she had the feeling she was being watched. "But why did you stay hidden?"

Fanth shifted his feet uneasily. *I know Flyers attack. I want catch by surprise.*

She threw her arms around his neck and hugged him fiercely. "You saved my life. I should have listened to you." She let go and took a step backward. "But I don't understand why you followed me. I thought you didn't want to leave your territory."

He stared into her face, as if trying to see something there that he couldn't quite make out. *Jackie makes Fanth remember. If Jackie goes, Fanth forgets.*

She eyed him sharply. "I make you remember? Remember what?"

Again, he shifted his feet. *Others like you.*

She felt a catch in her throat. "Others like me? You said there were no others like me."

Only sometimes—in night sleeps . . .

"You've dreamed about them?"

His eyes clouded and he scratched a place behind an ear

with a claw. *Makes itch to think.*

Something strange was going on here. How could Fanth dream about humans if he had never seen them? Jackie could sense a feeling of buried knowledge that Fanth couldn't reach. She felt sympathetic, but frustrated. He had been on the edge of a revelation and had closed his mind to it. Something was blocking his memory. Perhaps if he stayed she might be able to get him to open up.

"If you're willing to leave your females, I'll be happy to have you join me. As a friend," she added after a moment's thought.

Females not real, Fanth grunted, seemingly indifferent to their fate. Jackie gave an inner sigh of relief. There would be time to tease out Fanth's dream memories.

They searched the area until they found her knife and spear. Then they discussed the best direction to take. "I still need to find others I can talk with," she told him. "I want to learn as much about this world as I can. Where can we find friendlier types?"

Fanth pointed to where the oversized sun hung high in the western sky. Jackie nodded and they set out again, heading west through the tall grasses, the towering mound of rock on their right. From time to time she'd glance in its direction, alert for flying specks in the distance. But no more of the hostile creatures were sighted. Despite the one's dark threats, they had, apparently, had enough of Jackie and Fanth for now.

"Fanth," she said, "what do you know about a being the Flyer called the Master?"

Fanth shook his shaggy head. *Only know Flyers attack all who pass. Sometimes fly over other territories.*

"These friendly ones you are leading me to—would they be likely to know anything about the Master?"

Ask when there, Fanth replied and she could pull nothing more from him for the remainder of the day.

By sunset they stood at the edge of another forest, its trees casting shadowy projections towards them as the red-gold sun sank lower in the sky. The vegetation here differed greatly from the sparse growth that covered Fanth's territory. The trees grew smaller and were thick with under-brush, more like the woodlands in the eastern portions of the United States. Strange, she thought, that the plant life should change so much in so short a distance, and for no obvious reason. Again, it reminded her of planned terraforming. But who in these primitive lands would have the technology to accomplish such transformations?

According to Fanth, it would take them another full day's travel to reach the friendly ones he had spoken of. There was no point in continuing on this late in the day so they camped on the edge of the woods, building a fire on a rocky patch of ground where it was unlikely to spread.

Fanth located a shallow stream nearby he remembered from a previous excursion. He stood knee-deep, cupping his hands to splash water over his chest and down his thighs—washing away blood and grime. Jackie followed him in, shivering in its flow, dabbing gingerly at herself with moist-ened hands. Surprisingly, her back where the trident had raked her didn't hardly feel sore.

They replenished their supply of drinking water at a point upstream from where they'd bathed and settled down by the fire. Jackie hadn't eaten since morning and was acutely aware of the emptiness in her stomach.

"When are we going to have our next meal?" she asked, hoping to prod Fanth into food gathering.

Tomorrow, he projected.

With no prospects for food, she found she could put the thought of it out of her mind without too much effort. That surprised her. She had never been one to skip a meal easily. More evidence of her ability to adapt to the demands of nature.

They sat there as the world grew dark around them, listening to the small sounds of night things, wrapped in thoughts that they kept to themselves. The bright band of the Milky Way glittered brilliantly in the now moonless sky.

"Do you know there are other worlds up there among those little points of light?" she asked.

Fanth growled deep in his throat. *No other worlds for Fanth. All forgotten.*

"What do you mean 'forgotten'?" she demanded, alerted by the phrasing of his mental message.

Fanth tired—no more talk. He stretched long-limbed arms up toward the heavens, then rolled over and turned his back to her, his auburn pelt catching highlights from the fire's blaze. Frustrated, Jackie lay awake, staring into the fire, as if she might find in its dancing flames the answers that kept eluding her.

—CHAPTER—
11

Jackie woke to Fanth's clawed hand, gently shaking her by the shoulder.

When day come, not good sleep in open this near Flyers. We go now.

The morning dew moistened her bare feet as they hiked along the edge of the forest. The thick undergrowth appeared all but impassable. She had just about convinced herself they would have to hack their way in through the brambles with spear and blade when Fanth grunted and pointed a curved nail at a point twenty yards ahead. As they drew nearer, she saw there was an opening into the heavy foliage. No well trodden path, but a game trail of a sort that might be used by deer or other large animals.

Fanth plunged ahead and Jackie followed, keeping far enough behind to avoid back-springing branches. Her skin, largely exposed by her skimpy covering of pelts and hide strips, was all too vulnerable to thorns and twigs.

"You say the inhabitants of this territory are friendly?" she asked as she carefully pushed aside a branch. "What sort of creatures are they?"

Young, Fanth replied. *Much play.*

"They're children?" She had wondered why there were no babies or juveniles among Fanth's tribe. "Are they Hairy Hunters?"

You see soon.

"I'd think you could tell me something about them. And about this place we're headed for. Will you be able to find us food? I haven't eaten since yesterday morning."

You see soon, he repeated.

Jackie lapsed into an irritated silence. She was having little luck in digging information out of Fanth. And there was so much she needed to know. The Flyers had certainly been no help. And it seemed doubtful that any sort of young creatures would be either. There should be adults here too, but Fanth hadn't mentioned any. She sighed in frustration. If these creatures were anything like Fanth's females, they'd be worthless.

Several hours later the narrow trail ended on the shores of a large, almost circular pond, three to four hundred yards across. They stepped out from the trees into bright sunshine.

Their waters, Fanth announced.

Jackie shaded her eyes. "I don't see any signs of life."

Fanth grinned toothily. He threw his head back and let rip a wild howl. A series of answering yips came from across the lake. *Fanth!—Fanth!—Fanth!* the greeting clamored wildly into her consciousness. She looked off across the pond. Two dark heads cut through the water, trailing a wake behind them. They drew together. Suddenly sleek brown bodies were rolling and splashing, like seals at play.

Come, Fanth projected with gruff overtones, *I bring visitor.*

Amused by their antics, Jackie turned to Fanth. "They are very different from you. What do you call them?"

Swimmers, Fanth replied. *And friends.*

The pair reached the shore and splashed out of the water. Running upright on their hind legs, they dashed up to Fanth. Jackie watched as the dark-pelted animals flung themselves against her companion, then drew back to shake themselves dry, spraying water from their thick glossy coats. A new humanoid specie—the third she had encountered on this world. She studied them intently. Short and slender, they came no higher than her chin. And despite the thickness of their fur, it was evident that one was female and the other male.

After their vigorous demonstration of their affection for Fanth, they turned to look Jackie over, black button eyes alive with curiosity, noses wiggling to take in her scent.

"Do I get hugs too?" she asked, holding out her arms. To her delight they rushed forward to embrace her. "They're adorable, Fanth. What are your names?"

Krith, the male projected forcefully.

Krit, the female transmitted more shyly.

Fanth interrupted the introductions. *We hungry,* he projected. *You feed?*

Yes, yes, we feed! the two chorused, hopping up and down in their excitement. *Come to great rock.*

They turned about and plunged back into the water, making the same yipping noises they had made on Jackie and Fanth's arrival. Fanth motioned for Jackie to follow and started off around the side of the pond. A ways down the shoreline, they came upon a rocky deposit jutting out into the water, large enough to hold a house. There, the two Swimmers squatted around the beginnings of a fire that sent up wisps of pale-gray smoke. Lying nearby were several large fish, still flopping in protest to their removal from the lake.

Soon, the fish were grilling on hot embers pulled from the flames. Their tantalizing aroma, borne lightly on the lake-fresh air, made Jackie feel all the more famished. Before long she was sitting cross-legged on the flat rock surface, peeling back layers of fire-blackened skin and pinching off morsels of white flesh from the fine featherings of bone.

"Do you live here alone?" Jackie asked the dark-furred duo as they crouched over their own fish dinners, taking delicate bites with small, pointed teeth. Jackie hadn't seen any older versions of the twins about and was beginning to wonder how they came to be here.

Alone, Krith projected, with a touch of sadness. *All alone,* Krit echoed.

"How old are you?" Jackie asked.

They looked at each other, as if unsure how to respond.

Same age, Krith finally projected, *but I bigger.* Krit leaped at Krith and jabbed him in the ribs with webbed fingers. The two rolled around the rock surface, laughing as they wrestled.

Jackie pressed her lips together to keep from giggling. Fun was fun, but she had serious questions to put to these two.

"Please," she said, emphasizing the word. "Do you know anything about the territories near here? Do Flyers ever come this way?"

They stopped rolling about and lay looking up at her reproachfully, their high spirits dampened.

Krith sighed and rose to a sitting position. *Flyers not land here but others come—strange, scaly things with bad thoughts.*

Then we stay hidden, Krit added.

"Have you ever heard of one called the Master?"

They looked at each other.

Once when we hide, Krith said. *Those who come mind-talk of Master, one who sends them.*

Krit nodded. *Very powerful, this Master. Knows all that happens. Makes magic.*

The two crawled over to Fanth to sit by his side, as if

their troubled recollections created a need for protection. They had obviously been frightened by the intruders and their thoughts. But their account of this mysterious Master intrigued Jackie. The marvels of modern technology might well seem magical to primitive creatures. The Master might simply be someone with advanced technical capabilities. She needed to learn more about him.

"Did these others picture this Master being in their minds?" she asked.

They both nodded, their faces solemn.

"Can you picture him for me now?"

They exchanged glances, then set their gaze straight ahead, the black brightness of their eyes taking on a dulling glaze. An image of a face, darkened by shadows, formed in her mind, its features partially hidden within the folds of a loose cowl. But she could discern them well enough to recognize them as human.

Fanth's growl rumbled low from his chest.

Jackie suddenly realized she was holding her breath. She let it out now in a single exhalation. This world had humans. One human at least. And wherever humans traveled there would be spaceships. She turned to Fanth. "Did you see what they projected? The Master is human. He's the one I need to find. Him or others like him. They'll have the knowledge I need."

Fanth growled again. *Danger here,* he projected.

Master bad, Krith agreed.

Bad, Krit repeated. *Not like others before . . .* She paused. Her thoughts lost form, fading like wisps of smoke.

"Before what?" Jackie prodded.

Krit seemed to be losing her hold on whatever she had been thinking. She scratched her head with a clawed finger. *There are sleep memories . . .*

"You too?" Jackie said, thinking of Fanth's confused ramblings about seeing humans in his dreams. She glanced at Fanth. Even with his arms about the twins, his body appeared rigid and tense. Something clearly bothered him.

Jackie looked back at Krit, staring at the young creature as if she could penetrate the juvenile's thoughts with her gaze. "Picture your memories for me," she said, "show me what they hold."

Krit squirmed uncomfortably. *Sleep memories are strange. Disturbing. We never remember much.*

Only when we sleep, Krith agreed.

"But you can try," Jackie pleaded. "At least you can try to make them come."

The twins looked at each other. Finally they nodded, as if having reached an agreement. A few moments of concentration and they began to bring forth a confusing collage of images. There were scenes of cities with tall, glass-fronted buildings. Hundreds of humans moving in shifting crowds, down walkways that bordered wide thoroughfares filled with motorized vehicles. There were repeated images of a family: father, mother, son, and daughter; eating, talking, watching the tri-D. Other visions were of people in luxurious surroundings. The furnishings and appointments had an odd sort of familiarity. Something about them made the hairs rise on the back of Jackie's neck. She suddenly realized why. It was the interior of a Void liner.

Jackie heard Fanth's rumbling growl. The twins' imaginings had moved him too. A new image formed, the broad, ruddy features of a man dressed in a Void pilot's uniform, smiling reassuringly, a face such as one might see on an advertisement for space travel.

Jackie knew it well. This was her father.

—CHAPTER—
12

Shocked by the image of her father Krith projected, Jackie leapt to her feet to stare down at her three companions, her body trembling. They blinked up at her, as if confused by her sudden agitation.

"Where did you see this man?" Jackie rasped, her voice unrecognizably harsh in her ears. "Tell me!"

Krith and Krit drew back against Fanth, wide-eyed.

They are memories of dreams, Krith squeaked.

What we see in sleep, Krit added, *only that.*

Fanth pulled the twins closer. Jackie glowered at him. "How can these overgrown otters hold dream images of my father?" she demanded.

He blinked several times. *I, too, had such dreams. But the images of Krith and Krit are clearer—stronger. They bother me much.*

"They bother you?" An edge of hysteria constricted her throat. "What do you think they do to me?"

You asked them to show you, Fanth said, offering the statement as a mild rebuke.

Jackie fought to control herself—slow her breathing—clear her head. She took deep, surging inhalations of air, swallowing her frustration until her breathing slowed and steadied.

"I'm sorry," she finally sighed. "I appreciate your help, I really do. It's just such a shock—seeing my father through your eyes—so confusing. What can it mean?"

Fanth's eyes mirrored the blankness his mind projected.

Jackie dropped to her knees in front of the twins and took their hands in hers, careful not to squeeze the webbing between their fingers. "I know how hard it can be to draw out lost memories. But remembering makes things better. Will you let me help you to remember?"

The Swimmer twins looked at one another and nodded. *We will try,* Krith projected.

If you won't get mad at us, Krit added.

Fanth sighed heavily. *I too.*

Jackie released the twins' hands and placed her own hands over her heart. "I promise," she said.

Krith and Krit stayed snuggled up to Fanth. Jackie sat facing them. Holding back on her impatience, she talked to them in a soft, reassuring manner. She had once seen a hypnotist do something like this in a tri-D, to help a female victim of a shooting remember the face of the man who had shot her. She knew little about hypnotism, but hoped that her soothing monotone might relax Fanth and the twins to the point where they could access their memories more fully.

"Listen to me," she said. "Relax and concentrate on what I say to you." She repeated this several times, as persuasively as she could.

Eventually their eyes began to glaze over, as if their sight had turned inward. Their bodies slumped, bonelessly. "I want you to think back in time," she said. "Back to the last time you saw humans." All three nodded. They seemed to be responding. This hypnosis business might just work.

"Tell me where you are," she said.

Fanth moaned. *A strange place,* he projected, *many humans.* His thoughts came to her fuzzy and blurred, as if he were in a drunken state. Jackie couldn't make out the images he pictured in his mind, only vague shapes and an unintelligible murmur of voices. Suddenly he stiffened. *I see myself,* he said. *But I have no fur!*

"You've lost your fur?"

I have none. His body jerked as if grabbed and shook by a giant hand. *No! Not supposed to remember this!*

Jackie leaned forward. "You've got to remember. It's so important. Please Fanth, remember for me."

"No!" Fanth yelled aloud. He jumped to his feet, dislodging Krith and Krit, and looked wildly about. "I'm no hairy beast!" he shouted, now fully alert. He shook his head, vigorously, as if to clear his thoughts. "I'm a man!"

For a moment Jackie sat paralyzed, arms tight against her chest. Fanth? A human? Slowly, she rose to her feet. She laid her hand on his shaggy arm. "You spoke to me. Just now Fanth, you spoke aloud—in English."

He stared at her wild-eyed. "I did! I can!"

"You say you're a man? How did you get like this?"

He paused, projecting confusion. "I'm not sure. I was on a Void ship. A crewmember, I think. I remember wearing a spacer uniform."

"Who are you?"

He stiffened. His eyes unfocused as if his vision had turned inward. His face, contorted with strain, slowly relaxed.

"My name is Richfield," he said. "Dan Richfield. I—I'm a propulsion specialist."

Jackie took a deep breath. Each question seemed to unlock another portion of his memory. But her next, she was almost afraid to ask. Afraid what his answer might be. "What was the name of your ship?" she heard herself say.

"The *Golden Arrow,*" his voice trembled with emotion.

Her father's ship! This man was from her father's ship! How could it be? What could it mean?

Revelations were coming too fast. Her head felt light—her body unbalanced. But she couldn't stop now. She had to know what had happened. To the ship. To her father. "How did you get here?"

He shook his head. His mind projected confusion even while he tried to verbalize his thoughts. "There was some sort of problem. Just before we struck the Void. I was in Engineering, setting controls on automatic for the jump. The captain had called for a security detail. I remember being curious. And worried. A jump is no time for something to go wrong.

"I felt the normal pull when we entered the Void and feelings of contracting and expanding. But then there was something else. A different kind of pull. It squeezed my mind—hurt like hell. I couldn't think. I struggled to escape it, but it pulled me to it." A shudder rippled across his massive shoulders. "That's all I remember. From that point on I was a hairy beast without a past, living as an animal in that cave."

Jackie looked down at Krith and Krit, still huddled together at her feet, holding to each other as if desperate not to be parted. The force of Fanth's revelation had brought them out of their trance state. They stared back at her, eyes wide with wonder, lit with a growing comprehension.

"Has any of this helped you to remember more?" Jackie asked them.

They both nodded.

"Are you that boy and girl I saw in your projections?"

Krith started to project an answer, then caught himself. "Yes," he said, his voice a low whisper.

"You were on the *Golden Arrow*?"

Krith nodded again. "We were going to Draco-3 to be with our parents."

"They homesteaded a ranch there and sent for us," his twin added.

"Are Krith and Krit your real names?" she asked, remembering Fanth's disclosure.

Krith rose to his feet, pulling Krit with him. His mouth worked for a few seconds before he spoke. "I am Alpha Gilbert," he said, hesitantly as if the words felt strange on his tongue. "This is my sister Beta."

Jackie stared numbly at them, her mind drawing back into itself to escape the overload of shock. "I don't understand any of this," she said. "What transformed you? And how did you come to this place?"

Dan shook his head. "I don't even know where we are. It's not any of the linked worlds that I'm familiar with. Until you jogged my memory I had no sense of my past. Pulling it out was like sucking eggs. And painful."

"But what could make you like this? It just doesn't seem possible."

Dan laid his hands on the twins' shoulders. "The three of us are living proof that it is."

"But how?"

He rubbed his hand across his chin in a gesture Fanth had never used. "Pilots move huge ships through the Void by the power of their minds. If mental power can move matter, perhaps it can transform it too."

A mental transformation of matter? It sounded ridiculous. And yet, how else could she explain what had happened here? The implications were staggering. "Who could do such a thing?"

Dan paused before answering. "Manipulating reality on this scale would take a powerful mind. The most powerful mind on our ship would have been that of our Void pilot—your father."

"My father?" Jackie pulled her elbows tight against her sides and clenched her fists, resisting the urge to pound them against Dan's hairy chest. "My father would never have done this. Why would he want to trap all of you here?" And abandon his daughter, she left unsaid.

Dan stroked his chin. "I know—it doesn't make sense. But someone changed us and brought us here. Who else on the *Golden Arrow* would have the mental strength to do it?" His eyes lit with a new thought. "This being they call the Master—could he be your father?"

"That's the stupidest thing I ever heard!" Jackie said, with all the scorn she could muster. "I don't believe for one second that it's my father's face behind that cowl." Eyes blurred with tears, she spun about and stalked off toward the dark waters of the pond, determined not to even consider the possibility Dan had raised.

Jackie stayed away from the others, leaving them to sit around their fire, making enthusiastic use of the spoken form of the language they had so recently regained. She didn't feel like socializing. Several times, Dan came over to urge her to rejoin them. Each time she sent him away.

She crouched near the edge of the softly lapping waters, staring out as if she expected some mystical form to rise up from them, bearing the answers to her questions. Only she wasn't certain she was ready for answers if they bore any resemblance to what Dan had suggested. She grimaced. She was beginning to think she liked him better as Fanth.

A gust of wind came off the lake, chilling her barely clothed body. She shivered, but not entirely from the cold. The very thought that her father might be the one called the

Master made her cringe. He couldn't be her father. Now she wished more than ever that she had been able to see the face of the image the twins had projected more clearly. Despite her denials to Dan, she couldn't imagine how any of the crew or passengers could have overcome a ten-plus Void pilot in a contest of mental wills.

But why would he abandon his ship in the Void? To escape into his own fantasy world? The death of her mother had left him depressed for a time. But he seemed to be coping. Could he have had deeper feelings he kept to himself? Doubt raged within her, discounting her strongest beliefs.

She looked up into the thickly starred heavens. The pale gold disc of the Hunter and the silvery orb of the Flyer hung high above her. Heedless in their unending race across the sky, they offered little comfort.

Once again, she wished she had CAP's unbiased, unemotional logic to guide her. Then a thought crossed her mind. She could try taking on CAP's perspective. Think as he would. List the facts and see what logical conclusions she could draw from them. At least she could try.

Taking on her computer's persona, she reviewed what she had learned about this world. Fact one: the crew and passengers of her father's ship had been transformed into animal-like creatures shortly after their ship entered the Void. Fact two: she had also been transformed—first into a bodiless mind, then to her present state. Fact three: they all had been pulled from the Void and placed here. But how had they gotten here?

She grimaced. Bad premise. It assumed that they left the Void. Maybe they hadn't. Maybe this world somehow lay within the Void. How could she tell?

The scientific method. That would be CAP's approach. Identify alternative possibilities and test them. She thought for a moment. Things can be transformed inside the Void. That much she knew. She had been transformed into a bodiless entity—Dan and the twins into animals. If matter can be manipulated in the Void by a powerful mental power, as Dan suggested, and if they were still inside the Void, she should be able to change things too.

A chill of excitement passed through her. When Fanth had chased her she had run faster and stronger than she had ever done in the past. At the time she had thought it was fear motivating her. But maybe not. Maybe she had been adapting to meet her needs. She couldn't be sure about that, but she knew how to tell. She stared down at her right hand and concentrated. Slowly, a strange tingling developed at the base of her fingertips. Her hand trembled so badly that she had to hold her wrist with her other hand to steady it. But she had to try this—to uncover the nature of this world she had stumbled on. Her future and her father's depended on it.

—CHAPTER—
13

The lively conversation of Jackie's companions halted abruptly as she approached them. Dancing flames from the campfire lit their eyes like those of wild beasts, reminding her how cruelly they had been deprived of their identities.

Dan looked up at her. "Are you okay?"

After being used to Fanth's abbreviated mental projections, it seemed odd to hear him speak aloud and in complete sentences, although she still received his mental projections along with the verbalizations.

"I'm fine," Jackie said as she dropped down opposite them. "It threw me when you suggested my father might be responsible for all this. And I still don't believe that he did it. But someone had to. And unless we discover how and why, we may be stuck here forever. I want to find out what happened. Will you help me?"

Dan crouched ape-like by the campfire, peering into her face. "Whoever changed us and brought us to this place intended to wipe out our pasts. We were made to forget. If we hunt him down and confront him with our knowledge, what do you suppose he'll do to us?"

"I can protect us," she blurted, and immediately wished she hadn't. It sounded like a line from a bad melodrama.

Dan bared his fangs in what Jackie took to be an amused grin. "You'll forgive me," he said, "if I don't put a whole lot of faith in the protection you can offer against someone with the power to create all this."

Jackie held out her right hand and spread her fingers. In place of her nails, a set of two-inch claws sprouted from her fingertips. "A powerful being may have created this world," she said, flexing her fingers to show them what she had done to herself, "but I know how to change it."

In the flickering light of the campfire, Dan and the twins stared at her, as if they couldn't quite take in what they were seeing.

"How did you do that?" Dan finally asked.

"I'm no Void pilot, but my mental level is on a par with my father's. I've a ten-plus rating."

Dan swallowed nervously, as if finding it difficult to digest this new bit of information. "If your mental powers are that strong, why didn't you use them against me or the Flyers?"

She smiled wryly. "Like you, I assumed this world to be real. I had no idea I could change it. Looking back, I can see where I may have modified some things. But I didn't realize what I was doing." She wiggled her clawed fingers. "I can do much better when I put my mind to it."

The twins pressed in to examine the transformation.

"Good claws," said Alpha.

"Nice and sharp," Beta agreed.

"But how did you make them grow?" Dan asked, keeping his distance.

"It just takes concentration. I think about what I want to happen and it happens. I grew these in only a few minutes." She held up her hand and transformed the nails back to a more normal size.

"Have you transformed anything else?"

"I haven't tried yet," she admitted. She turned and focused her gaze on the fire. After a bit, its color changed from flaming reds and yellows to a cold, icy blue. She shook her head to negate the effect and the blaze reverted to its previous coloration.

"You did it, you did it!" the twins yelled, hopping up and down in their excitement.

"And us?" Dan said, rising to his feet, his voice a hoarse whisper. "Can you change us, too? Back to what we were?"

A wave of uncertainty washed over her. The idea of changing others disturbed her. What if something went wrong? "Are you sure you want me to try?"

He only nodded, but the eager glint in his eyes told her how badly he wanted her to make the attempt.

"Okay," she said. "Hold still and I'll give it a try." His Adam's apple quivered beneath the furry cover of his throat, but he held his position, as unmoving as a knife-thrower's assistant. Jackie first concentrated on eliminating his Fanth identity. Slowly, under her gaze, his entire body fogged over, becoming an opaque mass of gray matter. It was then that she realized that she had no idea of what this man looked like as a human.

Before she could give way to panic, Dan projected an image of himself for her to work with. Sighing with relief, she concentrated on the image, giving it solidarity in her mind. The fog of gray, shapeless matter that had been Fanth slowly shifted, molding itself into a recognizable shape. Even as she watched, color tinged the grayness and form took substance. Within half a minute, a heavy-built, square-chinned man in a spacer's uniform stood before her. A powerful-looking man, built like a football player, but with a kind face and sensitive eyes.

Gingerly, he raised his hands and ran them over his face. Then he looked down at the rest of his body. "By heavens, you did it!" he said, his eyes wide with amazement.

Dizzy from her concentrated effort, Jackie took a step

backward. This Dan person was suddenly a stranger to her, someone she had never seen. The twins were all over him, touching his skin, stroking his uniform and peering delightedly into his face. Expectantly, they turned to her. "Change us too," they pleaded.

She felt exhausted from the unfamiliar mental effort. Her head throbbed as if in the throes of a migraine. But she hadn't the heart to put them off. Several more minutes of intense concentration transformed first Alpha and then Beta into the slim, freckled redheads she had seen in their imaging. Babbling excitedly, they rushed into each other's arms in a prolonged hug. Then they started toward Jackie. Her world seemed to spin. The next thing she knew, she was on her back with Dan crouched over her.

"Are you okay?" he asked.

"I think so," she said, holding a hand to her head. "What happened?"

"You passed out. The mental effort must have been a little too much for you."

She sat up, rubbing her temples. "I guess I overextended myself. My head feels like someone used it for a drum."

Dan knelt behind her. "Maybe I can relieve some of the tension." Gently, he massaged her neck and shoulders, probing at the sore muscle tissue.

At first she found his attentions disconcerting. She had to remind herself that this man was not a stranger but a trusted companion she had come to rely on. As the small knots of pain dissipated under his fingers, she found herself relaxing.

"Better?" he asked.

"Mmm," she let her shoulders slump. "I'm glad I got rid of your claws, though. My back would have been shredded."

He chuckled. "You could probably have patched your-self up easily enough."

He's right, she thought, I could. But I need to learn to use my abilities a little more efficiently so I don't wear myself out. She turned to face him. "So have I convinced you we should go looking for the individual responsible for all this?"

His expression turned serious. "Just remember, whoever made this world has as much mental horsepower as you—maybe more—and a lot more practice using it. Don't assume you can barbecue the top dog around here just because you can turn his fires blue."

Jackie grinned. "That's what I need you for—to keep me from becoming overly confident. But there was no one on the *Golden Arrow* with a higher mental rating than I have. Only my father could match me, and he'd never do any-thing to hurt me. So again, I ask—will you help me find out who's behind all this?"

He grinned back. "That I will. Now that I have my memory back, I have no desire to return to those brainless hairy females."

That raised a point that had bothered her since she first discovered the Hairy Hunters. "What did you mean when you said that your females weren't real?"

He shook his head. "They never had any will or under-standing of their own. They were like constructs, created for my enjoyment." Dan's face reddened and she guessed he was thinking of the uses he had made of these creatures.

Relieved to have that mystery cleared up and feeling more in control of herself, Jackie turned to Alpha and Beta. "Did you two pick up anything about the location of this Master being?"

"Those he sends seem to come from the west," Alpha said.

"He's like a spider," Beta said, hunching her body and spreading her fingers. "He sends out his spies along his web to find out what's happening."

Dan grimaced at Beta's spider imitation. "I guess we continue west, then, into his web. The question is how?"

Jackie frowned. "What do you mean?"

Dan shook his head. "If I've learned anything as a spacer, it's that successful operations require effective planning."

"What do we need to plan?"

"First of all, what form we should take."

"What's wrong with the way we are?" she asked, thinking of the mental energy it had cost her to turn them back into humans and the headache she had suffered from doing it.

"Several things." Dan ticked the points off on his fingers. "If we go strolling into his territory as we are, his flunkies will spot us immediately. And human bodies aren't all that well equipped for fast travel or hard brawling."

Jackie sighed her defeat. "So what do you suggest?"

"Flyers," he said immediately. "The Flyer we fought threatened to tell the Master about us. That implies they report to him. Given that, no one will be suspicious about seeing Flyers in his territory. Then too, flying is a fast way to travel. And it gives us flexibility. We can fight or make a quick getaway as we need to."

"Flyers it is then," Jackie said. "We can make our transformations tomorrow once we find a place to try our wings. Anything else?"

"Just one more point. Going after the Master is bound to be dangerous. I'm wondering about Alpha and Beta."

"Of course we'll go," Alpha said.

"Yes," Beta echoed. "I'm not missing out on the chance to fly like a bird."

Jackie thought for a moment. "They may be better off staying with us where we can protect them. If the Master sends creatures here to find us because of what we did to his Flyers, the twins could be in big trouble."

Dan nodded. "Okay then, they come with us. We'd better plan on an early start in the morning. If I'm to become a bird, I want some flying lessons."

"Do you think we should post a guard tonight?" Jackie asked.

"Don't worry," Alpha said. "The creatures never come at night."

"Only in the daytime," Beta agreed. "And we always sense their thoughts in time to hide."

"Then I suggest we bed down now," Dan said. "We're going to need a good night's sleep."

They positioned themselves close to the fire, the twins back to back. It wasn't long before Jackie heard the steady breathing of her companions. But, although she lay curled in a sleeping position, she felt too excited for sleep. It occurred to her that she might not even need to sleep to replenish her energies, not if her mental powers could do it for her. Instead of sleeping, she tried out her newly found powers, changing rocks that lay within her field of vision into all sorts of shapes, textures, and colors. Her powers were limited. She couldn't make the rocks larger or smaller, but she was becoming more effective at making transformations. With practice, she found she could do it with less mental effort so the changes didn't tire her so much.

By the time she grew bored with her exercise, she was surrounded by a broad ring of the brightly colored abstract shapes she had created. Then, for a while, she experimented with expanding her mental sensitivity. She found she could reach out to touch the simple minds of the night

127

animals foraging in the darkness. That too, she quickly tired of, finding little of interest in the thoughts of insects, frogs, and mice. Their emanations spoke mostly of fear, hunger, or contentment.

Having little else to do, she lay back and considered the strange circumstances in which she found herself. I'm like Alice in Wonderland, she thought, going through so many changes; I hardly know how to tell if I'm still me. What gives us our identities anyway? Certainly not appearance—I can change that at will. But my thoughts and feelings change too, each time I take on a new role.

An involuntary shiver coursed through her body. Changes came too easily in this place. Dan and the twins had totally lost their identities along with their memories. She had temporarily lost hers in the Void. Now, all of them seemed to be themselves again. But were they? How could all this be real if—

Her body tensed as she picked up the faintest hint of a thought projection. Something was sneaking up on them.

—CHAPTER—
14

Jackie lay perfectly still, reaching out to hone in on the tendrils of thought that had brushed against her mind. She closed her eyes and blocked her ears with her hands, focusing all her concentration on her mental receptors, straining to raise her sensitivity. The creatures were muting their projections. Even with her sensitivity enhanced, she could barely receive them.

How old do you judge the tracks? one of them projected.

Less than a day, Pack Leader, another responded. *Unless they travel by night we should come on to them soon.*

Travel by night? Not likely, the one addressed as Pack Leader said with an edge of smugness. *Who but the Master's Stalkers have the keenness of sense to follow a trail in the dark and the endurance to keep to it without sleep or rest? These outlanders must hold a great importance to the Master. Never have I seen him so upset about their doings. When the Flyer imaged the creature he fought, the Master emitted waves of fury, striking out at all around him.*

Flyers, another mind interjected. *They brag so about the tidbits of information they bring in. But in these forested territories they are all but useless.*

Just remember, Pack Leader projected sternly, *arm your blowguns with the stunning darts. The master wants the hairless creature brought in alive.*

Stalkers, they called themselves—sent here by the

Master. Capable of tracking in the dark. If she hadn't enhanced her receptivity she might not have sensed them until it was too late.

She began to pick up their perceptions of sight, sound, touch, and smell along with their thoughts. They were following the trail she and Fanth had taken to the lake. There were six in number, slim, wiry creatures with slick, brown fur, much like a pack of giant ferrets except for their eyes—round, yellow orbs that glowed strangely, eyes that could pierce the darkness. Through the eyes of one, Jackie watched another bend low to peer at footprints and sniff the faint scent that clung to them. She shuddered. They seemed perfect hunters, thoroughly focused on their task, relentless in their pursuit.

She rose quickly, moving to the side of the fire where Dan and the twins slept. She touched Dan's arm, then laid a finger on his lips as his eyes snapped open. "Don't project," she whispered, damping her own mental projections. "There are creatures coming up on us that can sense our thoughts. They call themselves Stalkers."

His eyes widened, but he nodded and made no attempt to communicate mentally. Jackie woke the twins and repeated her warnings. "We need to get away from here," she told them. "Are there other paths than the one we followed when we came here?"

"Two," Alpha answered as he sat up to look about, acting more curious than fearful.

"One west and the other south," Beta added, as she sided up to her brother.

"We'll take the western one," Jackie decided. "We must leave now. The Stalkers will be on us at any minute."

"It's so dark," Alpha protested, "how will we find our way?"

"We can take one of the sticks from the fire," Dan said. "Jackie can make it glow brightly when we need to see, and dim it when we need to hide."

Jackie grimaced. "Of course. I keep forgetting to make use of my powers."

Dan pulled a smoldering clump of wood from the fire and blew on it. The embers brightened and spat. Jackie took the faggot and held it up to cast a dim glow. "Now where's that path?" she asked the twins.

They had no sooner gained the western path than the band of Stalkers broke into the clearing on the opposite side of the pond. Feeling a chill in the hollow of her chest, Jackie mentally doused the already dim light from the faggot and along with Dan and the twins, crouched down among the bushes and trees that lined the path. "Remember," she whispered, "no projections."

From what she had picked up, the Stalkers were elite forces of the Master, trained to track and kill. She doubted she could defend her friends against all of them at once. She wasn't familiar enough with her mental powers to use them effectively as weapons. And even if she could use them to kill, she wasn't at all sure she could bring herself to do it.

She needed a way to escape without confronting the creatures. But how? They had already searched the twins' sleeping area. From the still smoldering fire, they knew that her group couldn't have gone far. Now they looked for fresh tracks, examining the ground with glowing eyes and twitching noses, pausing to listen for the faintest sound of a breaking twig or crunching rock.

Jackie's brain worked furiously. What if she made it appear that her group had taken the southern path? There was no need for her to actually create the tracks. She could just place an image of them in the Stalker's minds. She could tell from their reactions if her ruse had worked.

She heard a noise, padded footsteps only a few feet from where she crouched.

Here! a Stalker projected. *A fresh print.*

Eyes squeezed tight and fists clenched at her side, she sent out a subconscious message to the other Stalkers, showing them tracks that headed toward the southward path.

I see other footprints over here, one of the Stalkers announced.

Did they split then? Pack Leader asked. *Have we spoor in two directions?*

Entering the mind of the nearer Stalker, Jackie broadcast a perception of the path that showed no more tracks leading in their direction.

No more prints this way, the Stalker projected. Jackie sensed his puzzlement.

All fled south then, the leader said. *And their tracks are fresh. They can't be far ahead.*

The tenseness eased in Jackie's shoulders. Her ploy was working. The crack of a twig alongside her broke the stillness like a rifle shot. In the clouded darkness, lit now only by a handful of the brightest stars, she could barely see Alpha's upright form. He had, apparently, stood up to take a look at the departing Stalkers. Jackie grabbed him by the shoulder and yanked him back down.

What was that? the Pack Leader demanded. Jackie could sense the Stalkers' alertness as they strained their ears to pick up on the slightest sound. One of them started back in Jackie's direction. She projected a noise like a small animal, scurrying off into the underbrush.

The investigating Stalker gave a growl of disgust. *Just*

some bush crawler, he snarled.

Let's be off then, Pack Leader ordered. *The sooner we bring in this creature, the happier the Master will be with us.*

For close to an hour, Jackie's group crouched at the entrance to the western path while Jackie projected images of tracks leading southward. She kept this up until the thoughts of the Stalkers began to fade. The side of her mouth curled as she thought of what the Stalkers would think when the tracks suddenly ended—as if Jackie and her friends had taken to the air.

Jackie's group needed to be well away from here by the time the Stalkers retraced their steps. The thick band of stars was still covered by clouds. Jackie held up the burned-out torch and concentrated on making it emit a bright glow. Easier than drawing sparks from flints, she thought.

"Our disappearance should confuse them for a while," she said. "I wouldn't want to be in their shoes when they have to explain it to the Master." She projected an image of Stalkers prostrating themselves on the ground before the hooded figure. The twins giggled appreciatively but Dan ordered them to silence.

"Alpha almost gave us away tonight," he said. "If either of you are that careless again, the Stalkers won't have to explain why they didn't catch us."

Alpha hung his head under Dan's rebuke. Jackie felt sorry for him, but Dan was right. There was no telling what dangers they would face in approaching the Master. For their own safety, the twins had to recognize the need for caution.

Unexpectedly, Dan now turned on her. "And why did you take such chances with them—letting them come so close to us. Why didn't you just kill the buggers?"

For a minute she didn't know what to say. "I—I thought

it better to evade them," she finally blurted. "To be truthful, I'm not sure I could bring myself to kill them."

He gave her a questioning look.

"I think they must be more of the crew and passengers from my father's ship, transformed, like you and the twins."

"I've thought of that, too," Dan said. "But whoever they are, they aren't playing games. Those two Flyers almost killed you."

She lowered her head. "I know. And you killed one of them to save me. I tried to kill them too. But I didn't realize that they were humans. Maybe that shouldn't matter to me but I'm afraid it does. I'll avoid any more killings if I possibly can. Hopefully, I can protect us in other ways."

Dan rolled his eyes but didn't argue further.

They managed several hours of travel before the sky began to lighten. Jackie now wore a spacer's jumper that she had created, similar to Dan's. It had occurred to her that she no longer needed to depend on a skimpy arrangement of pelts that might come undone at any inconvenient moment. And in the company of humans she felt a need to be better covered.

To throw off the Stalkers, she created a small whirling dust devil to follow behind them, wiping out all traces of their passage from the dry, sandy soil. Alpha and Beta kept glancing back at this tiny tornado, fascinated by its swift swirling dance.

Jackie laughed to see them so excited. She was definitely becoming more adept at manipulating matter. There had been no more headaches like those she had suffered from the earlier transformations.

The sound of rushing water up ahead alerted them to the fact that they were approaching a stream. The forested trail they followed soon came along side it. The twins ran to the water's edge to drink and scamper along the banks of the stream, looking for fish. Seeing some, they plunged, fully dressed, into the water. But they quickly found that their human forms were not so effective at catching the elusive creatures.

"Come on," Dan called. "We don't have time to waste. The Stalkers might still be following."

"Wait a minute," Jackie said. "We'll need to find something to eat sooner or later anyway. Maybe I can help things along."

Jackie felt certain she could go without food indefinitely, just as she had gone without sleep on the previous night. She was less sure about her companions. She could probably relieve them of their feelings of hunger, but the lack of nourishment might still weaken them. Using her mental powers was proving to be a tricky business. With time, she'd be more sure of herself, but for now, it was better not to take chances.

"Can you spot me a fish?" she called to the twins.

Beta pointed to a place in the stream where a boulder partially blocked the flow, forming an eddy of quiet waters. "I see one there," she said. "But without my claws I can't catch it."

Jackie stared down at the shadowy form and concentrated on holding it immobile. "Try now," she said.

Beta leapt into the water and plunged her hands below the surface. She came up holding a trout-like fish the length of her freckled forearm. Jackie repeated the process several times with both Alpha and Beta, letting them find a fish, then holding it in place while they grabbed it.

Dan frowned at the four fish that lay flopping on the grassy bank. "We can't cook them," he said. "Smoke from a fire would be a dead giveaway."

Jackie thought for a minute. "Get some rocks from the stream," she told him. "I can heat them mentally and we can cook the fish without a fire."

The plan worked well. Jackie mentally drew the water out of the twins' sodden clothes and then joined them and Dan in an impromptu meal, relishing the taste of the succulent flesh even if she didn't need the sustenance. They tossed the remains back into the stream, leaving no evidence of their passage.

"This mind power is great stuff," Jackie told Dan as they proceeded along the path. "When I was a little girl, one of my favorite fantasies was being a fairy with magical powers."

"You're catching on fast," Dan said agreeably. "I hope you can do as well with turning us into Flyers."

"As soon as we find some open country. I'll have us making like birds before you know it."

He nodded but his eyes held a worried look. "I just hope it's soon. From what you said, the Stalkers are awfully anxious to find us. And blow darts will be hard to defend against."

A few more miles of brisk walking and Dan's wishes were realized. Their path brought them to the edge of an open meadow, surrounded by the same thick forest growth through which they'd traveled since leaving the lake. Before Jackie could warn against it, Alpha and Beta went dashing out into the open, chasing each other through the sweet-smelling meadow grasses.

She had been monitoring for thought projections and hadn't picked up anything so far. Even so, the twins needed to be more careful.

"Come on back," she called. "This looks like as good a

place as any to start our flying lessons."

The two stopped in their tracks, turned, and raced back to her side.

"Are we really going to fly?" Alpha asked, wide-eyed.

"Will you change us into Flyers?" Beta wanted to know.

"Something like that," Jackie told them. "But first we need to do some experimenting. I'll start with Dan. You two pay attention so you can learn from his experience."

"So what now?" Dan asked.

Jackie looked him up and down. "I remember what the Flyers looked like when we fought them. I'll try and make you look as much like one as possible. But I can use your help."

He looked surprised. "How?"

"Try to picture the Flyers in your mind as you remember them. Two memories are better than one, and your impressions can help. After all, they were all I had to go by when I changed you back to your human form."

He grinned. "I'll give it a try." He closed his eyes and sent her a mental picture of a Flyer soaring above her head.

Some of the features seemed a little off to her, the wings a bit too narrow and the legs too short. She modified them to match her own recollections, not worrying about less important details like the curve of the hooked nose or the exact shade of the white plumage. The important thing was to make Dan into something that could fly.

She concentrated on his body, making it blur into a gray shapelessness as she had done before. Then she reformed it according to the Flyer image he had helped her construct. A convincing replica of a slender, long-armed, long-legged white-feathered Flyer took shape before her. A pair of enormous wings sprouted from his shoulders. His yellow eyes took on a look of confusion as a mild breeze lifted his wings, making him lurch forward. He quickly folded them and shifted his stance to a more stable position.

"He's a bird-man," Alpha said.

"A Flyer," Beta corrected.

"That," Jackie said, "remains to be seen. How do you feel?" she asked Dan.

Once again, Dan's giant wings unfurled and he had to catch his balance. "More awkward than I expected. I'm as clumsy as a gooney bird."

The twins giggled. "What's a gooney bird?" Beta asked.

"Another name for an albatross," Dan said. "Their wings are so long that they wobble from side to side when they take off or land. Sometimes they tumble head over heels." He drew back his own wings. "I wonder how Flyers get airborne?"

Jackie paused in thought. "I suppose they could leap off cliffs, like people with hang gliders. But there aren't any cliffs nearby. You'll just have to get a running start like your gooney birds."

Dan's bird-like features remained unreadable, but he projected a cautious optimism. He flapped several times experimentally, then lowered his head and bounded off across the meadow, waving his wings wildly and making short hops that held him up for no more than a few seconds. Alpha and Beta ran along behind, shouting encouragement. Jackie had to cover her mouth to keep from laughing.

He came to a halt on the far side of the clearing. Jackie jogged over to where he stood, bent over with his hands on his knees, sucking in air. Alpha and Beta stood beside him, looking sympathetic.

"I had no idea flying required so much ground work," Dan puffed. "It looks easy when you see Flyers gliding on air currents. Maybe you didn't get me quite right."

Jackie looked him over critically. "I might be able to increase your wing span a bit. And I can strengthen your legs and expand your lungs."

She made the changes and he tried again, time after time, clearing a few extra yards but never doing better than a short glide. Finally he collapsed to the ground, his chest heaving from the effort.

"It's no use," he wheezed. "I can't get my butt into the air to save my soul."

Jackie frowned. "There has to be a way," she said, wishing once again she had CAP to confer with. "Flyers can fly, so why can't we? You were right about the Flyer form being perfect for our needs. And flying is the best way to rid ourselves of those Stalkers." She looked about nervously. No telling when the devilish things might show up again.

Once more, she examined Dan's Flyer body, searching for anything about him that might differ from the Flyers they had encountered.

"Maybe you should make him smaller," Alpha suggested.

"Like a real bird," Beta added.

Jackie shook her head. "I can't change the size of things, just their shape and appearance. Besides, size shouldn't matter. Flyers are human-sized, and they fly quite nicely."

"That's the real puzzle," Dan said. He had dropped to the ground where he rested with his wings spread out behind him. "The stupid creatures aren't actually designed for flight. Birds are light because they have hollow bones. Flyers are heavy. The one I fought weighed a ton. And the Flyers' wings don't replace their arms like true birds—just attach behind their shoulders. The arrangement shouldn't work."

Jackie nodded slowly. "Perhaps we're attacking the wrong question. Instead of asking why we can't fly, we should ask why they can."

Dan shook his head. "We can't afford to spend time on fool questions that get us nowhere. By now the Stalkers could be closing in on us. I say we leave now."

"We do and they're almost sure to catch up with us eventually."

"Let us try to fly," Alpha said.

Beta nodded her agreement. "We're smaller and lighter."

Jackie smiled at their enthusiasm. But even if it worked for them, it would be no help unless she and Dan could fly too. "Not yet," she told them. "I want to take a crack at this flying business myself."

—CHAPTER—
15

Concentrating, Jackie closed her eyes, lifted her arms, and formed an image of a Flyer in her mind. Dan, she knew, had lost confidence in her. She had lost some confidence in herself as far as flying went. If she couldn't create proper Flyers, what else might she not be able to do? She felt a desperate need to reassure Dan and to regain her belief in herself.

She must have goofed somehow. Perhaps Dan's mental images had thrown her off. She would try making the transformation without his input. She felt a tingle of change run through her body: facial muscles constricting, a bulging at her back, and a soft sprouting of downy feathers all over her. It wasn't painful but it felt strangely different. Her wings unfolded and she stumbled off-balance as the breeze tugged at her pinions.

She leaned forward and flapped a few times as Dan had done. Her wings worked, but they didn't feel strong enough to lift her. She tried a short run. Up to speed, she broke into a low glide but couldn't get any lift. What was she doing wrong?

Wrong question, she reminded herself as she started back to the other side of the meadow where Dan and the kids waited. What were the Flyers doing right? As Dan had pointed out, they weren't built like birds. What other sorts of creatures fly? Some squirrels can glide from tree to tree.

Bats fly with a rapid wing motion, much faster than a Flyer could flap its feathery appendages. Insect wings beat even faster. None of this seemed relevant.

Of course there was Peter Pan's sidekick, Tinkerbell. She used pixy dust—fairy magic. Jackie had once played the role of Peter Pan at the Conservatory, running about the stage, pleading with the audience to help save Tink's life by shouting: "We believe in fairies!" Silly stuff.

Her train of thought jarred to a sudden stop. Could it be as simple as that? A question of belief? This was a world where thoughts took on the stuff of reality. Jackie had assumed that once a reality was created here, the normal laws of physics still applied. But maybe not. Maybe the physical and mental aspects of nature were so intertwined that they worked together.

Tentatively, she raised her wings. I can fly, she told herself. I believe this. I only need the beat of my wings to raise myself off the ground. Not like a bird, but like something magical.

She rose on her toes, light and springy, and bent her knees. Then, throwing out her arms, she leapt into the air. Two strong strokes lifted her six or seven feet above the ground. Her wings made a whooshing sound as they beat the air, lifting her even higher. She started to circle and, for the first time, looked down. Immediately, her confidence left her. She was so high up. And she had no idea what she was doing. She could fall—even be killed!

She felt heavy—awkward. Wings rigidly locked into place, she held her breath, fearful that the slightest movement might disrupt her balance and send her crash-diving to the ground.

A sharp pain in her mouth made her realize she was biting her tongue with her beak. Stop thinking like this, she told herself. Believe that you can do it.

She forced her wings to resume a steady beat. Slowly, she relaxed as she felt their rhythm, carrying her like a buoyant swimmer only through air instead of water. Again, she allowed herself to look down. Below, she could see Dan and the twins, pointing up at her and jabbering.

The twins were projecting excitement at her success, images of her in flight, and demands to be included in the fun. *Us! Us too!* they pleaded.

Again, Jackie lost concentration. Her wings skipped a beat. She tried to get back her rhythm and overcompensated. Suddenly she was plummeting downward. Frantically, she forced out her wings to break her fall. The ground came up with a jarring thud. A sharp pain stabbed her right ankle. She cried out as her legs gave way beneath her and she collapsed to the ground.

Almost immediately Dan and the twins were kneeling over her, asking if she was all right. She rolled over and held her ankle in both hands, moaning with the intensity of the pain.

"Is it broken?" Dan asked.

"I don't know," she wailed. "Just let me be until I can make it feel better."

With that, she ignored her companions and concentrated on easing the throbbing in her ankle. Then she strengthened the muscle tissue and reduced the swelling that had already started there.

"Help me up," she told Dan, "so I can try and put some weight on it."

He worked an arm under her shoulder and slowly hoisted her to her feet. To her relief, she was able to stand. She could even walk if with a limp.

"All right," Dan said, amber bird eyes glowering from

beneath feathered brows, "how did you manage to pull that off?"

Jackie could sense his embarrassment over her success after his failure. Well, partial success perhaps. Her landings were going to need work. Unable to smile in her Flyer form, she projected a "happy face" with dots for eyes and an upward curve for a mouth. "It's all about fairies," she said. "I just became a true believer."

She quickly explained how she had managed to convince herself that she was capable of flight. "It should be even easier for you and the twins. I can simply enter your minds and share my belief." She turned to the twins. "But flying takes concentration. I know this is exciting stuff, but you can't distract us with a lot of projections while we're learning how to do it."

They hung their heads and looked so downcast that she had to give each of them a hug. "You'll probably do much better than me anyway. Come on now, and I'll give you each your own set of wings."

She converted the twins into Flyer forms, noting again how much easier these changes were coming to her as she became more practiced. Her head ached slightly, but nowhere near as bad as before. With some concentration she found she could ease the headache too. She could deal with almost any sort of pain if she put her mind to it. Her ankle felt almost healed.

Next, Jackie sat Dan and the twins in front of her and probed their minds, implanting an unquestioning certainty that they could raise themselves on their wings and soar over the landscape. Soon, all four of them were high above the trees, testing themselves in glides and dives, awkward at first but smoother and more graceful with practice.

It was then she picked up the edge of a thought projection from the forest below. The Stalkers were again on their trail, already at the stream where Alpha and Beta had caught the fish. It wouldn't do to have them come across a foursome of fledgling Flyers, practicing an ability that should have been instinctive to them. Dan and the twins were too far away to call to so she chanced a projection.

Follow me, she transmitted, heading off in a westerly direction.

Why are we—? Alpha started to ask.

Silence! she ordered.

Dan drew close, his wing tips almost touching hers. "Trouble?"

"We've got Stalkers in the neighborhood. We'll have to perfect our flying skills while we travel."

It was still early morning and the air felt fresh and cool in her face as they winged across the sky, high above the trees. They flew in a rough V formation, like geese, taking advantage of the shielding effect of their bodies. Jackie kept the lead, since she could enhance her own strength and endurance beyond what she could do for the others. She also nudged up her vision and her mental receptivity, keeping alert for signs of life below. But either the lands they passed over were uninhabited or whoever was there stayed out of sight and kept their thoughts to themselves.

Suddenly, the landscape changed. Growth typical of eastern North America gave way to tropical rainforest. Still dense, the trees took on a broader spread and their leaves a brighter, glossier green, their tops mounding like waves. Jackie was struck by the unnaturalness of the transformation. This was truly an artificial world. She remembered a girl from the Academy who could always find some sort of far-out explanation for any offbeat fact that anyone brought up. She smiled. Even that girl would have one heck of a time accounting for this place.

The faintest hint of a thought brushed against her mind. *Did you project something?* she queried Dan, too far away to call to.

No. What did you pick up?

I'm not sure. What about you, Alpha? Beta?

No. Nothing. Their replies arrived almost together.

Jackie made a slow circle, soaring high above the place where she had felt her mind touched. *I'm almost sure I caught the thread of a thought. There may be other creatures down there. Perhaps they know something more about the Master. Let's see if we can make a landing.*

In all those trees? Dan protested. *We'll shred our wings in the branches.*

Birds land in trees all the time.

She spiraled downward, knowing that the others would follow. But as she drew closer to the thick canopy of glossy leaves, none of the uppermost branches looked strong enough to take her weight. Still, she persisted. She was curious as to what sort of creature she had sensed. And after insisting that they could land in the trees she'd look foolish if she suddenly changed her mind. Dan would think she didn't trust her own judgment. She wanted to show him that she knew what she was doing.

What she needed was an opening to drop through so she could grab onto the lower, sturdier limbs. When she saw a place she thought she could fit, she raised her wings and plunged in, feet first.

Leaves and twigs whipped against her as she pierced the top layers. Her hands clutched at a branch that bent and gave way. Something solid caught her hard in the stomach, whooshing the breath from her.

She lay doubled over, gasping from the cramping pains

that racked her stomach, fighting to fill air-starved lungs. Only then did she think to concentrate her mental powers. The pain in her stomach lessened and her constricted passages opened to admit air. She sucked it greedily into her lungs.

Feeling a little better, she raised her head to get a view of her position. She had dropped further down than she had intended and smacked into a large, lateral branch. She worked an arm around it and threw over a leg to bring herself up into a sitting position. Gingerly, she ran a hand over her feathered ribs. Nothing felt broken. She flexed each wing, just to be sure she could still control them.

A shadow fell across her and she looked up in time to see Dan make a more effective landing just above her. Well sure, now that she had cleared the way for him.

"You okay?" he asked, a note of concern in his voice.

"Just scraped a little," she said, not wanting to admit how badly she'd been shaken up. "We better warn the twins to be careful."

We found a bigger opening, Alpha projected from nearby.

We used to climb in trees a lot, Beta added. *We'll look around and let you know what we see.*

Oh fine, Jackie thought, everyone landed safe except me. *Stay where you're at for now,* she told them. *I need to sort out our situation.*

She was getting something again. Cobwebby tendrils of thoughts held back and not expressed. Whoever it was seemed awfully secretive. Then an object whizzed past her nose and shot through the leaves. Another missile flew over her head.

"Ouch!" yelled Dan. "I just got hit by a piece of fruit."

Jackie sharpened her sight, compensating for the darkness of the surrounding forest. In several places below her she saw movement in the branches.

Hey, cut it out! she projected sharply. *We aren't here to harm anybody.*

Master's Flyers get gone, an unknown mind responded. *This our territory.*

We aren't Flyers . . . Jackie started to say then stopped, realizing the ridiculousness of such a claim. A chorus of throaty hoots rose from below. *What I meant to say is we aren't the Master's Flyers.*

Another chorus of hoots greeted her. *All Flyers from Master. Go away.* Another missile, probably another piece of fruit, struck the branch she sat on with a dull thud.

She looked up at Dan. "You think these are some of the tree-dwelling Climbers you spoke of?"

"That would be my guess."

She thought for a minute. "You know what they look like?"

"The ones I've seen are ape-like creatures with long red-orange hair. But slimmer than most apes, something like a scrawny orangutan. They're strong, judging from their ability to swing through the trees. I'd hate to be set on by a bunch of them."

"They seem to have a thing against Flyers." She checked herself again for physical damage. She seemed to have pretty much recovered from her mishap. "Form an image for me," she said. "I want to change myself into one of them."

—CHAPTER—
16

Hand over hand, Jackie worked her way downward through a leafy tangle of branches and vines, looking for the ape-like creatures that had pelted her with fruits. She now resembled one of them. Long arms with orange-red hair supported her body weight with little effort. Her powerfully molded hands clung to each branch she grasped with a strength and surety that surprised her.

As a child she had loved swinging from bar to bar on the overhead ladder in the park playground near her home. Light-bodied and wiry, she had been better on the bars than most of her friends. But even then, she'd been able to hang in place for only ten minutes or so before tiring. Now, she felt she could dangle from a branch all day without straining her arms.

She saw movement among the leaves off to her right and headed for it. A ruddy-coated creature, much like herself, swung into view.

"Listen," she called. "I come to talk with you."

The creature stared at her from beneath a heavily ridged forehead that gave it the appearance of frowning. It opened its mouth in a display of large, sharp fangs. Another of the creatures slipped into view, then several more. Soon, they surrounded her. They kept their distance, but eyed her aggressively, as if ready to rush in at any moment. Jackie held to her position and let them look her over. The one she'd first seen was apparently their leader. It advanced within a few feet of her, shoulders hunched, eyes glaring.

What are you who looks like us and talks with noise? it projected.

"A friend."

Not of us, it insisted. *Where from then?*

"I was one of the Flyers that landed above you. I changed my form so you can see I'm not really one of them."

They shrieked mentally. A great surge of motion rippled the surrounding foliage as they shook the branches with wild abandon. The leader pounded its chest with its free hand, projecting fear and hate.

"I'm here to help you," she said, bewildered by the outburst.

You come from the Master, the leader projected. *Not wanted here.*

"We aren't from the Master," Jackie said emphatically. "I want to free us from him. But I need to learn more about him. Won't you tell me what you know?"

No talk with shape-changer, the leader projected. *Go away.*

Jackie seethed with frustration. How could she get through to these creatures? "You've all been changed, if you only knew the truth. You were on a spaceship and were transformed from humans to what you are now."

Lies, lies! the accusations erupted all around her. The Climbers bounced up and down, violently shaking the branches in their rage. One broke off a piece of branch and hurled it at Jackie. They were keyed-up to the point of attacking.

There was no time to work them through to their pasts, and she didn't want a confrontation. There were too many

150

for her to handle without someone getting hurt. With a final backward glance, she turned and headed upwards toward the top of the canopy. She could hear them scrambling after her.

We're leaving, Jackie projected, both to cue her friends and to appease the Climbers behind her. But the angry creatures only hooted and threw more fruit and branches.

Alpha and Beta had already launched themselves upward from their precarious perches. Jackie could see them circling above her, out of range of the Climbers' missiles. They had found their own ammunition. From the air they pelted the Climbers with broken pieces of branches.

Don't, Jackie projected. *It's not their fault. They think the Master sent us.*

Dan held his position and waited for her. He spread his wings to protect her from the upward arcing projectiles as she transformed her coppery fur back into feathers and grew another set of wings of her own. She worried that he might be injured by one of the hurled objects, but although a few of his feathers fluttered loose from lucky hits, no serious harm was done.

Her transformation completed, she unfolded her wings. "Let's get out of here," she said. She and Dan sprang into the air together and quickly beat their way above the trees.

"So much for trying to get allies," Jackie said. "I hope we'll have better luck with our enemies."

Dan laughed. "At least we look like our enemies. That should help."

Jackie didn't answer. She hadn't come out of this very well. Dan seemed to be taking her mishaps in stride but she couldn't help but wonder what he was thinking—if he was having second thoughts about her ability to deal with the Master when she couldn't even handle a troop of Climbers.

True, it should help if they could pass themselves off to the Master's people as Flyers. But even for that they weren't yet properly equipped. In their hurry to escape the Stalkers she hadn't the time to make them a set of the wooden tridents Flyers carried. Her mental powers were a far more effective protection than any such weapon, but they still needed the tridents for the sake of appearances.

Not about to repeat a crash landing among the trees, she waited until their flight carried them to the edge of the lush jungle growth. Beyond it, the land stretched into the distance, gray and rocky, barren of vegetation. Jackie swooped down to land at the jungle's edge. Her companions followed. At her request, they helped her collect broken tree limbs into four small piles. She concentrated on each of the piles, one at a time, first collapsing it into an unstructured mass, then restructuring the mass into the shape of a trident.

Alpha and Beta immediately started a mock duel with their weapons. "No time for that," Jackie told them. "Does anyone have any idea what lies ahead in this open territory we're heading into?"

Dan shook his head. "I've never been this far west."

"Neither have we," Alpha added.

Beta shivered, and turned away. "I don't like a place without trees. Do we have to go this way?" She absently scratched at a place on her shoulder, parting the soft feathers to get at the skin beneath.

Poor things, Jackie thought. It must be scary for them, having to leave the security of their lake and forest. Even while flying, they had, up to now, the comfort of knowing that trees were beneath them. But no more. Still, they had to go forward. There could be no turning back.

She glanced up at the sun, already past its mid point in the purple-hued sky. "We must continue on if we are to locate the Master's stronghold. At least we'll be able to see what's below us now. Perhaps we can find creatures less hostile to Flyers that we can mingle with and question about the Master. And don't worry. I'll protect us from any dangers we run into."

The twins smiled and nodded but Dan looked back to the forest, as if he were remembering how easily they were driven off by the Climbers. Well, she hadn't wanted to hurt them. She didn't want to hurt anyone. It would be a different matter, she told herself, if her friends were in serious trouble.

With their newly constructed tridents cradled in their arms, Flyer fashion, they rose into the sky once again, following the sun. It wasn't long before Jackie sighted a twisting line of green up ahead, cutting across the gray, rocky landscape.

I'll bet there's a river hidden in all that vegetation, she projected to the others. *A likely place for creatures to gather. Keep your eyes open.*

I could fly down and take a look, Alpha offered.

Better we keep together. Until we find out what's down there I don't want—

Flyers! The word rang in her head like the tolling of a great bronze gong. *Land and report!*

Jackie hung back to let Dan draw up to her. "Did you hear that?" she called without projecting, just loud enough to be heard above the beating of their wings.

"Hear it?" Dan said. "It nearly blew out my brains. Must be some of the Master's forces. Want to make a run for it?"

"We may be able to pick up useful information. But be ready for a quick getaway if anything goes wrong."

She motioned the other two closer. "We're going down. Stay close and don't project. And whatever you do, don't forget yourself and try to talk."

Alpha and Beta nodded agreement. They followed her as she drifted toward the river, looking for some indication as to where they were supposed to land.

Over here, you ignorant bird brains! The thought was almost painful in its intensity. Looking toward the trees that edged the river, Jackie saw movement beneath an opening in the foliage. A dark figure stepped out from under leafy branches to wave at them. She banked in that direction, spiraling downward in a wide, sweeping arc. She continued to circle, several hundred feet above the treetops, trying to get a better look at the squat humanoid figure that gestured up at them. As far as she could tell, it was alone.

Come on! Get your tail feathers down here and quit playing games! You know the routine. Its command left a hollow ringing in her head.

Without further hesitation, Jackie and her companions swooped down to land within a dozen yards of where the creature stood. Up close, the large, rounded head, the bulging eyes, and the broad, lipless mouth reminded her of a giant, upright frog or toad. A wide, protruding stomach contrasted comically with scrawny legs and arms. The thing was entirely naked but for a long, red silk loincloth draped around its stomach and between its legs. Its entire body was smooth-skinned; a yellowish green mottled by patches that varied from dark green to black. She couldn't be sure of its sex. It had no breasts, but that didn't mean much since it wasn't really a mammal. But it showed a swaggering bravado that she associated with males and she thought of it as such. She imagined that it must have a relatively powerful mind to be able to send out its thoughts so forcibly.

She folded her wings and approached the creature, trying not to show her revulsion for its appearance and hoping that the others were doing the same. Thank heavens their bird faces held little in the way of expressions.

You call us? she projected in the cryptic style used by the Flyers she had encountered.

Of course I called you, the thing responded. *No Flyer passes the river boundary without reporting in. But why are there four of you? It only takes one to report and we need as many Flyers out looking as we can field. I've never seen things so stirred up. I'm up to my eyeballs in reports from every territory within a week's ground travel. No one's seen anything of this new creature the Flyer Arven spotted. A group of Stalkers were sent out by the Master to nab it but it somehow eluded them. The Stalkers are on their way in now to report. I wouldn't want to be in their fur when they have to explain why they failed.*

The loquacious Toad-Man stopped to scrutinize Jackie through watery, red-veined eyes. *I don't suppose you have sightings to report?*

Not yet. Soon.

His gaze shifted to her companions then back to her. *You won't spot anything if you're not out there flying.* He shook his head. *Going back to my earlier question, why are all four of you here?*

Improvisation had always been Jackie's strong suit in drama class. But here, she didn't know the rules. She only hoped she didn't blow it for them.

Master sent for us, she told the creature. *Has special assignment.*

Then why haven't I heard anything about it? The creature scratched its stomach and made a noise halfway between a sigh and a belch. *I know,* he said before Jackie could think up a convincing reply, *not up to creatures of our ilk to question the intentions of the Master. If he has an assignment for you, it's best you be on your way. It would have sped things up, though, if you'd told me this from the start.*

Thought you knew, she said, trying to portray an air of injured innocence.

The Toad-Man glared at her, sighed/belched again, then scrunched his eyes closed and hunched down, as if preparing for a leap. Jackie took a step back, half expecting him to jump at her. Instead, he sent out a mental blast that almost knocked her off her feet. *Escorts here!* he bellowed mentally, *front and center!*

—CHAPTER—
17

Escorts! Jackie winced internally. She hadn't counted on this.

Here they come now, the grotesque Toad-Man said with a self-satisfied edge to his projection, *the Master's personal Gargoyle guard. The Master sent them here to be on hand and the lazy buggers have done nothing but hang out in the shade. At least now I can put them to work.*

Jackie followed the direction of the Toad-Man's gaze. There, flying toward them, came four dark-skinned, leathery-winged creatures. She watched their approach with a hollow feeling in her stomach. They flew fast and maneuvered effectively. Not an easy bunch to out-perform. And they carried spears, longer and more deadly looking than the tridents.

There's no need—she began, but the Toad-Man cut her short.

Master's orders. While the creature he's searching for is on the loose, no one comes near his castle without a complement of escorts. He turned to watch admiringly as the winged creatures swooped in for a landing, some fifty feet away. *Big, aren't they?*

They were indeed, she decided as she eyed the creatures. Each of the four was easily as large as Dan, himself a broad-shouldered six-footer. Her group would stand no chance in an even struggle.

The Toad-Man must have had similar thoughts for he

looked over at Alpha and Beta and shook his head disparagingly. *Those two look awfully small for Flyers. Where are they stationed?*

Eastern territories, Jackie replied quickly. *Many trees. Small Flyers better there.*

Really? The Toad-Man spat out a stream of greenish juice. *Never heard that before.*

Jackie tensed, ready to yell for Dan and the twins to take to the air if the Toad-Man should challenge her. But he only shook his ungainly head.

How do they expect you to do your job if they don't give you all the facts? he grumbled, more to himself than to her. *Oh well, Master knows best.*

As the Gargoyles approached, Jackie began to appreciate the appropriateness of the name given to these creatures. Their features were indeed demonic. While each had its own distinctive characteristics, they all were as ugly and repulsive as the Toad-Man. In fact, they went him one better. They looked mean and brutish as well as ugly as they swaggered up scowling.

Okay, Slime-Ball, the one in the lead addressed the Toad-Man, *what did you call us for?*

The Toad-Man spit again. *Like I said, escort duty. You're to take this bunch to the castle. The Master sent for them. Don't ask me why. I just try to do my job without being told fly-poop about what's going on.*

The Gargoyle leader projected his disdain for the amphibious humanoid. *And why should the Master tell his plans to one such as you? Does an eagle tell the ant where he flies?*

He might if he expects the ant to look after his interests. The Toad-Man took a step backwards as the Gargoyle leader's leathery face worked itself into a truly hideous frown. *But never mind, Master knows best.*

And don't forget it! Get too uppity and you're likely to end up a stuffed decoration in a castle niche.

The Gargoyle leader turned to face Jackie's group, lowering his head with its great peaked ears until his blazing yellow eyes and broad, fanged mouth hovered inches from her face. *As for you, birdbrains, you're to follow in close formation and keep your beaks shut or you'll get your tail feathers pulled. Do I make myself clear?*

Y-Yessir, Jackie responded, surprised that she could stammer mentally. Like the Toad-Man and the Stalkers, the Gargoyles appeared reasonably fluent in their communications. Perhaps those closest to the Master were given that capacity.

The monster spun about and leapt upward, aggressively beating the air with its leathery wings. The other Gargoyles quickly followed. Jackie nodded to her companions and they took to the sky, straining to keep up with the Gargoyle group. Taking the leader at his word, they flew close together, their wings almost touching.

"How do we handle this?" Dan asked, speaking softly enough so as not to be heard by the Gargoyles up ahead and taking care not to project his thoughts.

"We'll go along for now," Jackie replied in kind. "At least we're being guided to the very place we want to go. Don't worry, I'll come up with a way to shake off our keepers before we get there."

She could, of course, simply allow the Gargoyles to bring them before the Master. But she didn't want to approach the Master in that way. If he was, in fact, her father, she wanted to meet with him in human form—to confront him with the reality of what she was and what she meant to him. Perhaps, in the matterless vacuum of the Void, he had lost his identity, as had the others. Jackie had helped her friends to remember. She could help her father too—if she could get him alone.

And if the Master wasn't her father? She still preferred to face him by herself. She should have no trouble defeating him in a straight battle of minds. According to Dan, no one on the *Golden Arrow* but her father had a ten-plus rating.

Of course, getting the Master alone might not be easy. What if his people attacked them? How might she use her powers to protect herself and her friends? Could she really bring herself to kill others if it was the only way?

The countryside unfolded beneath them, desolate, rocky, and inhospitable. Probably meant to be that way, she thought. No creature could work its way in toward the Master's stronghold without being spotted by his Gargoyles or ground forces. From time to time she saw small groups of ground creatures moving westward, probably coming in to report their findings. She wondered if the Stalkers had reached the castle yet and how the Master had reacted when he heard how her group had escaped them.

On several occasions they passed over other observation areas where they were challenged by Toad-Men. Their Gargoyle leader simply sent back a mental message that their party was responding to a direct order from the Master. From him, that was enough. The Master's iron control probably made it inconceivable to his subjects that anyone would invoke his name this far into his territory unless they served his needs.

Having an escort had made their crossing relatively easy, but losing their bodyguard might be another matter. Jackie still wasn't sure how best to do that. She didn't want to confront them directly. The Gargoyles were physically powerful creatures and any attempt to fight them would place her friends in danger. Besides, despite their grotesque appearance, the Gargoyles were humans from her father's ship. She would get rid of them peacefully if she possibly could.

Time to experiment. Ideally, she should get to them in a way they wouldn't think to attribute to her. So what could she do? She thought long and hard, discarding possibilities such as freezing their wings or knocking them unconscious, actions that would surely injure or kill them. But what about their vision? If she could blind them temporarily her group could easily leave them behind. Without sight, they'd be forced to land. But in this open country they should be able to make a blind landing without damaging themselves too badly.

She concentrated on their eyes, working with what was there, envisioning the film of liquid that would normally lubricate their eyes turning opaque. Slowly, carefully, she decreased the clarity of their vision.

One of the Gargoyles cursed. *What's wrong with the air? It looks as if I'm flying through a cloud of fog. Everything is blurred.*

Same for me, another complained.

Enough! their leader ordered. *Try going higher to get above it.*

He picked up the pace of his wing beats and headed upward, the others following. Jackie led her group after them. The Gargoyles didn't have much trouble keeping their heading, despite her efforts. Blinding them might be harder than she had thought.

It's even worse up here, one of the Gargoyles projected angrily. *So thick I can hardly see.*

Something strange is going on, the leader replied, suspicion clear in his thoughts. *I'm taking us down until we can figure it out. Follow us,* he ordered Jackie.

"This is our chance," she called to her friends. "They

don't know what's happening. Just keep on and ignore them." She edged into a climb, feeling a rush of relief at their newfound freedom.

Hey, you flying vermin! the Gargoyle leader hailed them. *I told you to follow us down.*

"Keep going," Jackie urged, "by this time they probably can't see past the ends of their noses."

Why you carrion-eating scum, the leader blasted, *get back here or I'll personally yank you out of the sky and pull every feather from your carcasses.*

"Big words for a blind bat," Alpha muttered.

"Watch out," Beta yelled, "they're after us."

Jackie glanced over her shoulder and saw, to her horror, that Beta was right. The four dark-winged creatures were following them, their spears thrust out before them.

"I don't understand," she said. "They said they could barely see."

"Maybe the Master's influence is weakening your mental powers," Dan said, sounding worried.

The Gargoyles gained rapidly. They were definitely faster than her friends. Something would have to be done, and soon.

"Stay with the kids," she told Dan. "I'm going to see how much my flying skills can be enhanced."

Without waiting for him to respond, she headed into a sharp turn. Maneuverability, she thought. If I put all my eggs into that basket, I may be able to give them a few surprises.

She flew back toward the oncoming Gargoyles, keeping above them and concentrating all her energies on her reflexes and her ability to make sudden twists and turns without slowing. Then, folding back her wings, she dropped into a steep dive, directly at them. Her maneuver caught them by surprise. The Gargoyle she targeted barely avoided having

162

its backside whacked by her trident as she plummeted past him. If she could only delay them long enough to give her friends the head start they needed, she was certain that she could outdistance the Gargoyles by enhancing her speed.

She braced her wings and turned sharply. The Gargoyles were above her now. One peeled off and dived after her. The other three continued on after her friends. That wouldn't do. She rose to meet her pursuer, as if she meant to join him in aerial combat. Coming from above, he had all the advantage. At the last minute she twisted aside. The creature let out a mental blast of frustration and rage as he shot past her.

Ignoring him, she concentrated on changing her attributes. Now, all that mattered was speed. She had to catch up to the other Gargoyles before they reached her friends. She just couldn't understand why her blinding ploy hadn't worked. How could they continue to track her group so effectively? It made no sense. Not that much on this stupid planet did.

Her wings cut the air like feathered knives as she sped after the three dark forms up ahead. She had hoped to surprise them, but the one she eluded projected a warning to his fellows. Well, she should have expected that. The three ahead came about to face her, cautious now in the face of her unexpectedly superior airmanship.

Once again, she concentrated on maneuverability. She would dodge in among them, keeping just out of their range. The question was whether she could keep them occupied long enough to do her friends any good.

The Gargoyles spread out as she came at them, preparing to engage her from three different positions. They raised their spears above their heads. The pinfeathers rose on the back of Jackie's neck. They clearly intended to impale her, here and now.

—CHAPTER—
18

The closest of the three Gargoyles, its eyes narrowed to yellow slits, drew back its spear. Jackie shrieked and threw herself into a tight turn. Apparently not willing to chance a miss, the creature held back its throw. Instead, all three surged in after her. Again, she banked sharply and lost some of her lead.

She gasped, faltering in her flight as a sharp pain stabbed her wing, near her right shoulder. Stunned, she watched the spear continue its arching fall toward the ground, realizing it must have passed through her wing's thin flesh. The pain was distracting, but the damage was even more serious. With all her effort being spent on out-distancing or out-maneuvering her pursuers, she couldn't concentrate on repairs. And with a tear in her wing, she wouldn't be able to elude the Gargoyles much longer.

She looked back over her shoulder. The Gargoyle she had left behind had caught up with the others and all had closed to well within throwing range. One more lucky hit and she'd be finished. Their furious flapping flight as they pursued her reminded her of giant bats. Bats had terrified her as a child. She had feared that, in the dark, the wildly gyrating creatures would tangle themselves in her hair. To calm her, her father had explained that bats navigate amazingly well by sound waves, a sort of built-in sonar . . .

Of course! How could she have been so stupid? The

Gargoyles must use something similar to bat-sonar. Navigating by sound would allow them to patrol the Master's territory by night as well as by day.

Frantically, she concentrated her attention on the inside of the Gargoyles' ears, visualizing the creation of a waxy substance to cut off their hearing.

Now what the devil's the matter? the leader projected. *I'm losing orientation. I can hardly pick up on that cursed Flyer.*

Watch out! another warned, *you're flying too damned close. Your wing just clipped me.*

Jackie glanced back. They had slowed, as if unsure of themselves. She threw herself into another tight curve.

I've lost the damn thing, the leader groused. *Can't hardly tell which way is up.*

Jackie didn't wait to hear more. Concentrating on speed, she streaked off toward the black specks in the distance that were her fleeing friends. *Wait for me!* she projected with a force that even the Toad-Man would have appreciated.

Her friends slowed for her and she quickly caught up with them, despite her injury.

"You had us worried," Dan called to her as she approached. "I was about to go back and try to help. What happened?"

"Tell you later. At least we won't be bothered by those overgrown bats for a while. Let's land for a bit. I've got some wing repairs I need to concentrate on."

The flat gray planes had given way to rolling foothills, rock-strewn and barren of life. But the outcrops of large boulders that dotted the hillsides offered some concealment. Jackie brought her group down within the sharply jutting shadow of one of the larger rock formations. As Dan inspected her wing, the twins started to chase each other around in circles, reenacting Jackie's fight with the Gargoyles.

"Settle down!" Dan bellowed, "we don't want to draw any more attention."

Reluctantly, the twins gave up their play and flung themselves down, giggling over some shared secret. Dan turned back to Jackie.

"The tear looks pretty well closed."

She nodded. "Once I gave it my full attention, it healed fairly rapidly. I guess my powers are holding up."

He squeezed her shoulder. "You let them get too close."

Jackie sighed. "I was trying to find a way to take them out without killing them."

He made a clicking sound with his bill. "Why didn't you melt their spears?"

She grimaced with embarrassment, grateful that her face was hidden by a covering of feathers. "I was concentrating so hard on blinding them that I never thought to do something about their weapons. And then, when I couldn't blind them, I thought maybe I was losing my powers." Her head drooped. "I guess it's not enough to have special abilities— you have to know how to use them."

"The important thing," Dan said, "is you're learning. You won't make the same mistakes again."

She looked up into his eyes, feeling the full force of her near failure. "This time I barely saved our necks. Next time we might not be so lucky. Maybe you should take the twins back and let me go on by myself."

He shook his head, projecting determination. "We're in this together. If you fail, we all fail. And we may be of some use to you yet. Besides, I feel much safer with you around, even if you are still learning."

"Us too," Beta said.

Alpha waved his trident in the air. "And I want to be there when you get to pulverize the Master."

A surge of relief washed over her. She had dreaded losing the companionship of her friends, even though she felt she had to make the offer. Smiling, she rose to her feet. "We better get going then. I'm not sure how long the Gargoyles' ears will stay plugged."

Dan lifted his wings. "First," he said, "we should make another change of form."

Jackie frowned in surprise. "I thought we agreed that our Flyer bodies were ideal for this."

"That was before we knew that Flyers aren't allowed about unescorted. We don't want another squadron of Gargoyles sent up after us."

She thought a moment. "I could change us to ground creatures, like the Stalkers."

"It would slow us down too much. You want to get to the Master before word of us gets to him. Change us into Gargoyles. They, apparently, have the freedom to fly over this territory on their own."

She would have made a face if her Flyer features had permitted it. Bad enough to be chased by overgrown bats without being one. But she saw the sense in Dan's suggestion.

"I don't want to be a bat thing," Beta said. "They're ugly and mean."

Jackie turned to Dan. "Suppose just you and I change into Gargoyles. That way, if we're challenged, we can say we're escorting two Flyers in to see the Master. It gives us an excuse to be going to the castle."

"Good idea," Dan said. "Now you're using your head."

She wasn't sure whether Dan was complimenting her most recent idea or disparaging her past ones, but decided to take his comment as a compliment. After her near fiasco, she needed all the confidence building she could get. She transformed herself and Dan into replicas of Gargoyles while the twins watched and giggled. Then she changed her trident and Dan's into spears.

"Can't we have spears too?" Alpha asked, eyeing his trident disapprovingly.

"Flyers use tridents," Jackie replied. "You want to stay a Flyer, you carry a trident."

Jackie and Dan found it a little awkward to adapt to the flying mechanisms of their new bodies. Their featherless wings had a different feel to them than those of the Flyers. Keeping their balance proved difficult. Several times they had to call for the twins to slow down and wait for them to catch up. But the same shoulder muscles were involved in moving their wings and positioning them to guide the direction of their flight. Again, she discovered the main trick was to take on a proper mental attitude. Think of yourself as a Gargoyle and you fly like one.

Without their escort, they had to navigate on their own. They kept their westerly heading, guiding on the sun, and soaring high above the rocky hills. Jackie hoped they'd be able to see the castle the Toad-Man had spoken of from their high elevation and not pass it by.

To make it appear that the twins were under their care, they kept the two between them as they skimmed over the hills. Several times they were hailed from below by Toad-Men. Each time they projected back that they were escorting Flyers, and flew on without further challenges. From time to time, they saw land creatures, headed on a parallel course, an indication that they still traveled in the right direction.

The bloated sun hung low now in a red-violet sky, sending dark purple fingers of shadow slithering across the rocky slopes beneath them. In the distance they could see a foreboding rise of mountains, with peaks ablaze from the sinking sun.

What now? Jackie projected to Dan.

He scanned the distant ridge, then pointed to a particularly high peak in the middle of the range. *Over there,* he projected. *I think I caught a light reflection near its base.*

They aligned their flight in the direction Dan indicated. As they neared the rocky heights, Jackie enhanced her vision to get a clearer view. A structure was built into the base of the cliff, like the pueblos in Arizona. As they drew nearer, she saw it was, indeed, a castle. A multitude of towers and peaked projections rose from it.

It looks more like something out of a fairy tale than a fortress for repelling invaders, Dan observed. *But then, if the Master relies on mind power for protection, he doesn't need to fortify himself all that well. He certainly has no opposing armies to worry about.*

Fortified or not, the design of the castle gave Jackie a feeling of defiant withdrawal, as if its owner had fled from the world and planted his back against the mountains, raising sharp-spired towers to intimidate any who might come against him. She tried to picture her father creating such a stronghold. The image just didn't fit the man she knew. Could there be a side to him she was completely unaware of? Realizing that the answers to her worries now lay before her, she felt a paralyzing reluctance to continue with their quest. She was fearful, she realized, of what she would find there.

Good place for a Halloween party, Alpha noted cheerfully, breaking into her gloom-strewn thoughts.

His disruption of her unproductive musings brought her to the point of decision. She had no choice. Not if she ever wanted to see her father again. She had to go on—to discover whatever it was that awaited her.

"Twins," she called, "no more projections. We don't

want to give ourselves away."

As they drew closer, Jackie saw that a long flight of stairs wound up to the castle from the mountain's base. Land dwellers would have to reach the entrance by climbing those stairs. But Flyers and Gargoyles could come in from above. To land where? Her group would have to make the approach confidently or be viewed with suspicion by those guarding the castle. She couldn't just fly about the place and look things over. But perhaps they could come in high, circle down slowly, and try to locate the proper landing site on the way in.

She glanced back. The two slim Flyer figures were strung out behind her with Dan's gray-winged Gargoyle form bringing up the rear. Waving an arm at them to follow, she flew to a point high above the castle. From her present viewpoint she could see an outer wall, braced by a succession of conical capped turrets that surrounded an inner complex of larger, onion-domed towers that rose high above the outer wall. Scores of creatures could be seen along the walls, others within the courtyards.

She began a downward spiral. One of the twins veered off to the side, angling for a better look. "Get back here!" she said sharply. A Gargoyle escort wouldn't allow Flyers to flit about gawking.

The highest of the inner towers was joined to another, slightly lower tower that ended not in a peak but a flat surface. It seemed the most likely place to receive guests from the air. Jackie straightened out her spiral and headed directly for it.

Took your own sweet time, a voice boomed inside her head as she braced her wings to land. The unexpected projection startled her, causing her to stumble and fall to her knees. Muttering under her breath, she regained her feet as her friends landed beside her. She scanned the flat roof of the tower for the source of the projection. The adjoining tower of the complex extended several stories above her. Carved in its side and level with the surface where she now stood, was a large, arched opening, fifteen feet high and half that in width. Out of its shadows stepped another of the Toad-Men, looking much like the one she had previously seen.

What makes you so all fired anxious to bring in these Flyers that you don't even bother to announce your arrival? the green-skinned creature projected with a surly overtone.

Quiet, Wart-Face, Jackie said, adopting the haughty attitude of a Gargoyle leader. *We have orders to bring them straight to the Master.*

The Toad-Man eyed her suspiciously. *And just what unit do you belong to? I'm not aware of any order to—ooug!*

The creature's mental challenge ended in a grunt as she constricted the cells of its brain, cutting off its oxygen. It raised its hands to its throat and stared at her through eyes that bulged comically in disbelief. Then it spun about, making for the open doorway. It collapsed just inside the entry.

Alpha ran over to look down at its limp form. "Is it dead?"

"Just unconscious," Jackie said, hoping that her assessment was correct. It was. The creature was still breathing.

"Your powers are holding up well," Dan said, "even on the Master's doorstep. But we'd better get inside. The guards might become suspicious if they spot us standing out here gawking like tourists."

They moved through the great, arched doorway and into a large room that took up an entire cross-section of the tower. It looked like a reception hall, perhaps for receiving the Master's agents and taking their reports. The only furnishings were ornately carved benches, positioned at different locations around the room. The ceiling stretched high above their heads, plated with a greenish coppery metal worked into a collage of grotesque, misshapen faces. There were no windows. A huge wrought iron chandelier hung from the roof's center, illuminating the room with flickering rings of black candles that gave off an oily, pungent odor.

Drab colored tapestries, with scenes of the creatures of this world battling with dragons and other mythical beasts, hung from the curved walls. No human figures were displayed. A huge crystal staircase spiraled down from above, continuing on to whatever levels lay below. Its sparkling surface pulsed with inner lights that swirled and shifted like something alive.

Jackie stretched her neck like a nervous cat to peer up the stairwell. No living creature was in sight. She opened herself to projections but received only a mixed jumble of impressions from distant guards. Nothing near.

She pointed up the crystalline stairs. "My guess is his quarters are up there. Anyone who calls himself 'Master' would probably want to be high enough to look down on everyone else. I'm a little surprised, though, that he doesn't have more flunkies around here guarding him."

Dan, his spear at the ready, kept his gaze fixed on the staircase, as if there were something inherently distrustful about such a fanciful structure. "Maybe he doesn't think he needs them."

A powerful voice resonated from the landing above, vibrating the chamber with its hollow ring. "You win the prize for that guess, Gargoyle, but you're not going to like what you get."

—CHAPTER—
19

A man in a brown, hooded monk's robe stepped forward onto the top stair. Jackie looked up at him, her breath caught in her throat. He appeared of medium height, the same as her father. His bulk, shrouded as it was in the folds of his loose robe, was harder to judge. And his face remained darkly shaded by his cowl. No part of his body was visible to her. Even his hands were hidden by the loose dangling sleeves of his robe. Given the manner of his dress and the hollow sounding ring that disguised his voice, it seemed he wished to remain unknown.

Jackie stared at him, searching for the least clue that might hint at familiarity. "Who are you?" she asked, her voice almost a whisper.

A throaty chuckle, almost a cackle, burst from unseen lips. "Everyone knows who I am. Who you are is the question. Not one of my Gargoyle guards, I'm guessing."

Impatient with his verbal fencing, she took a step forward. Without taking her eyes from him she concentrated her powers on her appearance. Throughout her body, she experienced the sensation of transformation. Giant bat wings shrank back into her shoulders. She stretched out her arms, watching the dark Gargoyle skin lighten and take on her normal flesh tone. Her black, leathery uniform transformed into a blue wool jumper, the school dress she had worn at the Conservatory, an outfit her father would surely recognize.

"Do you know me now?" she asked, softly, insinuatingly.

For a moment the cloaked figure hesitated. Raising a hand to his face, as if to shield his eyes from an unexpected sight, he took a step backward. "I—I don't know you," he stammered, his voice puzzled and unsure.

"My name is Jackie Claver. My father is Jack Claver, a Void pilot. Doesn't that mean anything to you?"

The face beneath the cowl remained dark and obscure. "Who or what are you? Not of this world I can see. What do you mean, coming into my territory and taking on the forms of my servants without my permission?"

"And why should anyone need your permission to take whatever form pleases them?" Jackie snapped, irritated by his haughty presumption.

"You question my authority?" he rasped.

"I question your treatment of the inhabitants of this world."

"The world is mine. I'll treat its inhabitants as I please. I am the Master—the giver of all things."

"You play that role, but who are you really? What right have you to do this?"

The form beneath the robe stiffened. Arms lifted, shrouded hands trembling, whether in anger or fear Jackie couldn't tell. "I've had enough of you. It's time you felt my power."

A pressure descended on her shoulders, forcing her to her knees. A frightened squeak from behind her told her that her friends felt it too. Angry, she grasped this Master being with her mind, constricting his brain cells as she had those of the Toad-Man. The Master screamed and raised uncovered hands to his head. The pressure lifted from Jackie's shoulders. But a new force issued from him, pushing back her own mental projection with irresistible strength.

Bitch-girl! The thought rang out like a gong inside her head. *I'll teach you to play mind games with me.*

A sudden tightness grasped her skull. Hands to her head, she fought against it. But slowly, the force increased. Jackie felt like a baby, trying futilely to push away the powerful hand of an adult. Her last thought before blackness overcame her was for her friends. She had let them down again.

Consciousness returned with the sensation of a breeze against her face and feathers brushing her nose, making her want to sneeze. She opened her eyes to find a slim Flyer form bending over her, fanning her with a wing. She moved her head aside and the fanning stopped.

"Dan," Beta cried, "she's coming around."

Beta disappeared and Dan's Gargoyle face loomed above her. "Thank heavens," he said. "You've been out for hours." She raised herself on an elbow and looked about. Dan and the twins were with her in a large, stone-walled room. There were no windows, but large, curved doorways gaped open in two adjacent walls. A strange soft glow emanated from a sort of phosphorescent lichen that covered the walls with a fine webbing. A plank table with two benches straddled the middle of the room. Against one wall an old-fashioned water-pump sat on a sink with a stone foundation. A scattering of clean, dry straw covered the floor. Its pungent odor hung strong in the air.

Jackie looked down at herself. She still wore her human form and her blue jumper. She remembered changing to it just before . . . She shook her head.

"Where are we?" she asked as she pushed herself into a sitting position.

Dan helped her to her feet. "The master's dungeon. It's in the lower portion of the castle. Not exactly a hell-hole, but a prison nonetheless." He pointed to one of the open doorways. "That one leads to sanitary facilities, primitive as they are. The other exits on a corridor. But we can't use it."

"Why not?"

"Some sort of force field. Can't get past it." He eyed her questioningly. "So what do you think? Is the Master your father?"

A pang of remembered disappointment returned to her. She had expected an answer, one way or the other. Instead, she was as confused as ever. "I—I really don't know. He showed nothing of himself to me. But his mind is unbelievably powerful. Much stronger than mine."

"This is his territory," Dan pointed out. "That might be a factor."

"Maybe, but I feel there's something more." She walked over to the open doorway that led to the corridor. A faint shimmering of light could be seen across the open space and she felt a prickling sensation as she neared it. Tentatively, she raised a finger to the opening. A low-level shock made her finger tingle. The sensation wasn't particularly painful, but try as she would, concentrating all her powers, she couldn't force her finger beyond the edge of the door.

"Rats!" she said. "I can't penetrate it. Maybe I can remove it."

She now concentrated on trying to turn the force field off. Dan and the twins watched expectantly while she focused her attention on the opening. After a few minutes, sweat formed on her brow. Her teeth hurt and she realized she was clenching them.

"I can't touch it," she finally admitted, chewing on her lower lip. "It's too strong."

"What about the walls?" Dan asked. "The force field doesn't extend much past the opening. Can you melt the stones or change them into something we can dig through?"

She nodded. "I can try."

She concentrated on a portion of the wall that faced the corridor. But her best effort was no more effective than it had been with the force field. She only burned away some lichen from the rock surface.

"He's done something to make the walls super-strong," she said. "I can't change them."

A thought projection entered her mind. *There's no escape from the Master's prison—count on it.*

She looked up to see a repulsive looking Toad-Man standing just beyond the opening. This one lacked the air of authority and self-importance of the previous Toad-Men Jackie had encountered. His eyes held a doleful expression and he stood stooped, as if accustomed to cringing. Patches of discoloration that might have been bruises marred his glossy green hide.

I've orders to see you all live long enough for the Master to question, the amphibian-like humanoid projected. *After that, I guess it won't matter. Anyway, I've brought you food.*

He set a large metal tray on the floor with four shallow bowls of something that looked like a dark stew.

"And how are we supposed to get it through the force field?" Dan asked.

The Toad-Man stared at him. *Do you always make noises with your mouth like that?*

"It's called talking," Dan said. "Something humans do."

Well I've never seen a Gargoyle do it. He knelt to push the tray forward. *The field only blocks in one direction,* he explained. He stood up, shaking his head. *I can't believe that Flyers and Gargoyles would be so stupid as to go up against the Master. This odd-looking pink-skinned creature might not know any better, but those who serve him should know well enough not to cross him.*

"We aren't servants of the Master," Alpha said. "We're humans, like her."

"She can change us into any form she likes," Beta added.

The Toad-Man looked from one to the other. *She has that power? Was it her who knocked out old Sqwergal, up on the landing platform?*

"As a matter of fact it was," Dan said. "This is one powerful lady."

The Toad-Man looked her over with more respect. *Who are you?*

"Just one of these," she said, trying to stir his memories by projecting images of other humans, but from the blankness of his face she could see that he wasn't responding. She tried to exert a mental control over him. Again, no good. The field apparently blocked her from using any type of mental manipulation.

She grimaced and turned away. "I'm of the same race as you, if you only knew it. So are all the intelligent creatures on this planet."

The Toad-Man belch-laughed and shook his head. *The Master said you were all crazy. I guess this proves it. Well, enjoy your fantasies. They may be the only entertainment you'll have for a long time to come. You and that other pink-skinned idiot.* He turned away. Jackie could hear the slap-slap of his broad, webbed feet on the pavement of the corridor.

She looked to Dan. "What other pink-skinned idiot is he talking about?"

He scratched one of his enormous ears. "There may be other prisoners. While you were unconscious we heard somebody whistling. I thought it was one of the Master's flunkies, but maybe not."

As if on cue, a mournful whistling was taken up by someone outside their cell. Jackie ran to the doorway and pressed herself flat against the blocking field, straining against its tingling vibrations, feeling the blood pounding in her head. "Down in the Valley," she said, recognizing a song her father had sung to her a hundred times or more when he had carried her up to bed at night.

"Daddy?" she shouted, frantic to capture the whistler's attention. "Daddy, is that you?"

—CHAPTER—
20

The whistling stopped.

"You damned sadist!" an angry voice bellowed from beyond their cell. "Stop playing games with my mind."

Jackie's knees went weak. She leaned against the wall and slid down it, onto the stone floor.

Dan crouched over her, supporting her with his arm, his leathery Gargoyle face set in lines of concern that contrasted oddly with its demonic appearance. She looked up at him, unable for the moment to speak, overpowered by a wild jumble of feelings. Relief that her search for her father had ended coupled with a rush of confusion as to what his being here might mean.

"Is that whistler who I think he is?" Dan asked.

"It's his voice—I know it is. He must be a prisoner here too."

Dan frowned, looking more properly demonic. "Maybe not. Maybe the Master is playing his head tricks on us."

Jackie brought a hand to her mouth. An impersonation of her father was something she hadn't considered. She tried to reach out mentally to penetrate the mind beyond her cell, but again, found herself blocked. She couldn't get into the head of whoever was out there any more than she could enter the mind of the Toad-Man. Rising to her feet, she leaned against the wall and faced the shielded doorway, her lips close to the opening.

"Father," she called to him, "it's really me. After you disappeared I talked your friend Crow into taking me into the Void to try and link up with you. But Crow had a heart attack and died, leaving me trapped here." A silence. "I'm a ten-plus like you. Who else would know that?"

Again a silence—followed by a despairing groan. "Oh my God, he's got you too." There was an odd slurring to his speech, but the voice was definitely her father's.

"Why did you do it?" he said accusingly. "Why the hell were you stupid enough to follow me here?"

Jackie stiffened, stung by the words of rejection. So many times over the last month she had imagined how it would be when she finally found her father—how he would take her in his arms, hug her and kiss her and tell her how proud he was of all that she had accomplished. This was hardly the greeting she'd expected.

But was this really her father? As Dan had said, the Master could be playing tricks with them. Well, she had proven her identity—let him prove his.

"If you're really my father," she called to him, "tell me something no one would know about but you."

There was a pause. "You played Peter Pan," he said, speaking slowly, as if he had to think about each word. "You told me you cried after the performance because I couldn't be there."

"It is you!" she cried, her body trembling.

"But why?" he moaned, "why did you come here?"

"To help you escape."

"What happened to that damned computer thing? I thought it was supposed to keep you out of trouble."

"It wasn't CAP's fault. I ordered him turned off."

"Shouldn't have come," he muttered. "No way to escape—

no way. Tried a thousand times—ten thousand times. He's a devil."

"The Master? Who is he? How can he be so powerful? Where did he come from?"

"Who knows? From Hell for all I know."

Jackie frowned. There was definitely something odd about the way her father was speaking. Odd, but at the same time naggingly familiar. She wanted to look him over—see what sort of condition he was in. She thought for a moment. "Which side of the corridor are you on?"

There was a pause. "My sense of direction isn't all that great just now," he finally said. "But I'd guess the same side as you."

He sounded close. They might be in adjoining cells. She couldn't melt the wall that led to the corridor, but maybe she could melt the one between them.

She fixed her eyes on a spot in the wall dividing her cell from the next and concentrated on dissolving a small portion of it. After a minute of full effort without results she called to her father. "Has anything on your side been affected?"

"What are you talking about?" he muttered. "Why should my side be infected?"

His speech sounded so slurred. She was suddenly reminded of Crow returning from one of his binges. Her face flushed with indignation. "Are you drunk?" she cried.

He barked a laugh. "Constantly. What the devil else is there for me to do? Drinking is the one remaining talent I employ. I can change water into wine—or any other alcoholic beverage for that matter. Took me a hell of a long time to get the taste just right, but time was something I've had plenty of. Crow would have loved my bourbon."

Jackie wrinkled her nose in disgust. She had never known her father to drink this heavily. And from the way he talked, he kept himself this way most of the time. It was hard for her to believe he would let himself fall apart like this. Embarrassed, she glanced over at Dan and the twins. They looked sympathetic but offered no suggestions.

"Just how long have you been a prisoner here?" she asked.

"I stopped counting the days a long time ago, but I'd guess at least two years. After I singed the tail feathers off a couple of this Master character's Flyers, he sent his Stalkers out to get me. The stinking weasels knocked me out with their blowguns and brought me to this cell. Couldn't break out no matter how I tried. Then the Master himself comes to question me. He's stronger than me mentally—unbelievably strong. He pulled everything out of me he wanted to know. Then he just left me here to rot—the bastard. Just left me here to rot."

Jackie blinked back tears. Two years he had been here? His ship had only been missing for a month. Her time. But her father had reached the Void nineteen days before she did. Could those nineteen days have translated into two years? No wonder he had turned to drink.

"Listen," she said. "If you can make water into alcohol you should be able to change it back to water—even after you drink it."

"Why would I want to? Boozing is the only pleasure I have."

She clenched her fists in frustration. "I need you sober so we can put our heads together and think of a way out of here."

"No way out," he said, "no escape. Tried everything."

The sound of muffled sniffles came from the adjoining cell. She couldn't believe it. Her father was crying.

At that, her reserves crumbled. Her legs gave way beneath her and she sank against the cold stone flooring, burying her head in her arms, and letting her own tears flow. A hand touched her lightly on her shoulder and she looked up through watery eyes to see Dan's gray Gargoyle face peering down at her.

"Are you okay?" he asked.

"Nothing's been okay since we came to this awful place," she wailed. "My father's given up completely—become a drunk. And I can't get us out of here." She wiped her eyes with the back of her hand. "There's nothing more I can do."

"That doesn't sound like the feisty little fighter who brought me here. Don't let your old man get to you. Just because he gave up, doesn't mean that you have to."

She buried her head back in her arms. "I tell you there's nothing I can do. Just leave me alone, Dan—please."

He drew away. Her disappointment was a physical thing that ate at her innards and clawed at her throat, painfully constricting her stomach and chest. Emotionally numb, she sank into a state of depression. She stayed motionless, only vaguely aware of the cool hardness of the floor beneath her and the cramping of her back and leg muscles from sitting so long in the same position.

From time to time, the voices of Dan and the twins came to her, vague concerned murmurings she ignored. She had nothing to say to them—no assurances to offer. She had brought them here; confident she could protect them from whatever dangers they met. Protect them. What a laugh. Her overconfidence had, once again, tripped her up—brought her down—and her friends with her. Exhausted, she drifted into sleep.

The sound of whistling awoke Jackie. She lay there with her eyes closed, wondering how long she had been out. Her father was rendering "Down in the Valley" again. The song that once had been so comforting to her had become his personal lament. Her lips tightened. Just one more thing he had robbed her of in his escape into an alcoholic fog. He still had his mental powers. Enough to be able to transform things inside his cell. He just didn't have enough power to break out.

The thought set something off in her mind. She leapt to her feet and moved to the opening protected by the force field, ignoring Dan and the twins who were asking her if she was okay and what she was doing.

"Dad!" she called. "Dad, listen to me!"

The whistling stopped. "Why? What do you want?"

"I have an idea. But I need you sober to hear it."

"No point," he said. "Better off as I am."

She stamped her foot in frustration. "This is important."

"What's so all-fired important about it?"

"You need to clear the alcohol from your brain so you can think straight. Please."

"Okay, okay," he said. "Stop the nagging. Can't stand nagging. I'll sober up for you for now. Just don't expect me to like it."

A few moments of silence passed. Then he groaned.

"Are you okay?"

"One hell of a hangover, but I guess I'll live."

"You can get rid of the hangover. Just concentrate on feeling better. I need your faculties in order. I might just have a way to get us out of here."

"Believe me," he said, "there's nothing you can think of that I haven't tried a dozen times myself."

"But now there's two of us," she said, her voice edged with a building excitement. "We may be able to increase our powers by working together."

Her father snorted. "Our jailer wouldn't have placed us this close together if he thought we could help each other."

"From the way his flunkies tell it, he's a complete loner—doesn't share his planning with his people. Combining powers isn't something he'd be likely to consider. Anyway, it won't hurt us to try. What have we to lose?"

Her father sighed, sounding much put upon. "What have you got in mind?"

"Melting a place in the wall between us. Only this time we'll try doing it together. We can work on both sides at once. I'll pick a spot, say a foot back from the passageway and a foot up from the floor. You find the same spot on your side. When I say go, we'll both concentrate on melting the stone at that location—you on your side, me on mine. Find the spot? Ready? Now."

She counted off the seconds to herself as she concentrated on her chosen spot. One chili pepper, two chili peppers, three chili peppers—her count continued. At thirty-three chili peppers, the stone took on a dull glow. Heat radiated from its surface. At forty-five chili peppers, the rock face began to sag, like a melting candle. She intensified her effort. Now the rock flowed like partially molten volcanic lava, oozing slowly across the face of the still solid stones, leaving a fist-sized opening.

"Let's bring it up now," she said.

Slowly, they worked the opening upwards, enlarging it as they went until it was level with her eyes. Her father, bleary-eyed and dressed in a rumpled spacer's uniform, stood on the other side, peering between the still glowing edges of the hole. "Jump me blind," he said, "we did it."

The twins hopped up and down, squealing. Jackie felt like joining in but shushed them instead. The last thing they needed was to draw attention to themselves.

"We need to finish widening it now so you can come through," she said. "Working together, we may be able to make another hole out into the corridor."

His eyes narrowed. "Better you should join me in my cubicle. I don't like the looks of your cell-mates."

For a second she stared at him blankly. Then his meaning struck her. "Them?" she said, turning to look back at Dan and the twins. "They are friends. I made us look like Flyers and Gargoyles so we could fly over the Master's territory without arousing suspicion."

Her father blinked several times and ran a hand through his already disheveled thatch of brown hair, dusted with gray at the temples. "You figured out how to do that?"

Jackie nodded.

He stared at her as if he were having some trouble accepting the truth of her claim. Finally he shrugged. "Okay then, let's finish opening the wall."

It took several minutes to make the hole big enough and several more to let the molten stone cool to the point where her father could crawl through without burning himself. Jackie ran up to him and threw her arms around his neck. He held her to him, his grasp less firm and steady than she remembered. She leaned back and looked into his face. He was clean shaven at least—probably had stopped his beard from growing so he wouldn't have to bother with it. But he looked unhealthy. His skin had paled in confinement and his features slackened. The whites of his eyes were red-veined from steady drinking. Still, their blue depths held a familiar warmth. And there was no smell of liquor about him. He had done as she asked and freed himself of the alcohol. She was thankful for that.

Holding onto his hands, she took a step back. "You may know my friends. The Gargoyle is Dan Richfield, a propulsion specialist from your ship. The twins, Alpha and Beta, were passengers."

He inclined his head. "I remember seeing a pair of twins on the ship," he said. "And, of course, I know Dan." He eyed Dan's intimidating Gargoyle form. "I must say I never would have recognized him."

She placed a hand on Dan's shoulder. "He saved my life in a fight with Flyers."

Her father reached out to take Dan's taloned hand. "I owe you then," he said, "big time."

Dan shrugged. "I've been more than repaid, Commander. Jackie gave me back my identity—my humanity."

Her father looked bewildered. "What about the rest of the crew and passengers?"

"All these different animal forms," Jackie said, "that's what they are—the crew and passengers from your ship."

He shook his head. "I didn't know. I thought I was the only one from the ship who survived—that I had somehow been transported to a world populated by monsters."

"How did you manage to keep your human form?"

He looked down at himself, as if for reassurance that he was, indeed, still human. "I'm not sure. I guess I was strong enough mentally to resist whatever changed the others."

"This being who calls himself the Master must be responsible for all this. Have you any idea who he is or what he's up to?"

Before her father could answer, Jackie heard a sharp intake of breath from behind her. She spun around. Their Toad-Man jailer stood outside the doorway, eyes bulging, mouth agape as he stared at the hole in the wall. *Look at this would you. The Master's going to throw a fit.*

—CHAPTER—
21

Jackie's joy at reuniting with her father deflated like a punctured balloon. The Toad-Man stood in the doorway, staring at the hole they had created between their cells. Jackie lashed out at him with a mental blast, but he stood there untouched, showing no reaction.

She clenched her fists in frustration. So close to breaking out. She felt sure that she and her father could have penetrated the wall to the corridor by working together, if they'd only had a little more time. But that green slime ball would broadcast a mental warning to the Master long before they could ever break through. He'd ruined any hope for their escape.

She glared at the Toad-Man disdainfully, refusing to let him see how much his untimely appearance had devastated her. "So go tell your Master," she taunted. "Be a good frog-face and maybe he'll toss you a fly."

The Toad-Man blinked several times. *So the rumors are true. You do have powers like the Master. His strongest barriers can't hold you.*

The vertical opening, almost a yard across, gaped between their cells. There was no point in her trying to deny it.

And you can change us, too?

A plaintive quality in the Toad-Man's projection caught her attention. She eyed him sharply. "Why do you ask?"

He looked about from one side to the other, as if to

make sure no one was within sight. *I've been thinking about what you said—about all of us being like you—human. I haven't been able to get it out of my head. If there really was a chance to be something more than this*—He paused. *I'd do anything to be free of the Master.*

Her father pushed past her to confront the Toad-Man through the open doorway. "How dumb do you think we are?" he thundered. "You frog types are the Master's top people. Why would you be willing to defect?"

Being close to the Master is no great advantage. He takes out his irritations on whoever happens to be around him at the time. And for some reason, I'm his favorite target. Even when he's in a good mood, he delights in sliding objects into my path to trip me or making little explosions erupt under my feet. He raised a webbed foot to display patches of charred skin on its underside. *I don't know why he picks on me like this. I've always served him faithfully. But I've had enough.* The Toad-Man looked down at his mottled rotund body. *You say you can turn me back into something else that I used to be?*

"Once I return your memories to you, I'm sure I can. I gave back human bodies to Dan and the twins. They don't have them now because I made them into Flyers and Gargoyles so we could approach the Master. But I can change them back at any time. And I can change you too."

For several seconds the giant amphibian-like humanoid stood in place, blinking and swaying on its thin bowed legs, as if indecisive. Then he closed his eyes in rapt concentration. The shimmering field across the doorway disappeared. Alpha and Beta dashed out into the corridor, spreading their wings and twirling in circles.

It can be turned on and off from the outside, the Toad-Man explained, *so we can bring prisoners before the Master at his command.*

Jackie nodded her understanding as she moved through the now unguarded opening. "Is there an easy way to leave the castle?"

"I still say it's a mistake to trust this creature," her father growled, even as he moved out into the corridor, looking about as if expecting the Master to pounce on him at any moment. "You can't trust any of the Master's cronies."

Jackie gave her head a quick shake. "He's earned our trust by helping us."

"If he intended to inform on us," Dan pointed out, "he could have already done so."

And if we're caught, I have just as much to lose as you, the Toad-Man projected. *So let's get going. We can't afford to stand here arguing.*

Without waiting for agreement, the Toad-Man took off down the stone corridor, leading the way with a rolling wobbly walk that, for all its ridiculous appearance, made good time. Jackie and her father followed close behind. The twins trailed them, walking side by side, their wings held down to keep from getting in each other's way. Dan, in his Gargoyle form, brought up the rear. Glancing back at them, Jackie had to remind herself that the winged monster in the rear wasn't one of the Master's own leathery-skinned guardians, coming after them.

Leaving the cell area, they quickly trekked on down a narrow passageway of windowless stone, dimly lighted by the same lichen-like growths that grew in their cells.

"Where are we going?" her father asked, seemingly dazed by the rapid progression of events. Not the calm, confident man she remembered. She had expected him to take charge, once she had freed him. But he acted so withdrawn and fearful, she didn't feel she could trust his judgment. Maybe it was the long-term effects of the constant drinking.

"For now," she said, "my only plan is to get away from here as quickly as possible. If I turn us all into Gargoyles, we should be able to fly out of the Master's territory unchallenged."

"Now just a minute," he said, "you're not turning me into one of these animals."

She pressed her lips together. This was a fine time for him to get stubborn. If he wasn't going to lead, at least he could follow. "Flying is the fastest way for us to get away from here. And no one will challenge the right of a group of Gargoyles to fly over the Master's territory. If we crawl along the ground as humans, we're almost sure to be caught."

"Any of the Master's flunkies who tries to stop me has had it," her father growled. "I'll burn their brains out."

"We can't do that," she said, horrified by his words. "These creatures are all people from your ship. It would be murder to kill them."

"Better to let them kill us?" he scoffed.

Before she could answer, the Toad-Man stopped his determined forward movement and raised his head. His eyes rolled fearfully.

I'm being summoned by the Master. I'd better answer and pretend that I'm coming.

"He's lying," her father said. "He's setting us up."

Jackie snorted in exasperation. "He could simply tell the Master that we're here if he wanted to. Go ahead and report," she told the Toad-Man.

She watched as the great bulging eyes glazed over and the rounded jaw drooped, as if he were going into a trance state. Then the Toad-Man shuddered and turned to Jackie. *He wants me. I'm not sure why. He may have discovered the empty cells. I told him I was coming, but I won't be able to stall him very long. We need to get away from here now—out of his range of control.*

He took off down the corridor at an even faster pace than before. Suddenly he stopped. Again, his eyes glazed over.

He's forcing me to come to him, he projected weakly. *I can't . . . resist.*

The Toad-Man turned and started back the way they had come, walking awkwardly, as if trying to fight against each step. Jackie grabbed for his arm but he shook her loose.

"I told you we couldn't trust him," her father said. "I'll put him out before he gives us away."

"No!" Jackie said. "Maybe we can shield his mind from the Master's projection." She ran after the Toad-Man. "Help me form a mental bubble around him," she called back. She concentrated on imaging a giant, transparent bubble enclosing the Toad-Man, impervious to communication. She could sense her father's mind supporting her, however reluctantly.

Again, she grabbed at the Toad-Man's arm. This time he didn't resist. She held him in place. Slowly, his eyes cleared.

"Better?" she asked.

The Toad-Man stared at her blankly. Of course, she thought. With the bubble surrounding him, the mental part of my message couldn't get through.

"We need to make the bubble bigger," she told her father, "large enough to hold all of us. Then we can communicate without the Master or his people picking up our projections."

"I still say we should knock him out and leave him here."

She gave her father a look designed to wilt vegetation.

"We're not leaving him behind! Come in closer," she said, waving to the others. Dan and the twins moved up to join her. Her father followed, still muttering to himself.

But he helped her to expand the bubble.

"Can you understand me now?" she asked the Toad-Man.

A smile split the broad, green face. He nodded, then turned and plunged on with his wobble-walk.

Jackie followed closely, lost in thought. She could understand her father's fear of being caught again—imprisoned or killed outright. But it troubled her that he was so ready to hurt others in order to protect himself. He panicked at any difficulty they experienced.

She began to question the wisdom of their plans. If they simply escaped from the castle and hid out in the territories, what would they gain? The Master would be after them more than ever. He feared them as much as they feared him—she had sensed this when he attacked her. He would sacrifice any number of his people to capture or kill them. And her father, in his present state of mind, would kill as many as came after them. A terrible waste of lives.

And even if they could somehow elude the Master's forces, what sort of life would they have? They would still be stuck on this planetary prison. To escape it they needed to find out how they had gotten here in the first place. And that, the Master must know. But how could they make him tell them? Drat! she thought, it's hard to think on the run.

The Toad-Man came to a stop. *This area gets a lot of foot traffic. We need to drop the bubble long enough to check ahead for projections before we continue.*

"We can try," Jackie agreed. "But we'll have to raise it back quickly if the Master tries to draw you to him again."

Acting with extreme caution, she and her father gradually allowed their protective enclosure to dissipate. No presence sought them out, but she could pick up a large number of projections up ahead. The Toad-Man shook his heavy head.

As I suspected, our escape has been discovered. A search party is forming. But we're near ground level here. If you two can bore another hole in the wall we can get out that way.

Jackie frowned. If they made a hole, the Master's people would know that they had left the castle. They'd be right on their tails. Still, the Toad-Man's suggestion might work, only not in the way he thought.

"Okay," she said, "let's give the wall a try. The rest of you keep a close watch at both ends of the corridor. Let us know immediately if anyone's coming. And hold back on your projections. Especially you twins. I know how excited you can get. We don't want to give ourselves away."

Once again, she and her father focused their united minds on a small section of the stone wall. Jackie counted the seconds in chili peppers, wishing she could somehow speed up the process. But the outside wall appeared as strongly protected as the one between their cells.

"Someone's coming," Alpha called. Jackie stopped her effort and turned in Alpha's direction. A pair of the ferret-like Stalkers was headed toward them. "Back me up," Jackie told her father. "But please, just knock them out. Nothing more deadly than that."

Alpha and the Toad-Man backed away as the creatures raised blowguns to their lips. Jackie constricted the brain cells of the Stalker on her side of the corridor, trusting her father to deal with the other one. The Stalker she attacked reached for its head, projecting pain, then dropped to the floor. The other doubled over, projecting far greater levels of pain, but remaining conscious. Jackie stopped the blood to its brain as well, just long enough to knock it out and end its misery.

Furious, she turned on her father. "What did you do to it?"

He shrugged. "I sensed he was male. He probably experienced something akin to being kicked in the crotch." He scowled at the fallen creature. "It won't kill him, but it might make him wish it did."

Jackie sighed and shook her head. This was not the best time to discuss humane methods for disabling the Master's forces. "Let's get back at the wall before more of them find us."

After ten more minutes of their combined efforts, one of the stone slabs started to melt. They kept up their concentration until they had an opening large enough to crawl through.

"Come on," her father said, "let's get out of here before the Master himself shows up."

Jackie pulled on her father's arm. "First we need to reestablish our isolation bubble. I've an idea for a change of plans, and I don't want to be overheard."

—CHAPTER—
22

Her father gaped at her, eyes round with disbelief. "What are you talking about? This is no time for changing our plans. Let's get out of here while we can."

"Yes," Alpha said, "let's leave."

"Before the Master finds us," Beta said and started forward.

Jackie held out an arm to stop her. "As soon as they spot this hole, they'll know we left the castle and come after us in force. But if we hide out here for a while, we can slip out later unnoticed while they are all out looking for us."

Slipping out wasn't exactly what she had in mind. But at this point she wanted to tell them only enough to get them to cooperate. She would need their help to make this work, and her father, she knew, would have a fit if he had any idea what she really intended. She didn't like leading him on like this, but she had no choice—not if they were to have any real chance for escaping the Void.

Dan placed a hand on her father's shoulder. "Your daughter's right. We'll have them confused as hell. Once the Master has his whole force out looking for us, we can come up from behind, like we're part of the search party."

Jackie felt a surge of appreciation for Dan's support.

Her father looked from the hole to her and back. "Well, maybe a short delay," he said grudgingly, "just long enough to throw them off our track. But we'll need a place to hide out while we're waiting."

"Can you find a place in the castle for us?" Jackie asked the Toad-Man, anxious to follow up on her plan before her father changed his mind.

The Toad-Man thought for a moment, then reversed direction. *Follow me,* he projected.

They retraced their steps through the winding corridors, following the Toad-Man's lead. The twins glanced back wistfully several times, but Dan's Gargoyle form, bringing up the rear, kept them moving.

Abruptly, the Toad-Man came to a stop in front of one of the many ironbound doors that lined the passageway they now traveled. After a final glance up and down the corridor, he flung the door open and hurried them into a large room stacked high with cardboard boxes. Open rows ran between the stacks, allowing for access. Jackie eyed the boxes in wonder. "What is all this?"

The mouth of the Toad-Man curled in disgust. *Canned goods,* he said. *Canned beans, canned fruit, stews, soups, canned whatever. It's all we get here at the castle except when Flyers or Stalkers bring in fresh game. And that doesn't happen often I can tell you. They only share it when they want something in return, like an update on the latest castle gossip.*

"But where does the canned food come from?"

From the Master—where else? Workers bring in the raw materials—dirt, rocks, whatever—and pile it up in the storage rooms. The Master transforms it into something like this. He opened one of the lower boxes and extracted a sixteen-ounce tin can. A bright yellow label read " 'Pork and Beans.' "

"This is what the Master eats?" The very idea seemed ludicrous to Jackie.

That's what he eats when he eats. He seems to like the stuff. He doesn't always eat, though. Sometimes he goes for weeks without anything. I don't think he actually needs food.

That went along with what Jackie had experienced for herself. She ate out of habit but could fast without suffering. Just another way of manipulating reality. But why canned goods?

"Are you sure this place is safe?" she asked.

As safe as any place in the castle. The storerooms are emptied one at a time and this one isn't due to be visited for several days yet. Unless they search the entire castle, we should be secure here for a while. And it's doubtful they'll bother when they see the hole you've bored through the wall.

Jackie expanded their bubble shield to allow them more freedom in moving around the room. The twins explored the contents of the cartons, giggling as they opened box after box to read the labels. The rest of them drew several cartons together to sit on while waiting. Jackie and Dan sat across from her father and the Toad-Man.

What now? the Toad-Man asked.

"We give the Master's forces enough time to find the hole and spread out all over the countryside looking for us," Jackie said. "An hour or so should do."

"The sooner the better," her father said. "Much as I dislike the idea of changing into a Flyer or Gargoyle, if it will let us distance ourselves from this place I say let's do it." He looked from one to the other, as if seeking agreement.

Jackie quickly changed the subject. "Before we settle on a plan, I think we should help our new friend regain his identity as I promised. This seems a good time to give it a try. If you're ready that is," she said, turning to the Toad-Man.

By all means, the Toad-Man projected enthusiastically. *I've been most anxious to find out more about myself ever since you raised the possibility.*

"Hold on," her father said, irritation in his voice. "This

can wait till later. We need to be concentrating on our escape."

"It won't take long," Jackie said, "Now that I'm experienced at returning people to their natural states." Ignoring her father's disapproving glare, she turned back to the Toad-Man. "I know that these aren't the best of circumstances, but we'll have to make do. The first thing we need is to loosen you up a bit. Too bad we can't offer you a drink to help you relax." She snapped her fingers, pretending to just have come up with an idea. "Maybe we can get you that drink. My father has had quite a bit of practice with that sort of thing." She turned to her father. "We don't have any water handy, but you ought to be able to manufacture a little alcohol inside his blood stream—don't you think? Just enough to give him a slight buzz."

Her father's glowering features brightened at her suggestion. "I don't see why not. If I can make if from water, I ought to be able to make it from body fluids. Anything to speed things up. Might even give myself a little something. It would make all this waiting a hell of a lot easier. Care to join us?" he asked Dan.

Dan frowned. "I don't know if this is such a good idea. We need to stay alert."

Jackie placed her hand on Dan's and gave it slight a squeeze. "It's all right," she said, "you and I can stay on guard." Dan gave her a questioning look but didn't object further.

"Can you open your mind to me while you add the alcohol to his system?" Jackie asked her father. "I'd like to see how you do it."

He was already concentrating on the transformation. "Just don't try this on yourself," he grumbled. "You're too young to be drinking."

200

Jackie monitored his mental process as he manipulated the Toad-Man's blood to form alcohol in his veins. The Toad-Man's eyes widened. *Not bad,* he projected. *I haven't felt this good in a long time. In fact, as long as I can remember.* The corners of his ample mouth turned up in a crooked grin and he slid off the carton to sprawl spread-legged on the floor with the carton propping his back.

Her father's mental projections ended. Jackie glanced at him and concluded from his glazed expression that he had added something to his own veins as well. Quietly, she assumed full control of the bubble. The alcohol should keep her father quiet for a while. If she needed to, she could reverse the process and sober him up quickly, now that she had a feeling for how this worked. But for the moment, she could concentrate on the Toad-Man, undisturbed.

From her seat on the box she leaned toward him and spoke in a quiet but authoritative tone. "Stay very relaxed and concentrate on my voice. Try to remember a time before you ever walked the halls of this castle. Before you came under the Master's control, you were your own person. Remember what you were and show that person to me."

Almost immediately, images of the interior of her father's ship and the humans who inhabited it began to flow through the Toad-Man's consciousness and into Jackie's. She watched as a drama unfolded, almost like a tri-D projection.

The people pictured wore the uniforms of officers. They stood in what appeared to be the control center of the *Golden Arrow.* They seemed agitated. The Toad-Man projected surprise, indignation, and anger. Soon, a slim young man in a wrinkled set of coveralls, too large for his lanky frame, was dragged in through a portal by two burly crewmen. Beneath the dark shank of hair that fell across the youth's forehead, dark feral eyes stared out, panic-stricken.

As Jackie watched, a sudden sense of danger pervaded the Toad-Man's projection. Something had gone terribly wrong. A great pressure engulfed everyone. The Toad-Man's projection cut off with the suddenness of a car crashing into a stone wall. He rocked his enormous head from side to side, looking dazed and bewildered.

Worried by his reaction, Jackie negated the effects of the alcohol in his blood. "Do you remember who you are now?"

He stared up at her, considerably sobered, eyes wide with wonder. "My God!" he said, "I'm Captain Paliki, commanding officer of the *Golden Arrow*."

Awkwardly, her father stumbled to his feet and peered down at the Toad-Man. "Captain Paliki? Can it really be you?"

The Toad-Man's nod was barely perceptible, as if his head was suddenly too ponderous to move. "Jack Claver, our pilot? I fear I have only just now recognized you. But then how would I recognize you if I couldn't even recognize myself? I would not have believed such a complete loss of identity to be possible."

"Captain," Jackie said, "just before you stopped projecting you showed us an image of a young man being brought to you. Who was he?"

The captain put his hands to his head, as if to help support it. "A stowaway. Just one of the derelicts that haunt the launch area on Maddoc-Port, trying to get a berth on a Void liner. There's no way we would ever take on one of these unfortunates as members of our crew, but they never seem to give up hope. This one must have sneaked onboard with a work party. My people found him just as we were entering the Void for our jump."

"What did you do with him?"

The toad-like face of the captain grew thoughtful. "Actually, it was right at that time that everything went blank."

Jackie turned to her father. "I didn't see you among the officers. Where were you when all of this was going on?"

He blinked several times. "In a sound-proof cubicle. Pilots are kept isolated during jumps so that nothing interferes with their concentration. I had no idea what had happened."

Jackie turned back to the captain. "Could this stowaway have anything to do with your being stuck in the Void?"

Slowly, he rose to his feet, sober now, but still shaky from the emotional impact of his revelations. "Him?" the captain scoffed, "he was just a derelict. A nothing."

"But you said it was right after your people found him that a powerful force took over your ship. Do you know for sure that it couldn't be him?"

"No one with an ability like the Master's would be likely to go unnoticed by the spacer industries."

Jackie shook her head. "That's not necessarily true." She glanced over at her father. "My mental powers were kept hidden for some time."

"This is all beside the point," her father said, sounding angry in his impatience. "Whoever this Master being is, we need to get away from him—now."

"But now that we've established my identity," the captain said, "I would greatly appreciate being transformed back into my own body, at least until we're ready to leave here. I find my present form most abhorrent."

Jackie concentrated on blanking out the captain's Toad-Man features while he provided the image for his transformed self, much as she had done with Dan and the twins. The result was a somewhat stiff-looking medium-sized man dressed in a blue officer's uniform and wearing a sandy colored, well-trimmed beard.

Her father eyed the transformation critically. "You've got him too young. The beard should be grayer. He should have jowls and more wrinkles and be twenty pounds heavier."

"This will do for now," the captain quickly said. "And thank you my child. I would have hated to end my days in the guise of a giant frog."

Jackie smiled at the obvious relief the captain showed at regaining his natural form. "I have to agree that you're much improved."

"And I'm most anxious to stay that way. How soon do you plan for us to leave? I would think that by now all the Master's forces should be out looking for us."

Her father grunted agreement. "Can't be too soon for me."

Jackie pursed her lips. It was time to drop the bomb. She only hoped she could handle the fallout. She cleared her throat. "I've been thinking things over," she said, "and I think we should take on the Master."

—CHAPTER—
23

Jackie's five companions stared at her as if they couldn't quite believe what she was saying. Her father was the first to speak.

"Are you crazy? We've both tried to stand up to this joker and each of us has been flattened by him. Unless we get away from here now we may be flattened permanently, or back eking out the rest of our miserable lives in his dungeon. And this time he'll know enough to separate us so we can't break out. I'd rather die than be jailed here for the rest of my life."

Jackie heard the panic in his voice. She had expected it, given his present state of mind. But she had to win him over—to convince him that this was their only chance to gain their freedom.

"As long as we're stuck on this planet we're in a jail of sorts," she said. "But you're right on one point. The Master would have to separate us to keep us from breaking out. Together, we're stronger than he is. We had to be stronger in order to break through his cells and block his transmissions." Jackie gestured at the bubble surrounding them. "If we face him together, are able to control him—we can force him to tell us how he brought all of you here."

Wild-eyed, her father ran a hand through his hair. "What kind of crazy scheme are you hatching in that head of yours? We have to leave here now, like we planned."

"He'll just keep after us until he finds us. And sooner or

later, either he or his creatures will find us. If we run. But he won't expect us to confront him. If we go against him together, while his people are out looking for us, we'll have a real chance to bring all of this to an end."

"The Master is absolutely paranoid," the captain said, nodding agreement. "He'll never give up on hunting us down if he thinks we're a possible threat."

"But he's too strong," her father said, as if he could give his argument more force simply by repeating it.

The others might join Jackie in this, but it was obvious she wasn't going to win her father over. And without him they had no chance at all. She stiffened her resolve. If she couldn't talk him into helping, she'd have to trick him into it. Too many lives were at stake to let this chance slip by. She only hoped that, in taking advantage of her father's weakness, she wasn't pushing him beyond the limits of recovery—as she had with Crow. She sighed, thinking how much she wished CAP were here to advise her.

At least she knew what she had to do. She had paid close attention while her father formed alcohol in the captain's circulatory system and in his own. Now, unobtrusively, she nudged up the alcoholic content in her father's blood. A look of surprise crossed his face. He started to sway, then caught himself. She gave him the scornful look she had once used playing Lady Macbeth at the Conservatory. "I guess if you're that afraid of facing the Master, I'll have to do it on my own."

He blinked at her owlishly. "Can't do that," he said with a definite slur. "Master would whack you for sure."

"My friends and I are going to take on the Master whether you come along or not. If you're afraid, you can run off like a coward and hide."

Even though she was playing a role, her words bit deep,

paining her, as she knew they would her father. For a moment he just stood there, an expression of hurt confusion drawing down his features. Then he shook his head. "Can't let my little girl go get herself whacked," he said, heavily slurring his words. "Can't let the bastard do that to you."

"Well, I'm going after him. Are you coming or not?"

His chin rose belligerently. "You just take me to him. I'll teach him a lesson—show him that he can't whack my little girl."

Jackie's eyes filled with tears. She had achieved the effect she needed but she didn't like herself much for doing it. "Come on," she said to the others, having all she could do to keep her voice from cracking, "it's time that we make our move." She opened the door to the hallway and waved them on. "Captain," she said, "you lead the way. Take us to the Master's quarters in the tower—hopefully without running into any more of his people along the way. Dan, keep Dad back in the rear for now. Twins, stay between. And none of your play. We're in for some serious business."

Dan gave her a doubtful look but put out an arm to help support her father as he stumbled forward on shaky legs. With everyone sorted out to her satisfaction, she moved up beside the captain.

"Are you sure you know what you're doing?" he asked, quietly enough so the others wouldn't hear.

Jackie rolled her eyes. "I sure hope so. If I don't we're in big trouble. But I don't see any other way out of this."

They moved swiftly down long stone corridors, still shielded by their mental bubble, supported only by Jackie. She could maintain it on her own, now that the Master had given up trying to call in his Toad-Man. She hoped it would be enough to keep their presence from being detected.

She tried to keep her feet from slapping too loudly against

the hard pavement, but in the empty corridors the sound of every footstep seemed amplified. Every few minutes her father stumbled and giggled. This, in turn, set the twins tittering despite hard looks from Dan. But her ruse had apparently worked. The corridors were deserted. All the Master's people had taken out after them. But not the Master himself. He, she believed, would be holed up in his fortress, waiting to be brought word of their capture or death.

Who was this powerful being? she wondered for the hundredth time. Could he be the stowaway? A mere boy? Or was he something more insidious? Could some powerful alien presence have entered the Void to experiment with human travelers? A frightening thought.

And here she was, ready to lead her father and friends against him. Was she once again being overconfident? In one sense her father was right. The Master had easily defeated both of them before. Their combined strength had been enough to break through the barriers he had created, but that was without him there. Confronting him in person might prove a different story entirely. At least this time she knew what sort of chance she was taking. And considering the alternatives, facing down the Master still had to be their best hope for getting free of him and of this world.

They followed the captain through a series of twists and turns that ended up at the foot of the great crystal stairway. It was unguarded, but they ascended it cautiously, holding tightly to the rail and taking each step with carefully placed feet, making their way up toward the garish reception area where they had confronted the Master before.

All at once, a mental force broke over them like an ocean wave. Jackie staggered backward against the captain, feeling her hold on their protective bubble shield slipping away from her.

"Fools!" The word boomed from above as if fired from a cannon. "Did you think I wouldn't sense your mental barrier? You may have tricked my people, but your games won't work with me. I'll settle you now, once and for all."

Jackie glanced back at her companions. The twins in their Flyer forms crouched down, holding on to each other, amber eyes wide with terror. She ignored them, concentrating on her father who was being held up bodily by Dan. Quickly, she broke down the alcohol molecules in his body, sobering him instantaneously. "Help me," she cried. "Help me restore the barrier."

His eyes widened as he realized the full extent of their predicament. His mind frantically grasped for her—twined around hers. Together, they firmed the isolation bubble just as another mental blast slammed into it, shaking them with its strength. But their bubble held. Jackie shook herself and started up the stairs again, one step at a time, the other four following, each step taking them closer to the reception area. Somewhere above them the Master waited, ready to lash out with mental lightning bolts should they relax their guard in the slightest.

Still another blast rocked them as they gained the reception area. Jackie steeled herself against its force, then looked around the great hall. The Master wasn't there. He must be still higher up.

Holding together like a squad of Roman soldiers, they started up the next flight of stairs. Jackie glanced back at her father. The muscles of his face looked strained and his skin ashen, but he flickered a smile. She returned it warmly, relieved and strengthened by what it conveyed to her. Sober now, he was still with her. No matter what happened, he would play his part.

A rapid string of hits pummeled them, as if the Master

were trying to achieve with quantity what he had failed to win with sheer power. For a few seconds, the barrage brought them to a halt. Then he paused, apparently unable to keep up the level of his attack. They moved forward.

Jackie's head ached like a muscle pounded too long and too often. The force of the Master's blows was creating a tremendous tension in her mental defenses. Father's feeling this, too, she thought. I don't see how we can hold out against it much longer. Thank goodness we're almost there.

They reached the top of the landing with their shield still intact. Directly ahead lay a large open doorway.

"Father and I will go ahead," Jackie said. "The rest of you stay back."

Dan started to object but she held up a hand. "From here on out this is a battle of minds. Only the two of us are equipped for that sort of conflict. Take care of the twins."

Dan nodded and placed his leathery hands on the shoulders of his two feathered companions. Her father joined her and the two of them moved forward, mental fields meshed and probing ahead. Beyond the doorway Jackie could see a huge, open room with marble walls and flooring. Everywhere were tables and shelves of crystal, holding strange collections of objects: models of spacecraft, fanciful animal figures, and many other creations, almost toy-like in their construction. A variety of primitive hand-weapons hung from the walls.

At the back of the room, the brown-robed, hooded figure stood rigidly, arms extended, as if trying to physically push them back. As they entered the room, the Master shrieked and snatched up a massive broadsword, mounted on the wall behind him. The weapon looked too heavy for him to handle, but he held it, two-handed, before him, and swung it powerfully in a whistling arc.

Jackie halted, surprised by this turn of events. With all her concentration focused to counter the Master's mental powers, she hadn't expected a physical attack. Raising his sword, the Master charged directly at them, cleaving the air with broad, hissing strokes.

Jackie and her father leapt aside in opposite directions, barely escaping the sweeping cuts. "Help me stop the blood to his brain," Jackie cried. She felt her father's powers adding to hers. "Squeeze harder!" she yelled.

The Master raised his sword again and started toward her, his body trembling with the effort of holding back their combined attack. Suddenly, a dark winged form shot past her and slammed into the Master with a vicious body-block, doubling the Master over. The Master's sword flew from his hand, clanging against the marble flooring.

Dan, in his Gargoyle form, grappled with the Master on the floor. Taken by surprise, Jackie eased up on her own attack. But the Master was far from beaten. With a wave of his arm, he flung Dan aside and rose to his feet. His eyes locked with Jackie's and she felt a tremendous pressure mounting in her head.

"Block him!" she yelled to her father.

Immediately, they reestablished their shield, deflecting the gouging squeeze of the Master's mental fingers. Jackie staggered, reeling from the force of his attack. Their combined minds might be stronger than his, but the Master used his mental energy efficiently and was quick to take advantage of their slip-ups.

Feathered wings swept past her and the twins were in the room, snatching objects from shelves and hurling them at the Master. A sculptured spaceship narrowly missed his head. He whirled about to face the twin who threw it and Alpha dropped to the ground, writhing in pain.

The Master ducked as another object flew past his head, thrown by Beta. Then the bulky form of the captain charged forward to grapple with the robed figure.

"Now!" Jackie yelled. This time, they took full advantage of the Master's distraction. With vice-like projections, they squeezed his brain unmercifully. The Master screamed once and collapsed to the floor in a heap of robes.

They had won! It had taken the combined efforts of all five of them, but between them they had brought down this powerful, mysterious being. For a moment Jackie stared at the still form. The captain stood over it, breathing heavily from his exertions. But Jackie had others to consider. Turning back, she saw Dan stagger to his feet, at least partially recovered from his encounter. Alpha, however, lay motionless. Beta had dropped to her knees beside him. Jackie hurried over. The boy was unconscious but alive. She quickly set her healing powers to work on his body.

But as Alpha started to stir, her attention was diverted by a sudden premonition. She whirled about to see her father. He had retrieved the Master's dropped sword and now stood over the brown-robed body of their fallen enemy, holding the sword in both hands.

"Daddy!" she cried. "What are you doing?"

"Making sure this creep never hurts anyone again." He brought the sword upward.

"Stop," she yelled, striking out at him mentally. The sword rattled to the marble flooring and her father jumped back, shaking his hands as if they had been burnt.

"Why did you stop me?" he yelled. "This monster almost killed us. He may do it yet if we don't finish him off."

He bent down to grasp the sword.

"No!" Jackie said, and gave the alcohol content of her father's blood a quick boost. The sudden effects of the intoxicant made him lose his balance. He tumbled forward to sprawl on the floor.

"Hey!" he protested, sitting up and looking about with a bewildered expression, "wha's going on?"

Jackie ignored the slurred question. She couldn't, however, ignore the jabs from her own conscience. Again, she had taken advantage of his weakness. It was a rotten thing to do. But she just couldn't allow him to kill the Master, no matter how dangerous he was. There had to be a better way for dealing with this. While the captain helped her father to his feet, Jackie picked up the sword and handed it to Dan. "Hold on to this for now. And keep my father away from the Master."

Dan glanced down at the still form. "What if he recovers?"

"I can keep him unconscious for now. But I need time—time to think this through."

—CHAPTER—
24

Leaving Dan to guard the Master, Jackie returned to look after Alpha. The male twin sat supported by Beta, her arm around his feathered shoulders. His eyes were glazed and his body trembled with fits of spasms. "It feels like lightning hit me," he said. "I can't stop shaking. And every move I make hurts."

Jackie knelt and concentrated her mental powers on easing muscles painfully cramped by the Master's mental grasp. Soon the strain left Alpha's face and his Flyer body relaxed into a more natural state. Jackie gave him a quick kiss on the forehead and, leaving him under Beta's care, headed over to view the Master. Dan had drawn her father to one side of the room, but the captain stood by their fallen enemy's prone form. He watched in silence as she approached.

Facedown, with his head covered by his cowl, one could have mistaken the Master for a pile of empty clothes if not for the booted feet sticking out from beneath the robe. So much strength this one had shown. Her own mental powers combined with those of her father's had barely been enough to defeat him. Without the distractions from Dan, the twins, and Captain Paliki, the Master might well have overpowered them. A shiver ran down her spine. She crossed her arms tightly, holding herself together.

She felt no elation at their victory, only a dull confusion. Her father had been right; they could all have been killed.

And yet, with the Master lying crumpled and unconscious, she couldn't let her father do him in. She just couldn't. She might argue that they needed the Master's knowledge to help them escape from the Void, but that wasn't her real reason for sparing his life. She simply couldn't go along with killing a fellow human being while he lay helpless.

But what was she to do with him? They had a tiger by the tail that they couldn't turn loose. Jackie could keep him unconscious indefinitely, but he was no good to them that way. There were questions they needed him to answer.

A hand fell on her shoulder and she looked up to see the captain's eyes fixed on her. "What are your plans?"

She shrugged shoulders heavy with indecision. "At this point, only to take a look and see what we have."

Dan and the twins came over to join them, Alpha leaning on Beta's arm. Her father stayed slouched against the wall in an alcoholic stupor, singing muttered words under his breath. Guilt lumped in her chest. She reduced the level of the alcohol in his bloodstream.

"Come on," she called to him, "you may as well have a look."

He blinked several times as if surprised by the sudden change in his condition, and staggered over, maintaining a precarious balance.

The Master lay on his stomach, his face hidden by an arm. Jackie bent down gingerly and pulled the cowl back from his head, releasing a shock of thick, black hair. The captain grasped him by a shoulder and rolled the Master on his back. His head flopped to one side. Grunts of surprise greeted the sight. Jackie stared into a face no older than her own, dark lashes over a slender nose, and an ample mouth, framed by a tapering jaw and chin. A sensitive face, she thought. One capable of strong emotions. She reached down to straighten his head and caught her breath at the sight of a long scar etched into his left cheek.

"Well, I'll be damned," the captain muttered, "it's him after all."

Her father leaned unsteadily over her shoulder. "This is the stowaway?"

"He is," the captain said.

Her father swayed unsteadily on his feet. "How could this little creep be so powerful mentally without anyone knowing about it?"

Jackie looked to the captain, curious as to his answer. The captain shook his head, his features pinched with disapproval. "Testing for mental ability on Maddoc is supposedly mandatory. But the Maddoc-Port ground station is infested with these street urchins. Some of them must slip through the cracks. I wouldn't have believed the authorities could be so remiss, but this fellow's very presence proves just how lax they can be."

Jackie sighed. "He looks so young."

"Young or not," the captain said, "he remains a very real threat. For years now, he has kept us all in mental slavery. And he's likely to do it again, if we let him. I'm afraid your father is right. Allowing him to live will endanger the lives of hundreds of passengers and crewmembers. Our only safe choice is to eliminate him."

Beta's amber Flyer's eyes grew large. "We can't let him hurt Alpha again."

Recoiling from the thought of killing their now helpless opponent, Jackie searched desperately for reasons to keep him alive. "Look," she said, "we still don't know what kind of role he played in getting us here. We might well need his help in getting out."

Her father glared at her through bloodshot eyes. "And

how do we keep him from attacking us again?" he challenged, his voice still slurred from the alcohol.

The alcohol! The answer seemed obvious now that she thought of it. If she could control her father with alcohol, why not the Master? "I think I have a solution," she said. "But first, let's move him to some place more comfortable."

They found sleeping quarters nearby. They carried the boy there and laid him on a thickly stuffed bed with a quilt heavily brocaded in patterns of burgundy and gold. Jackie drew an ornately carved chair by the bed and gestured for the others to stay in the background. She wanted them out of the way but ready to help should she need them.

She seated herself in the chair and stared at the boy. He looked so helpless; she had to keep reminding herself of what he was capable of doing. She couldn't afford to underestimate him—not for a second. Proceeding cautiously, she manipulated the makeup of his blood, creating alcohol within his veins as she had done with her father, trying for just the right dosage to retard his reflexes without plastering him completely. Satisfied with her work, she removed the restrictions she had placed on his mind to keep him unconscious and drew a surge of oxygen to his brain.

Dark lashes fluttered. His eyes, she saw, were brown with flecks of green, clouded now with confusion. They widened as he focused on her.

"You!" he said. "You're the one who came after me."

Jackie increased the alcohol level just a bit. "Don't worry, we aren't going to hurt you."

An odd expression settled on his face. He licked his lips. "My tongue feels thick like . . . and my head . . . fuzzy . . . what have you done to me?"

"You're okay. You may feel a little woozy right now, but the effect is temporary. We're making sure you don't try any more of your power games with us."

He struggled to a sitting position, swinging his legs over the edge of the bed. Jackie rose to her feet. She could sense him gathering his mental powers to lash out at her. But the alcohol slowed his reflexes and made it difficult for him to concentrate. Jackie held his mind in hers with just enough pressure to let him know she could squeeze him blind if she had to. He scowled and ran a hand through thick, black hair, as if trying to wipe away the cause of his disorientation.

"What do you want with me?" he said, slurring his words together.

"First of all, I'd like a name to call you by. I'm certainly not going to be calling you Master."

He grinned feebly. "I make them call me that to let them know who's boss. My real name's Scarf."

"Scarf what?"

"Just Scarf. That's all anybody ever called me."

Jackie settled back down in her chair. "Then tell me, Scarf, why have you been keeping all these people fixed up like animals without memories of their pasts?"

He frowned. "They hate me. They'd kill me in a minute if I gave them half a chance."

Jackie pursed her lips. He sounded paranoid, but maybe he had reasons. "I'm not surprised they're unhappy with you, after the way you've treated them. But why did you do this to them in the first place?"

He blinked, looking confused. She eased up a little on the alcohol content to free his thinking.

"It was just part of my making this world. I made everything here, you know—everything."

"But how?" she asked. "How could you possibly do that?"

He blinked again. "It's hard to remember. I know I was surrounded by nothingness—scared out of my head. I wanted something to be there—anything. Then, all at once, this world starts to form up around me. After a while, I can see that it's me who's making it all happen. It's as if I'm taking things I've seen in pictures, or heard spacers talk about, or can see in the minds of others, and I'm bringing them all together. The animal forms were just a part of that—ideas I picked up and played with. I knew they weren't real, but I got a kick out of the way they looked and acted." He giggled drunkenly.

"And you forced them to serve you?"

"Hey," he protested, "I didn't force nothing. At least not at first. Some of them wanted to stay under my protection when they saw what powers I had. Others were frightened and took off into the far regions." He snickered. "But I made them all afraid of me. Even the ones who stayed."

"Why?"

He leaned toward her conspiratorially. "I didn't trust them. They'd been after me before . . . before all this happened." He passed a hand over his eyes. "I was scared then. Scared of what they would do to me."

"It seems to me you still are."

He glowered at her. "Hey," he said, holding up a wobbly finger, "I was doing okay until you came along. You and that guy I stuck in my dungeon. He was strong too—stronger than any of the others. But I was stronger." A smug smile raised the corners of his mouth, then turned into a grimace. "Then you two ganged up on me. It wasn't fair. I thought you'd kill me for sure." He gave her a sullen glare. "Why did you come here anyway?"

"That man you put in the dungeon is my father. I came here to free him and the others. But I don't have anything against you. I mean I don't hate you or anything."

His features took on a puzzled expression. "Yes," he said, "you're different. I never felt that you hated me like the others do. Still, you tried to use your mental powers on me. You and that other one." He lowered his eyes and shook his head, as if trying to clear it of confusion.

"You say you find it hard to remember how you got here. Maybe you wanted to forget. It seems you've made most of the others forget about their past lives. But I've helped some of them to get back their memories. I could help you—if you'll let me."

He eyed her suspiciously. "Why should I?"

"Remembering might help you to understand your situation."

He looked past her at the silent line of her companions, standing at the back of the room. "What about them? What are they doing here?"

"They're all my friends. You don't have to be afraid of them. They're here to help. And I'll protect you. I promise. Will you trust me on this?"

"So you can zonk me again?" he sneered.

She glared at him and leaned forward, hands on hips, her nose only inches from his. "Look, dummy, if I wanted to do anything to you I would have done it while you were still unconscious."

He grinned sheepishly. "Okay, okay, don't have a burnout. You feel straight to me. What do you want me to do?"

"For starts, I'll feed you some images of what happened just before you came here. Try to stir up your memories."

Jackie called for Captain Paliki to join them. "I need you to open your mind to him," she told the captain, "let him see what happened on the ship from your perspective."

"Are you sure that's wise?" the captain asked. "Whatever set him off before might do it again."

"I have him under my control now. Besides, we have to bring back his memories if we're ever going to learn how all this happened."

Paliki mentally ran through the scenes of Scarf's capture just before the jump. Jackie kept her eyes on Scarf's face. A nervous twitch pulled at the side of his mouth.

"Bring back anything?" she asked.

Scarf stayed silent for a while. "It's funny how it works," he finally muttered, "like rocks rolling down a hill. One memory starts another, and pretty soon you've got a regular rock slide coming down on top of you." He shook his head. "I've forgotten a lot."

"What do you remember?"

"I remember that lousy port town where I lived. I was nothing there—on the streets like an animal. I'd see the crews from the Void ships come down in shuttles and I'd follow them around, just to hear them talk about the places they'd been and the things they'd seen. Sometimes they'd give me stuff to eat. Stuff out of cans. It sure beat the slops I used to get from the garbage bins. Spacers were like gods to me. I wanted to be one—more than anything in the world. But I knew it wasn't in the cards. Not for a rat-brat from Maddoc-Port."

"Didn't you have any idea of your mental abilities?"

"Just that I could sense things sometimes. Like when my old man was feeling mean. I could usually keep out of his way. The one time I didn't was when I got this." He fingered the scar at his cheek. "After that I ran out on him—never saw him again."

"Why didn't the authorities ever test you?"

"The one thing my old man taught me was to keep away

from anyone who comes looking. 'Once you're taken in,' he told me, 'it's all over. You never come back.' I made damn sure no one ever took me in for nothing."

Jackie found herself sympathizing. How horrible to grow up alone, unwanted, and afraid in such a place. "How did you get on the ship then?"

"I'd been hanging around the bars, listening to spacer talk. The liner was in for repairs and there was a whole parcel of reps in the bar who had just come back on the shuttle."

"Reps?"

"Repair types. Technicians who work on the ships while they're docked. This bunch was all drinking heavy, but one was in real bad shape. I followed him when he went to the can. He was so zonked that he passed out in his stall." Scarf's lips parted in a feral grin. "He didn't even come to when I worked him out of his rep whites and took his badge."

Scarf gave a little hiccup, then continued. "The rep's uniform was a little baggy on me, and I had to smooth down my hair and clean myself up some so I didn't look quite so scraggly, but I must have looked good enough. No one even gave me a glance when I walked out of the bar. It made me feel real good to think I could pass for a rep. I headed out to the shuttle. I never believed I could get on the ship but the idea of walking around the base, having everybody think I belonged there, seemed mega-wild to me. When I saw a bunch of reps waiting to be taken out to the shuttle, I just kind of joined them." He grinned broadly. "It was like I belonged. The uniform made me one of them. I thought they might be on to me because my badge was different. Different companies have different badges. But they were all from different companies anyway, so mine being different didn't matter."

"And so you joined them."

He nodded vigorously and hiccuped again. "Next thing I knew we were riding a tram out to one of the beat-up looking little space shuttles they use to carry the reps to and from the orbiting Void-liner while it's being repaired. The shuttle had a few dents and needed some paint here and there, but it looked great to me. This was the closest I'd ever been to anything you could ride into space.

"I thought for sure they'd stop me when we boarded the shuttle, but they barely glanced at our badges and waved us on. We strapped ourselves in and the shuttle blasted off. I couldn't believe my luck. I was going to board an honest-to-God Void-liner.

"I felt a little sick during free fall, but managed to hang onto my guts. As soon as we boarded the liner we were met by a crewmember that took us to be briefed on our work assignments. I hung back and slipped away, first chance I had. I wanted to see as much as I could of the ship before they caught me. Every time someone passed I'd either stop and pretend to inspect some piece of equipment or just walk on like I was headed somewhere important. Nobody questioned me." Scarf hiccuped again and giggled.

"For goodness sakes," Jackie said, "with all your powers you ought to be able to control a case of hiccups."

Scarf held up a finger, waited for a minute, then gave her a nod.

"Didn't the police come looking for you?" Jackie asked.

He gave an exaggerated shrug. "I thought they would. I figured that the rep whose badge and uniform I took would report me. But either he was too embarrassed to admit how he lost his stuff or the cops didn't figure where I went. They never showed.

"Meanwhile, I found places where food dispensers were

kept and spaces where I could take naps without being
seen—mostly lockers where emergency stuff was stowed. I'd
wait until I'd see one being inspected, figuring that it
wouldn't be checked out again for a while. Each night I
holed-up in a different place. That's what gave me the idea
of becoming a stowaway. On my fifth day I heard the call go
out for all reps to leave the ship. I took as much food as I
could carry and hid myself in one of the lockers. I figured
that all I had to do was wait until we got to our next port
and walk off the ship with another bunch of reps.

"Blast-off roughed me up some because I wasn't
strapped down in cushioned seating, but I came through
with only a few scrapes and bruises. Once we were underway, though, another thought struck me. If all the repairs had been done here on Maddoc, there wouldn't be
any reps coming on board at our next stop. To get off the
ship unnoticed, I'd need a different outfit. I'd heard that
crewmembers go to duty stations during a jump so I figured
I could snag some spacer clothes then.

"When I heard them announcing preparations for the
jump, I made my move. But I guess that some
crewmembers aren't tied down to duty stations during a
jump. One of them spotted me in a passageway and next
thing I knew I was being dragged up to the captain by a
couple of security apes. They told me I was in big trouble—
that I might spend the rest of my life in jail. I was scared out
of my head."

He sat there for a moment as if reliving the experience.
"That's when everything went funny. We must have gone
into the jump because I had this weird feeling that I could
reach out beyond myself with my mind. I'd never felt anything like it before. It was as if I could go inside people's
heads and see what they were thinking. One set of thoughts

came across real strong. Someone was taking the ship through the Void to the next star system. I knew that when we got there I'd be arrested."

He looked to Jackie as if waiting for a response. When she made none, he shrugged. "So I just reached out and stopped him."

—CHAPTER—
25

"You stopped him from taking the ship out of the Void?" Jackie asked, brought up short by the implications of Scarf's statement. She exchanged glances with Captain Paliki, ignoring the murmuring from the side of the room where her father and the others waited.

Scarf blinked and nodded. "I kind of knocked him out with my mind. I just thought about it and it happened."

Jackie drew a deep breath. "What happened next?"

"I don't know. It seemed like everything started shrinking. I felt like a speck of dust hung out in a night that was blacker than any I ever spent down in the sewers. Everywhere was emptiness. Even inside me. Nothing to hold on to. It scared the living hell out of me."

An empathetic shiver ran down her backbone. She knew the feeling of losing yourself to the Void—only too well. "Was that when you decided to create your own world?" she asked softly.

"I didn't decide anything. I just did it. Even as everything shrank down to nothing, I could feel my mind growing. And I could sense other minds around me. I held onto them—kept them with me. But it wasn't enough. I needed something solid—something I could touch and hang on to. And then, suddenly, it started to happen. It was awesome—a whole world, rising up around me. And I could shape it—make it into whatever I wanted. I lost myself in it, became part of it." He was silent for a moment. "I'm part of it still. It's like I've always been here. At least it was until you jogged me into remembering. I'd almost forgotten how it all happened."

Like acting, she thought. You get caught up in your role until you almost become the part. But this was acting on a grander scale than anything she'd ever experienced.

Scarf peered at her uncertainly. "What are you going to do to me?"

Jackie sighed. It was the very question she had been asking herself. She glanced at the captain. He raised an eyebrow but stayed silent. This was her show. With her father out of the picture, she held the balance of power. And since she wasn't willing to let others decide what to do about Scarf, she had to do it for herself.

"I guess that depends on you," she finally said. "First of all, we're going to be changing everyone back to their natural states and returning their memories. Then, we'll be searching for a way to leave this place—to return to physical space. If you cooperate with us, you won't be harmed by anyone—I promise. None of this was really your fault. You hardly knew what you were doing."

Scarf's face stiffened. "You can do whatever you want with the others, but there's no way I'm going back. I know what those bastards would do to someone who hijacks a Void liner. They'd put me away forever. Even if I could hide out from them—I'd be right back where I was before, a Maddoc-Port rat-brat with nothing. Here, I can have anything I want."

"What about people?" Jackie said. "If we leave, you'll be the only one here."

"It doesn't matter. I've been alone for most of my life. Besides, I can create people for myself if I want to. I've done it sometimes just to amuse myself."

The thought of Fanth's females came to mind. "That's no kind of life for someone with your ability. You've got one of the most powerful minds in the galaxy. You could be a Void pilot. The space companies would fight for the chance to take you into training." She turned to the captain. "Isn't that so?"

The captain gave her a quick glance, then turned away. "There's always a need for those with the mental strength to jump the Void." His tone was unconvincing. Jackie was about to question him further when Scarf interrupted.

"No way they're going to make a Void pilot out of a hijacker."

She turned back to him. "The shipping companies will be as mad at me as they are at you. My friend and I had to steal a hopper to get here. We even stunned a clerk."

She heard a sharp intake of breath from behind her. Her father, she imagined. Not how she would have chosen to break this to him, but it was too late to worry about it now.

Scarf's eyes were small, dark circles surrounded with white. "You stole a hopper?"

"It was the only way I could search for my father. As you can see, our situations aren't all that different."

He shook his head. "They won't treat a Void pilot's daughter like a rat-brat. Anyway, you can't return to physical space once you're stuck in the Void. I've heard spacers talk about that plenty of times. No one has ever come back."

"But your powers are so much greater than most Void pilots. You created this world and brought everyone here. There must be some way for you to get them back out."

"I brought them here by accident. There's no way I can get them out."

"Won't you at least try?"

Scarf's mouth set in stubborn lines. He ran a hand down the edge of his cheek, tracing the line of angry tissue that marred it. "I won't make any more trouble for anyone here as long as no one makes trouble for me. But as far as getting them out of the Void, forget it. There's nothing I can do."

Jackie's father was bitterly opposed to releasing Scarf from his alcoholic stupor. "First chance he gets, he'll be on us again," he complained when he had a chance to take Jackie aside. "And this time we may not be so lucky." But despite his objections, she decided to take the former Master at his word. Scarf's background had left him bitter, but there was a frankness and openness about him that made her believe he would live up to whatever he agreed to. He was certainly open enough in refusing to help them leave the Void.

Still, she kept a close watch over him at first. But once he exchanged his cowled robe for more conventional clothing and began assisting them in returning the inhabitants of this artificial world to their natural states, she felt sure she had made the right decision. She was glad to have his former people see him helping to transform them back to their human forms. That could only help create better feelings all around. And maybe, she thought, if he experienced some gratitude from them he wouldn't feel so persecuted.

And Scarf's help was needed as, over the next several days, Gargoyles, Flyers, Toad-Men, Stalkers, and others of his people who had been out searching for Jackie and her friends began to return to the castle. Captain Paliki briefed the returnees on the changes that had taken place while they were gone. Jackie worked along with Scarf and her father, restoring memories and returning animal bodies to their human forms.

At first bewildered and confused, the newly transformed humans quickly adapted to the reality of their situation. Jackie saw to it that all were informed that their being trapped in the Void by Scarf was more accidental than intentional. If some of them harbored grudges against their former Master, they kept it to themselves, all too aware that he still retained his enormous powers. And as Paliki pointed out to them, if anyone had reason to resent Scarf, it was he, since Scarf had singled him out for mistreatment as the one who had been in charge of arresting him. If he could forgive Scarf, they could too.

As their stock of transformed humans grew, they began to consider how to reach out to the other inhabitants of Scarf's world. It was, Scarf had told her, mostly ocean, the only landmass being a solitary island that they now occupied. A big island to be sure. He had pulled an image of it from one of the passenger's minds. He wasn't sure of its exact size but claimed it took a Flyer nearly four days to reach the coast from the castle that sat at the island's center. Many of the crew and passengers had resisted Scarf's domination from the first. These had been sent away to fend for themselves on other parts of the island, far away from his stronghold. But Scarf, always suspicious, had his underlings keep a close watch over those outlying territories and make sure that those exiled there were kept where they belonged.

Their next task was to organize search parties to comb the outer territories for these exiles. The welfare of passengers and crewmembers was the captain's responsibility and he took charge of this effort, sending out groups of those already converted back into human forms. They could have traveled faster as Flyers, but Paliki felt they would be more likely to be trusted and listened to by the outliers if they went as humans. Remembering her rejection by the Climbers, Jackie had to agree. And their recruiting efforts proved effective. Just seeing a human was often enough to prod memories of past lives.

With the search parties underway, Captain Paliki formed a committee to consider possibilities for returning from the Void. The initial members included the captain himself, his head space science officer, a dark-skinned woman named Zuta who had been one of the Master's leading Stalkers, Jackie, and her father. Knowing little about the physics of space, Jackie assumed she was included in the planning because her mental powers might be needed. She, in turn, talked the captain into having Dan join them.

Dan, himself, was less than confident about contributing to their planning sessions. "Sure, I helped you fight Flyers and evade Stalkers," he said, "but I don't know micro-dust about getting us out of the Void."

"Who does?" Jackie countered. "But I've learned to trust your judgment. Besides, you always have supported me when I needed it—and I need that now. My father is being difficult. He doesn't even want me involved in this—claims there's no point to it since I'm not an experienced spacer." She sighed. "He never wanted me to have anything to do with space travel in the first place. And I think he's still angry with me for making him drunk to keep him from killing Scarf. I'd like to know I have someone on the committee who's on my side."

Dan put a hand on her shoulder. "For that, you can count on me. And don't worry about your dad. He'll come around. He's just not ready to recognize how competent his little girl has grown."

Jackie wanted Scarf to join them too, but he stubbornly refused, saying he saw little point in wasting time on what was bound to be impossible.

Their committee met in a room once used as a recreational area by the Gargoyle teams. They sat around a long gaming table, put there for the amusement of the Master's followers. The game, a popular pastime in Maddoc-Port, involved directing lightweight metal balls with electromagnetic controls. Her father had modified it into something more suitable for their needs, changing the top into a smooth, wooden surface. Captain Paliki sat at the head. Jackie, with Dan at her left, sat facing her father and Commander Zuta.

"I knew your young punk wouldn't help us," her father said. "I still don't trust him. He's dead set against leaving here."

"He's being completely cooperative in everything else," Jackie countered, "and perfectly open about telling us what he is and isn't willing to do. I'd be more suspicious if he simply agreed to whatever we asked."

The captain cleared his throat. "I suggest we stop worrying about Scarf and concentrate on the problem we're here to deal with. Perhaps we can start by having Commander Zuta brief us on current knowledge and theory concerning the Void's makeup. The better we understand it, the more likely it is we'll be able to devise a way to escape it."

Commander Zuta twisted her mouth into a wry smile. "I'm afraid no one understands the Void all that well. When it was first discovered in the year two thousand and twenty-two, scientists speculated that it might have been created by some form of advanced beings, simply because it made galactic space travel so convenient. But most theorists now recognize it as a natural phenomenon—created by the black hole at the center of our galaxy. Such singularities, it is thought, place so great a strain on the fabric of space that it forms rips in the ether, creating fingers of hyper-space that extend out from the center of the galaxy.

"The Void manifests a number of unusual effects. For example, the slowing of physical time. An atomic clock, taken into the Void for a minute-long jump, loses several microseconds."

"I thought time passes faster here," Jackie said. "The weeks that it took me to get here were like years to the rest of you."

"Very true," Zuta agreed. "It's one of the Void's contradictions. Mental perceptions in the Void are often the reverse of physical manifestations. Perceived time as you say, accelerates. Physical time, however, actually slows. It's believed, in fact, that it approaches a point of stasis."

Jackie frowned. "What about our sensations of physically shrinking and mentally expanding. Have you an explanation for those?"

"It's another contradiction. Our bodies and our environments seem to shrink in on us while our mental capacities expand. Of course, all movement within the Void is mentally directed. That's how we guide our ships from one entry point to another."

Jackie nodded. "And how I drew myself to this world."

"Only a projected mental image of yourself. It's my belief that this world and those of us who inhabit it are mental constructs. We share a world of dreams. That's why Scarf, you, and your father, are able to manipulate its reality."

Jackie stared at Zuta, stunned by the implication of her statement. "If we are just mental constructs, how do we return to our physical bodies and our ships?"

"That, of course, is the problem. It's unclear what happens to physical material in the Void. Perhaps it actually shrinks into nothingness, just as our shared experiences tell us. Whatever the case, there's no way I know of for us to return to our physical bodies."

Jackie tried desperately to find flaws in Zuta's argument. "When I change things I still have to work under some physical restrictions. I can't make things bigger or smaller, only change them into something else. Doesn't that suggest that there are some physical aspects to this world?"

Commander Zuta shook her head. "The physical laws under which this world appears to operate may actually be mental restrictions imposed by Scarf in its creation. Things behave as he conceived them."

Jackie sighed in frustration. Commander Zuta's conception of the Void was devastating. With their ships and bodies lost to them, how could they ever escape? A sudden thought came to her. "Even after I was lost in the Void, I somehow directed myself to this planet. Why, then, can't I direct myself back to my ship?"

The captain looked to Commander Zuta. She shrugged. "If our ships still exist, it might be possible."

"Why don't you make an effort to return yourself," Captain Paliki said to Jackie. "You too, Jack," he said to her father. "Concentrate on sending yourself back to the *Golden Arrow*."

"It sounds crazy to me," her father muttered, "but I'll give it a try."

Jackie watched her father close his eyes and take on an expression of concentration. Then she closed her own eyes and pictured herself back in her hopper with Crow's body beside her. She reached out with all her mental strength, straining to project herself out to her craft, wherever it might be. This might be their only hope of returning. Without their ships they would be lost here forever.

Nothing happened. Jackie was unable to sense anything

about her ship—felt no sensation of drawing out of herself. An ache of disappointment welled up inside her. She opened her eyes. Her father's eyes were already open. She looked at him inquiringly but he shook his head.

"I felt nothing," he said.

Jackie sighed and grimaced. "Neither did I."

"It appears, then, that our ships are lost to us," Commander Zuta said.

Jackie's fists clenched in anger, a reaction against the finality of Zuta's statement. In a world where almost anything could happen, there had to be other possibilities. Her mind searched desperately for the germ of an idea for getting them off the planet, no matter how bizarre or unlikely it might seem. And one came to her. She turned to Zuta.

"If I can mentally recreate my body," she said, "why can't I recreate our ships?"

Again, the wry smile. "Perhaps you could. But they wouldn't be real—only mental constructs."

"As long as they were in the Void. But what if we left the Void in them?"

The slender lines of the Commander's face registered surprise followed by interest. "I see your line of thought," she said, nodding to herself. "Since physical objects become mental representations on entering the Void, might mental representations become physical objects on leaving it? Unfortunately, we have no way of knowing what would happen to a mental construct projected into physical space—if, indeed it could make the transition. It seems unlikely."

—CHAPTER—
26

"What an idea," Jackie's father snorted. "Flying out of the Void in a make-believe ship. Now I've heard everything." He nodded to Captain Paliki. "I told you my daughter shouldn't be in on this planning session. She has no understanding of what's involved here."

His voice held the slightest of slurs, confirming Jackie's suspicions that he was keeping himself semi-intoxicated. Freed from the Master's prison, he was still bound by the need he had nurtured for drink. How much of that, she wondered, was her fault?

Still, she couldn't allow him to discredit her. To deal with their situation they needed someone with strong mental powers and her father's present condition left him unfit.

"From what I understand," Jackie said, "we haven't much of a choice. All we can do is work with what we have—that or give up completely. We should at least try to find out what it's possible to do with mentally-created ships."

Captain Paliki nodded. "At this point," he said, speaking slowly as if to give weight to his words, "it seems reasonable to experiment. What would you have us try?"

"As a first step, I'd like to create a replica of a ship and see if it can be brought into orbit." She turned to Dan. "Perhaps you could help guide its construction."

They exchanged glances. "I'm willing to try," he said. "My expertise is mainly in propulsion, but there are plenty of others who know about hull characteristics and control systems. Commander Zuta for one."

Zuta's eyes flashed as if she were excited by the challenge. "If, indeed, you are able to construct something as involved and complicated as a spaceship, I will be happy to participate in its design."

Jackie's father placed his hands on the table and looked from one to the other, as if they had betrayed him. "Look here now, if we really want to play around with mental creations of spaceships, I'm the one to do it. I certainly know a lot more about such matters than she does. How could she possibly expect to put together anything as huge and complex as a Void-liner?"

Jackie held up her hand. "Actually, I thought we might start with something a little more basic. A hopper should be simpler and easier to work with. And that sort of craft I've had some experience with."

Her father eyed her disdainfully. "You were a passenger in one once. You know nothing about the physics and mechanics that underlie a hopper's operation."

"I don't know much about biology either, but the physical forms I created worked out well enough. And as Dan pointed out, I have plenty of technical types to consult with."

Her father's face reddened as his voice rose. "And I'm telling you, you have no business fooling around with spaceships."

"I'm still in command here, Jack," Captain Paliki said quietly. "I've made my decision."

The meeting broke up with her father storming out of the room.

Jackie took the captain aside. "Thanks for supporting me. I don't think Dad's up to anything quite so demanding just yet."

The captain nodded. "He needs time to recover. The last two years have been hard on him—harder, perhaps, than for the rest of us. With no memories, we pretty much accepted things as they were. Finding himself isolated on a planet populated with impossible creatures, he must have doubted his own sanity."

Following her conversation with the captain, Jackie went looking for her father. She knew he was angry with her, but hoped she could somehow get across to him that she wasn't just doing this to spite him. She rapped her knuckles on the carved wooden door of the room assigned to him but got no answer.

"Daddy," she called, "I need to talk with you."

"Go away," a slurred voice croaked from inside.

He sounded as if he had been drinking heavily. It was because of her—she knew that. "I just want you to understand why I have to do this."

"I understand all right. You've turned on me is what you've done. My own daughter's turned against me. Never thought I'd see the day."

"That's crazy," she yelled back. "I haven't turned on you. I'm just trying to find a way for us to escape from the Void."

She banged on the door several more times but got no further response. Trying to touch minds with him, she felt only rejection. Slowly, she turned away, the lump inside her chest just as heavy and hard as any of the stones in the walls that lined the passageway.

Over the next several days, Jackie spent most of her time

with Dan and Commander Zuta, obtaining insights into the workings of a hopper. Since the craft would have to carry her off-planet as well as operate in space, it would be a modified version of the one she had ridden into the Void. It would be streamlined to cut air resistance with booster rockets for the initial lift-off, and a ceramic-plated hull to protect it from high temperatures during its return into the planet's atmosphere. Commander Zuta had the engineering skills needed to guide all aspects of its design, but Dan still proved to be a great help with its construction, especially with the development of its propulsion system.

Dan and Zuta imparted their knowledge to Jackie through direct mental transfers, making it easier for her to understand them and speeding her learning to a considerable extent. The material for the vessel she took from a large outcropping of rock near the base of the mountain, shaping it and transforming it into the types of structures and components they needed.

In the past, her transformations had been mostly of a superficial nature. External appearances had been altered or characteristics modified in a fairly simple manner. She changed things she could see or easily visualize. Even her transformations of people were mostly surface modifications of what was already there.

Building solid-state electronic circuitry and complex mechanical devices from scratch was another matter. Now she was dealing with insanely complicated mazes of connections that generated mysterious forces she could only roughly comprehend the nature of.

But her two assistants guided her at every step along the way, helping her to mind-picture everything from the intricate webs of circuitry and micro-components that carried electronic impulses to their allotted destinations, to the way that delicately balanced rocket fuels functioned to produce their desired effects. By the end of her task, she knew a devil of a lot more about spacecraft than she had ever wanted to. And she still didn't understand most of it. But it seemed to work. They checked system operations time after time until Jackie would have taken almost any risk in preference to having to perform one more check.

Dan and Zuta also helped her construct and test a pressurized spacesuit to wear during her initial flights in the hopper. Mental creation or not, individuals in this world could be injured or killed. Jackie had seen a Flyer die in its battle with Fanth. With something as risky as mentally created spacecraft, back up protection only made sense.

All in all, it took her nearly a month to construct the hopper and prepare for her attempt to place it in orbit around Scarf's planet. No one had bothered to name the artificial world of Scarf's creation, so Scarf's planet was what they called it when they called it anything. During the time of the hopper's construction, the population of the castle expanded rapidly as more and more outliers were brought back and transformed into their human forms. Scarf and Jackie's father were kept busy making the transformations and creating additional housing and food supplies for the newcomers. They both stayed away from Jackie, united for once in their disapproval of what she was doing.

But despite the continued efforts to gather in the outliers, many resisted being brought to the lair of the infamous Master. It was difficult to convince them how radically things had changed. Alpha, now fully recovered from his bout with the Master, and his sister, Beta, proved to be particularly effective recruiters. Skeptics were more likely to believe the young twins than to credit the adults who brought the same message. Those approached by the

twins often remembered them from the ship and were soon
won over by their openness and enthusiasm.

At last the day arrived when the hopper was ready to
launch. Jackie was to be its pilot. She had insisted on that.
And despite her father's continued objections, Captain
Paliki had concurred. Her father still wasn't recovered from
his alcoholism and Scarf still refused to be involved. That
left Jackie as the only one with enough mental strength to
be able to manipulate the reality of this world. If anything
went wrong on this test flight, she might be able to make it
right. If she was lucky.

On this first flight she would be taking the craft out beyond the planet's atmosphere, placing it in orbit, and then,
bringing it back. They were by no means certain that even
these relatively limited objectives would be possible. After
all, nothing about the world they experienced was real. The
sun that warmed them by day and the thick river of stars
that flowed above their heads at night were only illusions,
created to give the impression of a physical universe. What
reality they would experience in a spaceship high above the
planet's atmosphere was anyone's guess. That was part of
the reason that experimentation was required.

Dan had wanted to accompany her but she refused his
offer, arguing that there was no point in risking more lives
than necessary and that if something did go wrong she'd
rather have only herself to look after. Again, Captain Paliki
agreed. Jackie had expected him to. His primary responsibility was, after all, to his crew and passengers, and Jackie,
however much he might appreciate what she had done for
him, was neither.

On the evening before her flight, Scarf broke his self-
imposed exile and came to her private quarters. Jackie felt
surprisingly pleased to see him. His avoiding her had both-

ered her more than she had realized.

"Here to wish me luck?" she asked, waving him inside.

He turned to face her as she closed the door behind him, his eyes dark and troubled. "This experimenting with the hopper is crazy."

"I thought spaceships fascinated you. Isn't that why you ended up here in the first place?"

"But this one isn't real. What can you do with an artificial spacecraft?"

"Take it up and see what passes for reality above this world." He looked so serious she tried to reassure him. "This is just a first step toward learning whether we can use mentally-created spaceships to leave the Void. I'll only be taking it up into orbit."

"But it's dangerous. Why do you have to be the one to do it?"

She found herself becoming irritated. It was bad enough getting this kind of pressure from her father without Scarf laying it on her as well. "You may be satisfied to stay here on your little dream world, but the rest of us are determined to break out of it. And break out we will."

His face paled, making his scar stand out in contrast. "Do you seriously believe you can sail out of the Void on something you created with your mind?"

"I don't know. No one does. But at some point we're going to have to try." She paused and arched an eyebrow. "Unless you have a better idea for getting us out of here."

He drew back. "I'm not involved in this. Besides, it's pointless. Remember when you first entered the Void—how it shrunk you into a pinpoint of existence? Outside of this world, that's all any of us would be. Try to leave here, and that's what you'll become."

"Maybe so, but I have to try. I'm not willing to spend

the rest of my life in a mental cage, no matter how big or comfortable it may be. It isn't real."

He grimaced. "When you come from a background like mine, reality isn't all that hot." He paused, as if having difficulty finding the right words. "I just wish you could accept things as they are. You're the one person here who treated me decently—the only one I can trust. I—I don't want anything to happen to you."

Jackie was moved to see his eyes glisten moistly and sense the strength of his feelings. He seemed so vulnerable, despite the immense powers he wielded and the hard life he had led on the streets.

"You're not disliked by the others anywhere near as much as you think. They really appreciate what you've done in helping to restore them to their proper forms and to provide them with food and shelter. And so do I." She paused, somewhat overcome by the strength of her own feelings. "Besides, nothing bad is going to happen to me. We've tested this hopper every step of the way. I have a spacesuit and my mental powers to fall back on if all else fails. What could go wrong?"

Shaking his head, he turned away from her. "Out in the Void? Everything."

—Chapter—
27

On the morning of her flight, Captain Paliki, Dan, and Commander Zuta were all there to see Jackie off. So, to her surprise, was her father. He appeared completely sober and, for once, had nothing negative to say. He just held her to him, his tears hot against her cheeks.

"You be careful now, you hear?" he whispered in her ear.

Jackie only nodded, afraid she'd lose all her self-control if she tried to speak. This was no time for an emotional breakdown. She gave him a quick kiss, then turned away to climb into the bulky spacesuit that Commander Zuta had designed for her.

Jackie wished the twins could have been here. And Scarf. But Alpha and Beta were out helping to hunt down the few dozen stragglers who had not yet been contacted. And Scarf—well, he'd said his goodbyes last night.

She sank deeply into the padded seat of the hopper and proceeded through her flight checks, feeling a trifle awkward performing the operations in the suit. "Everything looking good," she reported.

Dan's voice came to her over her radio. "All cleared for takeoff."

Tentatively, she reached forward to energize the boosters. The roaring surge of acceleration flattened her against her seat as her craft hurtled upwards through the planet's life-sustaining atmosphere. The crushing weight of five Gs pressed the air from her lungs, making each breath a struggle. She found herself wishing that Scarf had been a little more positive in assessing her chances. His last words to her, that anything can happen in the Void, had taken on a prophetic ring. Not particularly helpful for building self-confidence or keeping up spirits. But maybe that's just as well, she thought. My biggest problems have come from being overconfident. That was something she had discovered more than once on this world that was, even now, dropping away beneath her.

At least her father had finally come around. She still felt a tingle from the warmth of his final hug. It had meant so much to her. It would have been hard to go off with nothing but bitterness between them.

And so far so good. This hopper was noisier than the one she and Crow had stolen from Earth's space station, and its vibrations more noticeable, but the boosters hadn't exploded and none of the panel lights on the console-board indicated problem readings.

"How's it going?" Dan's voice came to her.

"Looking good," she replied. "I'm beginning to think this thing can really fly."

"Just be careful. We want you back here in one piece." Dan spoke as if he was joking, but he couldn't keep a note of concern out of his voice.

"Don't worry," she said, grinning, "I've been trained by experts."

A short time later, with her weightless body held in place by webbing, she guided the hopper into orbit with short bursts from the auxiliary rockets. The controls were simple to handle and the ship's computer guided all her actions, so she felt confident in performing the necessary procedures.

In the monitoring screens, Scarf's planet loomed as a giant blue ball, dotted with pinkish clouds. Toward the center of its great encompassing sea, lay the single spot of land that held the entire population of the planet. Beyond the planet, the illusion of a star-filled galaxy continued to display itself. But there was a ghostly thinness to its appearance, as if its reality had lessened this far away from Scarf's influence. Beyond that, she knew, lay the true reality, the vast emptiness of the Void.

According to her indicators, all systems were still functioning properly. She made a final verification of cabin pressure, atmosphere, and temperature for herself by cautiously opening a valve in her spacesuit. Everything felt normal. For a moment, her spirits surged and she bathed in the warm glow of her accomplishment. She had met their initial goal of placing a mentally built spacecraft in orbit. She keyed her transmitter.

"Dan," she said, "you can tell Commander Zuta that the ship you two designed works just fine. I've placed it in orbit."

"Great news," Dan responded. "Now all we have to worry about is getting you back down here."

Jackie's satisfaction dampened as she considered the next step in their plan for testing the hopper. Jackie would launch a small, remotely operated drone and attempt to mentally guide it out of the Void. The problem would be in verifying the drone's passage into normal space. Even if it appeared to leave the Void, there would be no way to tell for sure whether it had made it through intact or simply ceased to exist on the other side. Commander Zuta had argued that they might learn something from this additional testing, but Jackie was doubtful.

She had promised the others that she wouldn't try

anything beyond what they had planned. But it would be so much easier on everyone if she just went ahead and attempted an escape from the Void in her hopper. Especially on her father. It had been hard enough for him to accept her role in the preliminary testing of this craft. His brief show of affection, just before she took off, was the first sign that he was beginning to accept her new role in his life. The warmth of that acceptance was something she hungered for. She didn't want to disrupt it with more conflict. But how much harder would it be for him when the time came for her to actually try and pilot a ship out of the Void? He'd fight her all the way on that.

She didn't really have to delay the final testing. Her hopper's controls were designed to allow for manual operation. If she made it out of the Void in one piece, she could return to it. And she was going to have to try breaking out eventually, no matter how many test flights they ran. Why put off the inevitable?

She suddenly realized that she had intended to do this all along. She hadn't planned it consciously, but at some level she had known she would make the attempt. She took a deep breath and keyed her transmitter.

"Dan? There's something else I want to try before I bring the hopper back down. I'll be out of contact for a while. Don't worry, I'll be fine."

Before Dan could answer, she switched off her receiver and settled back in her contoured seat to concentrate on Caliban as a destination, the same link that she and Crow had struck for. She wanted to do this right away, before she had second thoughts about making the attempt. There was no need to fire up the rockets. Travel within the Void would be purely mental. How she would be moving when she exited the Void, she couldn't guess. That would depend on how her orbiting velocity translated into normal space. For that matter, everything depended on how she and her hopper made the transition.

But if this worked out—if this ship she created in the Void transformed into a real-world physical representation, she'd be able to return to her father and the others with the news that their escape from the Void was truly possible. How excited they would be!

All except Scarf. She had to get through to him. If only he wasn't so stubborn. At times he could infuriate her. But at other times there was a mistreated puppy-dog quality about him that made her want to hold him. Nothing like those pampered pompous poops brought in as guests at the Conservatory.

Scarf had such potential. And vision. Even as a neglected street urchin, he'd set his sights on space. And he'd gotten there the only way he could. The thought of abandoning him, alone on his artificial world, was more than she could bear.

But now she had to focus on Caliban—split her mind between ship and destination, just like before. The seconds ticked by. One chili pepper, two chili peppers, three chili peppers . . . Was anything happening? Yes. Her perceptions had that same weird, ghostly quality as before. And she felt the simultaneous sensations of contraction and expansion. She must be crossing the Void now. But could she pierce it?

Her count continued to mount. Sixteen chili peppers, seventeen, eighteen . . . Her feelings of expansion and contraction intensified. One hundred, one hundred and one, one hundred and two . . .

Still no boundary encountered. This wasn't working. Her world was folding in on her. She was shrinking up into nothing, just like before, becoming a matterless point of consciousness surrounded by emptiness.

She fought back. She had gone through this before and survived. And now she knew something more about the tremendous mental power she carried within her. Concentrating with every ounce of energy she possessed, she willed herself to expand back into herself—to be back in her hopper, in control of her ship.

Gradually, a sense of reality formed around her. A vision of monitors, cables, and control panels solidified. She was back in her seat in the cabin of her hopper, held down by the seat's webbing. She could breathe air, move her body, stretch her muscles. Suddenly, she froze. Something was different. She wasn't wearing her spacesuit. She turned to look about her but stopped when she saw a still form in the padded seat beside her. It was Crow. She reached out to him, grasping his wrist to feel for a pulse. The hand was cold and lifeless. He was definitely dead.

Jackie? a voice projected from inside her head. *I just had the most peculiar experience.*

She jerked back her hand in surprise. "CAP!" she squealed. "Where in the universe did you come from?"

I'm not sure. Things faded out for a while and then suddenly returned. Does this have something to do with our presence in the Void?

She quickly brought CAP up to date on her experiences since they had been separated.

Incredible! CAP exclaimed. *I must have been out much longer than my circuits indicate. You have added a significant amount of knowledge to my data banks.*

"But how did I get back to this hopper? What does it mean? I tried to project myself back here and couldn't. Commander Zuta thought that our ships and bodies had lost their physical existence."

Obviously they haven't. Perhaps you couldn't project yourself here before because you were on Scarf's planet. The world he created might exert too much of a hold on you to allow you to return here. From what you tell me, his influence weakens with distance. By going into orbit, you may have freed yourself sufficiently to allow for your return.

She considered CAP's explanation. "You might be right, but there is at least one other possibility. What I'm experiencing now might just be something dreamed up by my subconscious mind."

It's real enough to me. But you can prove it to yourself easily. If this ship and everything in it are mental creations, you should be able to modify them.

Of course. If this was a mental projection, she could change it. And she knew the very thing to test her powers on. Crow's body. Having his corpse sprawled out beside her was unnerving. She couldn't keep from glancing at it, even during her interaction with CAP. She now attempted to change Crow's body—to make it into a wax figure. Nothing happened. She undid his webbing and tried to mentally float his body back into the compartment with the freeze-sleep containers. His body didn't move.

"This is real then," she murmured, not completely pleased with her discovery. She would now have to remove Crow's body by hand—unpleasant, but not as bad as leaving it there beside her. Thank God they were in free fall.

She released her webbing, grabbed Crow's wrist, grasped a handhold with her other hand, and drew his body from its seat. Even without gravity she found it difficult to maneuver his long, lanky frame around cables and equipment. She managed with a series of awkward tugs and yanks that brought her into closer contact with Crow's corpse than she would have wished. Thank heavens there were no signs of decay. And her own body showed no signs of muscle deterioration. It must be as Commander Zuta had speculated. Physical objects caught up in the Void remain in a static state—unchanging.

As she stopped to catch her breath, she felt a returning of the pressure from the Void that threatened to shrink her back into oblivion. She knew how to fight it now, but she still had to keep up a steady mental resistance.

She opened the hatch to the rear compartment with the freeze-sleep modules and sent Crow's body floating through. She then raised the cover of the lower freeze chamber, pulled Crow's body over to it, and pushed it into place, closing the curved glass door with a final thud. Sighing with relief, she sealed the chamber and set the temperature to freezing. At least she'd be able to preserve Crow's body if she was ever able to return it from the Void. Maybe give it a decent funeral.

CAP's projection interrupted her thoughts. *If you have convinced yourself that the ship is real, I'd suggest that we leave this highly abnormal environment while we still can.*

"I can't go, CAP," she said. "Not yet. I have unfinished business. I have to contact the others and tell them it's possible to return to our real ships." She paused. "I wish I could make a test run, though—just to prove that it can be done."

Why can't you?

"This hopper will be broadcasting its ID. As soon as we enter Caliban's system, their patrol ships will be after me. Heavens only knows if I could ever convince the authorities to let me return to save the others."

I wouldn't normally approve of modifying a hopper's identification system. But given our situation, I think it would be fair to consider this an emergency.

"You can cut out its ID broadcast? For heaven's sakes CAP, why didn't you tell me that before?"

If you recall, I was out of operation when you stole this craft. And I was hardly about to volunteer information that might get you into worse trouble than you were already in. But helping the crew and passengers of the Golden Arrow *out of the Void may be your best chance for avoiding prosecution.*

"CAP," she said, "there are times when I wish I could kiss you."

—CHAPTER—
28

Jackie immediately set to work under CAP's guidance, modifying the hopper's programming to eliminate the broadcast of its ID. She tried to stay optimistic and keep from dwelling on her previous attempts to break out of the Void. This time, she had CAP working with her.

With her hopper's signal silent, she was ready to try making it out from the Void. Remembering Crow's instructions, she split her mind, locking part of it onto her ship and the rest onto her original Caliban destination. She held on to that destination, frantically reeling in the rest of her mind, along with her ship, through the vast reaches of the Void. She could sense the two parts of her mental being coming back together, joining in a final burst of elation as she blasted through the tenuous boundary that separated the Void from real space and time.

The physical universe! She had actually returned to it. The proof lay before her. In the center monitor of her display she could see Caliban's red-dwarf sun, hardly more than a ruddy pinhead of light at this distance. Even more reassuring was the cessation of the Void's insistent draw. She was free of it.

She gave a deep sigh of satisfaction. "Now, CAP," she said, "how do we turn this thing around?"

That took some doing. As CAP explained it to her, her hopper had accelerated to a high rate of speed before it had entered the Void. While in the Void, it retained its potential momentum. Now, back in the physical universe, she was hurtling away from the Void in the direction of Caliban. To return to the Void, she'd have to decelerate and build up momentum in the opposite direction.

CAP guided her in maneuvering the hopper into a return position. Gravity hit her as she fired up her drive. She had set the hopper's thrust at two Gs. The doubled weight was uncomfortable, especially after being in free-fall, but the time saved made it worth putting up with. She wouldn't, after all, be moving around all that much inside the hopper.

Even at two Gs, it would take fifteen hours of deceleration to counter her momentum away from the Void, and another fifteen to return to it. With little to occupy her and only a few of Crow's energy bars left to curb her real-body hunger, it made for a long flight. She was decidedly relieved to experience the familiar tug of reentry and the ghostly perceptual distortions that told her she was back under the Void's influence once again. She cut the thrust of her rockets, welcoming the loss of body weight.

So, CAP projected, *you've proven you can do it. What's next on your agenda?*

She frowned in thought. "I guess to return planetside and tell everyone the good news. That means I'll have to leave my physical body again and you with it. But I won't be gone long—I promise."

No matter. For me there is no passage of time without your presence. But how do you intend to return to the planet?

"I figured on transferring back to the hopper I created and—" she paused. "Come to think of it, I'm not sure just how to do that. When I tried to direct myself back to the created hopper, I ended up here instead."

You may not need to transfer yourself to the created hopper.

His response puzzled her. "What do you mean?"

From what you tell me, the first time you were trapped in the Void you projected yourself directly to Scarf's planet. You should be able to do that now. Unless, of course, the experience was so traumatic as to prevent you from repeating it.

She grinned and nodded to herself. "I can handle it. After all the transformations I've been through, why should one more bother me?"

In that case, all you need do is stop fighting the pull of the Void. Let it take you in. Then you can project yourself back to Scarf's planet in exactly the same manner that you did before.

"CAP," she said, grinning, "I swear you're a genius."

After a quick farewell to CAP, along with another promise to return soon, she secured herself in her seat and waited. Soon, she felt the sensation of the Void drawing in on her, condensing her into a minuscule kernel of essence. Once again, her physical being was lost in a vast sea of nothingness. The experience still unnerved her, but not enough to distract her from her purpose.

Hanging fiercely to her identity, she once more directed herself toward the one individual to whom she was linked to by blood, mind, and emotion—her father. This time the link seemed clearer. Perhaps because Scarf was no longer an opposing influence, suppressing the essences of those under his domination.

Her focus on her destination was still only an approximation, but this time she ended up closer to her goal. She found herself standing naked in the barren, wind-swept foothills of Scarf's territory.

In the distance rose the dark ragged peaks of the mountain range that cradled Scarf's castle. The bloated sun hung low in the purple-hued sky. She could see beauty in those jutting peaks as they reflected the ruddy light of the setting sun—now that she was no longer threatened by what they held for her. They were a challenge she had met, a destiny fulfilled. And now she had knowledge that would allow her and the others to free themselves.

A cool breeze swept across her unprotected body, causing her to shiver. Anxious to get back as soon as possible, she assumed the form of a Flyer, taking comfort in her warm covering of feathers. Leaping into the air, she rose on the wind and headed unerringly toward the place where her father and friends waited for her return. She'd not keep them waiting much longer.

On her short flight to the castle, she saw a group of a dozen creatures below her, headed in the same direction. Still bringing them in, she thought. I wonder how long it will take to collect the rest of them. The more converts we win over, the more we have to send out searching for others. But those who have stayed hidden the longest may be the most difficult to find and convince to return.

She also wondered just how long she'd been gone in Void time during her brief return to normal space. Subjective time passed more swiftly in the Void and the weeks it had taken her and Crow to first reach the Void had seemed like years to those trapped there. According to Zuta, there was an acceleration factor involved. The longer one was in the Void, the faster time passed. How the thirty hours Jackie had just spent in physical space would translate into Void time, she couldn't be sure. But she knew that her father and friends would be worried.

She dropped out of the sky onto the same flat-topped landing tower where she and her friends had so recently first entered Scarf's castle. No sentries were posted to challenge her, but a slim young woman in a spacer's uniform emerged from the high arched doorway that led to the reception area. A short, heavyset male in civilian dress followed behind her.

"Ah," the woman said, "another returnee. All incoming are to report in for re-establishment of identities. Janson, here, will lead you to the proper area and assign you to temporary quarters after you're transformed."

For a moment, Jackie just stood there, bemused by the brusque, matter-of-fact manner in which returnees were being met and processed.

"I know that regaining your identity can be a bit of a shock at first," the woman said, apparently assuming her to be disorientated. "But most of us adapt quickly, once we're back in our own bodies. Has your memory been fully restored?"

Jackie couldn't resist the opportunity for drama. Holding up her arms, she transformed her Flyer's body into her human form, her feathers into a spacer's jumpsuit. Both the woman and the man stared at her in disbelief. The woman recovered first.

"My God, you gave me a start. You must be Void Pilot Claver's daughter. We feared the worst after we lost contact with you."

"Happy to say I'm fine," she replied. "I just had to return by a slightly different route than I left by. How long have I been gone?"

"About two and a half days. Your father's been frantic."

Jackie's lips tightened in a wry grimace. More guilt feelings. At least the time differential wasn't so great for shorter durations. And the news she brought should more than make up for the emotional trauma she had put her father and friends through. There was really no way she could have made things easier on them.

The woman continued to stare at her, wide-eyed. "What happened to your ship?"

Jackie grinned. "You'll find out soon enough after I meet with the captain. But first I want to see to my father. Do you happen to know where he is?"

The woman nodded. "Inside the reception area." She pointed toward the great curved portal. "He and Scarf are transforming a new batch of creatures from the outlying territories who straggled in only a short time ago."

Scarf and her father working together. She found the thought amusing. Maybe her dad was beginning to accept Scarf's conversion as legitimate. Or maybe they had found a point of agreement since neither of them had been happy about her conducting tests with the mentally created spacecraft. Scarf still wouldn't be happy when he heard her news.

"I'll go to him then," Jackie said. "Could you inform the captain of my return and tell him I can meet with him and the planning team whenever he's ready? Oh yes, and there are more stragglers coming. I passed over a group on my way in."

Jackie strode through the high arched doorway into the reception area to find throngs of Hairy Hunters, Climbers, Swimmers, and other creatures she didn't recognize, milling about in mixed groups, making use of their returned capacities for speech. At opposite ends of the hall, Scarf and her father sat in ornately carved chairs of a dark glossy wood. Before each of them stood one of the creatures, undergoing a transformation back into its human form. Other humans in spacer uniforms stood off to the side, there, Jackie expected, to escort the newly formed humans to their quarters.

Scarf saw her first and jumped up from his chair, leaving the Flyer he had been restoring only partially transformed with blurred features.

"It's you," he cried, "you made it back." His expression grew more serious. "You've been gone so long. What happened?"

Her father rose from his own transformation effort. For a moment he just stood there, as if he couldn't believe what he was seeing. Then he rushed over and gave her a massive hug. "Thank God you're safe! I had a premonition when you left that you might try to take your craft out of the Void. When you didn't return, I was sure that the Void had taken you. But as long as I could sense your presence I never gave up hope."

A feeling of warmth spread over Jackie and she hugged her father even closer. This was the first time he had ever admitted he could sense her presence, just as she could his. He eased back and held her at arm's length. "You did try to make it out, didn't you?"

She nodded, gulping back words that caught in her throat. Again, he pulled her to him. "I'm sorry," he said. "I've been such a fool. I just couldn't accept the fact that you weren't my little girl anymore—that you didn't need my protection. But after your mother died, I was so afraid for you." He let her go and ran a hand through his hair. "And I was frantic when you didn't return in your hopper as planned. We all were—even him." He nodded toward Scarf. "But you're okay?"

"I'm fine," she said, sniffling loudly as tears tingled against her cheeks. "Better than fine. And I have good news. But I'll save it for our meeting with the captain as soon as he's ready." She waved at Scarf who had stopped halfway to her, looking as if he didn't know what to do with his feet. "Go ahead with your transformations," she told them. "I'll help out until we're called."

Smiling and wiping at her eyes, she seated herself in another of the great, carved chairs and called one of the Climbers over to her. Her father and Scarf reluctantly returned to continuing their own transformations. But Scarf still looked troubled and kept glancing over in her direction.

Before long, the female spacer who had welcomed her back entered the reception hall and announced that the captain was ready to meet with Jackie and the planning committee.

"I'm coming too," Scarf said. He dismissed the remaining animal forms with a wave of his arm. "The rest of you will have to wait."

There were grunts and growls of disappointment. "Find them something to eat," Jackie's father told the spacer guides. "But keep them together until we're ready to finish them up."

He joined Jackie and Scarf as they followed the young female spacer down the crystal stairs. Jackie edged closer to her father. "You and Scarf seem to be working well together," she said, speaking softly so as not to be overheard by the others.

Her father darted a glance in Scarf's direction. "Someone has to keep an eye on him," he muttered, but the hint of a suppressed smile crossed his lips.

Captain Paliki, Dan, and Commander Zuta awaited them in the meeting room. Jackie quickly told them of her experiences. Her father's face paled when she described her failed attempt to bring the mentally created hopper out of the Void. But all except Scarf became positively jubilant when she reported how she had accidentally popped back into her material craft and taken it beyond the Void's boundary.

The captain's face turned thoughtful. "I wonder why none of the others trapped in the Void were able to effect such an escape."

"I wondered about that too," Jackie said. "When I first entered the Void and felt its effects, I tried to resist them but didn't know how. I panicked. This time, I knew how to hold myself together. I can only imagine that my experiences on this planet gave me the knowledge and confidence I needed."

"Our experience in the Void was unique," Commander Zuta added. "Scarf's creation of a stable world, Jackie's being drawn to it, her attempt to take a mentally constructed spacecraft into orbit, all contributed to her return to the physical world. Small wonder that no others ever duplicated her escape."

"That's true," Jackie said. "And my return to my physical hopper was purely accidental."

The captain nodded solemnly. "Still, you are to be congratulated on your perseverance. Without that, we might never have found our way out of here. Now it seems we only need to repeat your actions on a larger scale."

Commander Zuta looked doubtful. "Can we assume that? Jackie had only herself to worry about. We have the additional problem of transporting a great many individuals who lack her mental powers. We'll have to take them into orbit to free them from the planet's influence and return their minds to their physical bodies." She glanced pointedly at Scarf. "And this young man doesn't plan to return with us, but his physical body is still on our ship. If we take his body with us, what will be the effect on his mental construct?"

"Hold it right there!" Scarf said. "No one's taking my physical body anywhere."

—CHAPTER—
29

Everyone at the table looked to Scarf, their conversation brought to a halt by his declaration. It was the captain who finally broke the silence.

"We have no need to bring your body with us," he said. "We can jettison it into the Void before we leave."

"Sure," Scarf muttered, "toss me out like a piece of garbage. That's all I ever meant to anyone." Unconsciously, his hand went to his cheek.

"That's not true," Jackie objected. "We would be only too happy to bring you back with us if you'd only come."

"To be put in jail? Not this rat-brat."

"It doesn't have to be that way." Jackie turned to the captain. "You wouldn't file charges against him would you?"

The captain looked uncomfortable. "He is responsible for our being here."

"But it was mostly accidental. And the knowledge we've gained from all this might be used to help others who have been lost in the Void. That should help to make up for what he did."

The captain and her father exchanged glances. "If Scarf returns with us," the captain said, "I'll do what I can to see that he's pardoned."

Scarf's eyes blazed with distrust. "Spacer-crap," he snarled, "I can just imagine you standing up for me. I'll take my chances staying here. But if you're going to dump my body in the Void, the least you can do is give it some protection."

"Some of our freeze-sleep containers are portable," Commander Zuta said. "We can freeze your body in one of them and deposit the unit, body and all, in the Void. It should stay preserved just as well there as if it were on the ship."

"Will that answer your concerns?" the captain asked, obviously anxious to get past Scarf's objections.

"I guess it will have to," Scarf replied glumly.

"Then that's what we'll do."

Over the next few weeks, efforts to contact the remaining inhabitants of Scarf's planet and bring them to the castle were redoubled. Meanwhile, Jackie and her father proceeded to construct the ships they would need to carry them away from the influence of the planet so they could transfer to their physical crafts as Jackie had done before. Her father would transport the rest of the crew and passengers up to the *Golden Arrow*. Hopefully, he would be able to hold their mental essences together, just as Scarf had done when he created this planet. Both Jackie and her father would transition into the Draco-3 system, the *Golden Arrow*'s initial destination, and rendezvous in normal space, just beyond the Void.

Jackie worked on reconstructing her hopper while her father took on the larger task of building the giant shuttlecraft needed to carry the crew and passengers into orbit. Dan and Commander Zuta helped with both projects, bringing in the expertise of other crewmembers as needed. The construction of Jackie's hopper proceeded much faster this time because of her practice with their previous construction.

She finished the hopper well before the larger shuttlecraft was completed and spent the rest of her time assisting her father.

"Dad's a new man," she told Dan after a day of working on the giant shuttle. "I haven't heard him as much as slur a syllable since I returned from my test flight."

Dan nodded. "He's gotten himself back on track. But it was you finding a way out of here that gave him the motivation to do it."

Jackie felt herself flush with pleasure. Her faith in her father had not been misplaced. She might have had to nudge him along for a while, but he had come around at last on his own.

With Scarf, she had been less successful. No matter how she argued, he remained steadfast in his decision not to return with them.

"Haven't I proven myself to you?" Jackie asked, exasperated with his stubbornness.

A look of regret softened his features. His hand moved to his cheek. "I trust you," he said, "but you aren't the one who will decide whether or not to lock me away. And there's no way I can trust those others." He shook his head. "I know I can't ask you to stay here with me—but I wish I could. You have no idea how much I wish I could."

His words struck a sympathetic chord within her. She didn't want to leave him either. She felt drawn to him in a way she had never before experienced. And she knew she could help him with the space authorities if he'd only let her. But if he wouldn't let her, what could she do? She couldn't very well force him to come with her. And she couldn't stay here with him in this world of mental make-believe.

Finally, the day of their departure arrived. All four hundred and eighty-six passengers and crewmembers were accounted for. Five, including the Flyer Fanth had fought, had been reported to have died.

Jackie said temporary goodbyes to her father, Dan, the twins (so excited they could scarcely stand still long enough for her to hug them), Captain Paliki, Commander Zuta, and to the dozens of other well-wishers who came to thank her one last time for her role in giving them back their lives.

Standing outside her hopper, she could see the long string of passengers, lined up to enter the great shuttle her father had built. It sat three hundred feet away, near the base of the cliffs, its nose pointed up toward the sky. The big ship dwarfed her craft, more than ten times its length and five times its diameter. Even at that, it was less than a fourth of the size of the *Golden Arrow*. No private quarters or recreational areas were needed since all that was required of it was to carry its passengers and crew into orbit. Then, as soon as the Void took them, her father would transfer them mentally to the *Golden Arrow*. At least that was the plan—a repeat of what Jackie had done with her hopper. But as Commander Zuta had said, Jackie transporting herself back to her ship was one thing—her father, carrying along several hundred entities with him, was another.

Despite the difficulty of his task, Jackie strongly believed that her father was up to it. Her test flight out of the Void had had a profound impact on him. It was as if he finally had accepted the fact that her life was beyond his control and protection. And with his release of responsibility for what he couldn't control, he had resumed taking responsibility for the things that he could.

He'll bring them back, she told herself, if only to prove he can undo what Scarf had done.

It was then that Jackie noticed the lone figure approaching

her in the distance. It was Scarf. For a few moments her expectations rose at the thought that he might have changed his mind about staying. But the droop to his shoulders and the resigned expression on his face as he neared suggested otherwise. He had come to say a final goodbye. He looked so unhappy it brought tears to her eyes. She hugged him once and kissed him full on the mouth. His scar almost disappeared in the crimson flush that reddened his cheeks. He made an ineffectual attempt to pat her on the shoulder. Then, still without speaking, he turned and stumbled off, wiping his eyes with the back of his hand. Jackie's throat tightened. If only he could have put a little more trust in them.

But the entry hatch of her father's ship would soon be closing and she needed to enter her hopper now if she and her father were to blast off together and coordinate their efforts. They planned to link minds once they were well established in their separate ships, and make the jump together. Linking minds should provide an extra margin of safety if either of them experienced any difficulty. And it would ensure they ended up in the same general quadrant of physical space. Once there, they would join and moor the hopper to the *Golden Arrow* so Jackie could board it and ride it back to Draco-3. More was involved here than a desire to socialize. Jackie was still a fugitive in a stolen hopper. On her return she would need all the help and support she could get to keep from being arrested and imprisoned by the Space Security Force.

This time, she did without the clumsy spacesuit she had worn on her previous flight. Her hopper's design had proven trustworthy and she felt no need to wear the suit for backup. Her only anxiety was for her father. It was he who faced the uncertain transfer back to his ship, carrying all those people with him. For Jackie, it was practically a routine. What she had done before she could repeat. There should be no surprises—no problems.

As they had previously, all her ship's systems seemed to be working smoothly as her craft hurtled upward through the atmosphere. She could only hope that things were going as well for her father. She established herself in orbit and relaxed, allowing herself to be taken in by the Void's powerful pull.

But even as she started to close up on herself, she suddenly realized that she wasn't alone. Another presence held to her. Its mental grasp was preventing her from returning to her physical body.

Who are you? she projected, her very essence awash with fear and frustration. *What are you doing here?*

The presence clung to her like a drowning swimmer, grasping at anything within reach. Its fear-driven thoughts washed over her with waves of terror and desperation, shaking her self-control.

My world has collapsed. Without the others I can't hold it together. Help me! Please!

It was Scarf! Now a bodiless entity. In maintaining his world he must have relied on the others more than he realized. Without their presence—their mental support—he couldn't hold his creation together. He was terrified, afraid of being lost forever in the Void's emptiness.

And his panic was affecting Jackie, making it impossible for her to think clearly—to exert her willpower. If he hung on to her like this, his blind fear infecting her mind—possessing her—she would remain trapped here with him, unable to function. To regain control of herself, she had to make him turn her loose. But he was strong in his fear. She couldn't shake him off—couldn't break away. She had to reason with him—calm him—make him see that he had to let her go before he swamped her completely with his terror. Once that happened, they would be lost forever—a tiny knot of mindless dread, drawn into themselves.

Your body, she projected to him. *You must go to it. It's your only chance now.*

But they'll leave it behind in the Void, his projection came across as a wail. *In a portable freeze-sleep container. I'll be as good as dead. Worse.*

I'll have them take your body with them. But to contact them I need to get to my ship. You have to let me go.

No! Please! His plea shivered across her like a cold wind. *Don't leave me alone in this emptiness.*

Not for long, I promise. You said before that you trusted me. It's time for you to prove it.

His mental grip relaxed slightly. *I do trust you*, he projected. *But I can't let go. I can't face this aloneness.*

If you hold me here, we'll both be lost. If you care for me at all, you have to help me—release me so I can help you.

For what seemed an eternity there was no response. Jackie could feel her self-awareness ebbing away. She could no longer resist him—hold him back. His mind was taking her over—smothering her with his fear.

Then, abruptly, his grip on her lessened. The coils of terror loosened and unwound. Jackie sensed his withdrawal, like a shadow passing from within her.

Go to your body, she projected. *I won't abandon you. I promise. I'll get you out of here, one way or another.*

She reached out to her own body. Suddenly she was seated in her hopper staring at the view screens above the console board.

Welcome back yet again, CAP's voice spoke inside her head.

She undid her webbing. "Quick CAP," she said, "I need to contact the *Golden Arrow*. How can I do that?"

In Void space? I'm afraid you can't. You can radio them as soon as you leave the Void, assuming, of course, that you both exit into the same system.

"That's too late. I need to reach them now, before we leave. If I can't reach them by radio, can I go to them? Can you locate the *Golden Arrow* in the Void?"

Impossible. Remember that this isn't physical space we're dealing with.

She sank back in her seat. Her hands were trembling and she closed them into fists. CAP couldn't help her. But maybe if she mind-linked with her father, she could get a message through to him. Here in the Void, minds were more open to each other. It might be possible for her to convey something to him.

She reached out to her father. Feeling his presence, she tried to send a message to him: *Don't leave Scarf's body in the Void.* But there was no response—no sign her father had understood. And time was running out. They could leave the Void at any moment.

"I could let the Void take me again," she said, thinking aloud, "and draw myself to my father, like I did when he was on Scarf's planet. Except he's in his physical body now. I don't know if that would . . . Oh no!" she cried as a tremendous force tugged at her mind. "He's making the jump and taking me with him."

Stunned by the mental jolt, she tried to resist its pull. But the sudden shock of it was too much for her. Everything went blank. Then, just as suddenly, she was conscious again. She could sense CAP, projecting his concern.

Jackie! Are you all right Jackie?

"What happened?" she asked, shaking her head to clear it. For a minute she couldn't remember where she was or how she had gotten there.

Your father pulled you out of the Void with him, CAP told her. *You tried to resist him and blanked out. But we're back in physical space. You should be able to contact the* Golden Arrow *now on your ship's transceiver.*

Jackie felt no surge of relief. Scarf was back there somewhere inside that vast nothingness.

"Tell me how to set it up," she sighed.

She reached her father through a hierarchy of ship's communications personnel, each of them thrilled to be speaking to the individual responsible for their final escape from the Void and reluctant to turn her over to another. Even yelling at them and calling them addled-brained nincompoops failed to faze them. But eventually she heard her father's voice.

"Jackie? Thank God we made it. As soon as we get a fix on you we'll come about, match speeds, and lock on."

"Listen Dad," she said, her voice flat from emotional exhaustion, "I have to go back."

"Go back? To the Void? What in creation for?"

"Scarf couldn't hold his world together after we left. He's stuck in that deep-freeze unit you dumped. I promised him I wouldn't leave him behind."

There was a short pause. "Scarf's body is on board the *Golden Arrow*. We never dumped it. The captain was worried that it might be difficult to convince a review board that a young stowaway was responsible for his ship's disappearance without some sort of proof."

Jackie felt her breath catch. Hands held tightly to her chest, she shoved aside her anger at the captain's duplicity to voice the one question that mattered. "Did Scarf make it back into his body?"

Another pause. "Scarf might have returned to his body before we left the Void. We'll check on him as soon as we get you on board."

Jackie paused a minute to confer mentally with CAP. "I'll come on board," she finally said to her father, "but only with the understanding that I can take Scarf's body back into the Void if he didn't make it."

"You can't be serious. It would be foolhardy to go back there chasing after that delinquent. Besides, it was his choice not to return with us."

"I promised Scarf I wouldn't leave him there. Either the captain agrees to my conditions or I'll bring charges against him for abandonment. Captains are responsible for anyone who boards their ships, stowaways or not."

"No need for that," her father said quickly, "I'm sure the captain will comply with your request."

"I want a statement on the ship's permanent log that I can take Scarf's body. And I want you and Dan to witness it."

"Is all this really necessary?"

"He didn't keep his promise to Scarf, did he?"

Her father sighed in defeat. "Give me a few minutes." Soon he was back on the line. "Captain Paliki has agreed to your terms."

For a second, Jackie wondered if her father could be lying, simply to stop her from returning to the Void. But his voice held no hint of evasiveness. She sensed he was being truthful.

"I'll be waiting for you to pick me up then. But don't be embarrassed if I have a few choice words for your captain." Truth to tell, she wasn't sure if she wanted to jump all over Captain Paliki for going back on his word or hug him for taking Scarf's body with him. Much would depend on whether Scarf had been able to return to it in time.

"Shouldn't take us more than a couple of hours to reach you," her father said, sounding much relieved.

It took, in fact, only an hour and a half. Jackie watched the broad, gray mass of the *Golden Arrow* swell up in her view screen. Magnetic clamps clanged hollowly against the side of her hopper to draw it in. Twenty minutes later, she stood with her father, Dan, and a pair of Med Techs before the freeze-sleep unit that held Scarf's naked body, draped beneath the same sort of thin covering Jackie had been forced to make do with on board the hopper. The captain was reportedly involved with duties that required his attention elsewhere. Avoiding her, Jackie expected. She'd deal with him later.

Right now, she couldn't pull her eyes away from Scarf's rigid features, almost blue in their frozen state, and the tubes that ran down from unseen sources into his stiffened limbs and torso. Lights flashed on and off in rhythmic patterns and digital numbers changed in rapid succession, indications of his condition that were meaningless to her. His face, she thought, had gained some color. But that was merely a physical reaction to the revival treatment. Whether there was any mental activity going on behind those closed eyes, she hadn't a clue. Then his eyes opened. He looked up at her and smiled, and she knew that everything would be okay.

And it was. At least until they docked at the Draco-3 space station.

—CHAPTER—
30

Every possible excuse for celebrating and merrymaking was devised and carried out in the five days that it took for the *Golden Arrow* to proceed on to Draco-3. Jackie and Scarf were hailed as guests of honor. The twins also managed to get in on the festivities, enjoying their own celebrity status. Their return was, after all, a tremendous first. No lost ship had ever come back from the Void. And the information they brought with them about the nature of the Void would be invaluable.

Caught up in the excitement over their return, Jackie had begun to believe that their hero status might make them immune altogether to prosecution by the authorities. She found she was wrong. News of their exploits had preceded them to Draco-3. Within minutes of their docking it was announced that they had been boarded by members of the Space Security Force. Shortly after that, she and Scarf were summoned to the captain's quarters.

"Don't worry," Jackie told Scarf as they followed an escort of two junior officers up to the first level and down the main passageway that crossed the great liner. "I'm sure that Captain Paliki will keep us on board under house arrest until the authorities decide whether to prosecute us or give us medals."

"I doubt they allow prisoners to wear medals," Scarf said gloomily.

Jackie wrinkled up her nose at him. "Don't be so pessimistic."

Her own optimism dampened considerably when she entered the captain's stateroom and saw the grim expressions on the faces of Captain Paliki and her father. With them were two muscular young men, dressed in the natty black and silver uniforms of Space Security. The security pair stood apart from the others, faces devoid of expression. But the atmosphere of the room crackled with tension.

The captain dismissed the two junior officers then turned to face Jackie and Scarf, standing with his hands clasped behind his back. "It appears," he said, glancing at the security officers, "that these gentlemen have warrants for your arrest. I tried to persuade them to allow you to remain on the *Golden Arrow* until your trial. But the authorities seem to doubt our ability to hang on to fugitives clever enough to have escaped from the Void. Rest assured, however, we will do everything in our power to obtain your releases as soon as possible."

Jackie's father took her in his arms and kissed her. "Don't worry," he said, "there's no way they're going to put you away for this. We'll have you out in no time."

"Scarf, too," she whispered as she gave him a final hug.

"Scarf, too," he agreed.

"It's okay," she told Scarf who stood awkwardly, shoulders slumped, looking down at his shoes. "The captain is going to help us."

Scarf nodded, without raising his eyes.

The security agents attached bracelets to their wrists that would incapacitate them with a high-energy field if they tried to resist or escape. The agents then led them through the ship and down to level five where some of the passengers were already disembarking through a bridging hatch to the space station. With one agent walking before them and one behind, it was obvious to all that saw them that they were being taken into custody. Passengers and members of the crew stood to one side, frowning darkly at Jackie and Scarf's captors as their party passed through the ship's exit hatch into the outer rim of the space station.

They walked briskly along the corridor paying no attention to the lighted, color-coded lines that directed travelers to their destinations. With the agents leading them, they didn't need to worry about finding their way. A steady stream of people moved past them, many who glanced at them curiously, probably wondering where their agent escorts were taking them, Jackie thought. She wondered about that herself.

The agent in front stopped by an entrance to the circulator, the elevator-like conveyance that carried passengers around the outer rim of the station. Apparently their destination was not within the immediate area. A green light lit up over the entrance, indicating that a module was available. They entered it, hanging on to side grips as the module accelerated and decelerated rapidly between stops where other people got on and off. Their stop was the fourth.

The section of the outer corridor where they exited was lined with doors, all of them identical in appearance except for their identification logos. They stopped by one with an image of a five-pointed star with an eye at its center, symbol of Space Security.

Inside, their escorts turned Scarf over to a male guard and Jackie to a matron. The heavy-built woman made no attempt to communicate with her. She simply took her by the arm and led her firmly away, giving her barely enough time to call out a brief goodbye to Scarf. She continued out through a back door and along a narrow corridor, lined with sturdy metal doors—cells, Jackie guessed. The doors looked strong enough to withstand a rocket blast.

The matron stopped before one of them, unlocked it by keying a device on her belt, and motioned for Jackie to enter. The room was a small, windowless cell, furnished with cot, toilet, and sink. Jackie eyed it with disapproval. So much for hero treatment. She had enjoyed better accommodations in Scarf's dungeon.

The matron swung the door shut and Jackie heard the lock slip into place. "Well, CAP," she said, "it looks like you and I will be entertaining each other for a while."

The matron returned shortly with a change of clothes: smock, underwear, and slippers, all made from treated plastipaper. She waited in stone-faced silence while Jackie changed, then carried off her clothes.

Angered by the treatment she had received and for being so naive to imagine that space authorities would allow them to return to their previous lives without prosecuting them, she threw herself down on the cot. "What do you think they'll do to us?" she asked CAP.

It's difficult to say. You and Scarf both committed serious felonies, but there are mitigating factors. Between the two of you, you saved a passenger ship from the Void, an unprecedented feat. That's bound to create public sympathy. A lot will depend on how PanGalactic and the people you stole the hopper from evaluate their situation and interests. We can only wait and see what sort of deal they offer.

Jackie stretched and yawned. "I think we can do better than that. There are a number of possibilities we can discuss while we're waiting."

Jackie was left alone for the next two station sleep

periods except for meal times when her jailer brought her trays of flat tasting food. There wasn't as much as a radio unit in the cell—no chance to get local news. She wasn't greatly surprised that they kept her in isolation. According to CAP, they weren't required to provide her with legal representation because of her computer advisor. And space station commanders had the authority to limit a prisoner's right to visitors.

"They figure they can soften me up by keeping me isolated and scare me into going along with whatever scheme they dream up," she told Cap. "But after being strung out in the Void, I think I can stand a few days in a cell without panicking."

On the morning following her second sleep period, before she had quite finished the bowl of mush and the lukewarm, metallic-tasting coffee, the matron returned, carrying her clothes, cleaned and neatly pressed.

"Get changed," she told her. "Someone has come for you."

This time, the matron waited outside while Jackie changed. A much improved situation from her point of view. She then led Jackie to the room where she and Scarf had been separated. Her father stood there waiting for her. A male Space Security guard sat at a desk, engaged with a stack of documentation. The matron went over to the guard and said a few words before leaving.

Her father gave her a prolonged hug. "I've put up bail," he said. "You can stay with me until your trial."

"Where's Scarf?" she asked, looking around the room.

Her father's lips formed a hard line. "He's held without bail. The judge considers him a flight risk."

Jackie shook her head, angrily. "I'm just as risky as he is."

Her father glanced nervously at the guard. "Please," he

said in a low voice. "PanGalactic and the people you stole the hopper from both want to meet with you. At least talk with them and see what they have to offer."

Jackie drew back and eyed her father. His face was flushed but he didn't look or sound as if he'd been drinking. He's worried I might not like their offer, she decided. He's probably right. But then, they may not care for mine either.

"All right," she finally said. "I'll come along and listen."

Her father quickly led her out of the Space Security office, as if anxious to get her away before she changed her mind. They entered the circulator and got off three stops away at still another section of offices. They stopped at an entrance with PanGalactic's logo prominently displayed on the door, a pair of stars enclosed in a circle. From there, they passed into a lobby and were waved on by a prim-looking secretary into a large conference room with a table, carved from Castanian glow-stone, long enough to seat a dozen people. An impressive display of wealth and power.

Five people sat at the table. Captain Paliki, Commander Zuta, and Dan sat on one side. On the other side, Bradly Goodman of PanGalactic sat alongside a thin, dark, balding man who Jackie didn't recognize. Apparently PanGalactic had thought the situation important enough to fly Goodman up for the meeting. They probably also believed that her father and friends would help convince her to be reasonable. Well, she would be—on her own terms.

The thin, dark, balding individual, was introduced as Adi Kistna, a representative for Interplanetary, the people Jackie and Crow had stolen the hopper from. Jackie and her father settled into seats beside their friends, facing Goodman and Kistna. It struck her how calm she felt in contrast to her previous meeting with Goodman. The issues at stake were still critical, but she experienced no tightness of breath, felt no stabs of panic, had no need to retreat into a character role. Jackie Claver was quite capable of dealing with the situation as herself, thank-you-very-much. As a matter of fact, she hadn't felt the need to assume a persona for some time now. Probably a good sign.

Goodman led off the meeting. "I think you'll be relieved to know we've persuaded Interplanetary to drop all charges against you for taking their hopper," he said, his voice almost jovial in tone. "We feel the return of our Void-liner more than makes up for the inconvenience of the theft. We do have some documents for you to sign, restricting any publication of your involvement in this incident." He handed Jackie a holo-sheet, the thickness of a single page but capable of containing several hundred pages of readable text. Jackie doubted that this document held more than a few pages of legal claptrap. But it really didn't matter. Whatever was written on it would be unacceptable to her. She pushed the holo-sheet away without examining its contents.

"It certainly is accommodating of Interplanetary to forgive my transgressions," she said. "But tell me, what are PanGalactic's intentions for Scarf?"

Goodman blinked several times. "The hopper incident we can overlook. The Void-liner is a different matter. Its return has received far too much attention. The population at large may not know all the details, but they are aware that a hijacking took place and delayed the ship's passage. We cannot allow so major a crime to go unpunished. Mr. Scarf will be bound over for trial."

Jackie glanced down at the holo-sheet, then raised her eyes level with Goodman's. "I have no intention of signing off on this attempt at scape-goating. And furthermore, if you insist on prosecuting Scarf, I intend to call a media conference and reveal to the public how PanGalactic is covering up the fact that there are people abandoned in the Void who might still be rescued—that we have definite proof of this since a rescue has already been made."

Goodman's face paled. Jackie's father and the captain looked concerned. Dan looked amused. The representative from Interplanetary glared at her.

"Young lady," he said, "I don't think you understand the seriousness of your situation. If you refuse Mister Goodman's generous offer, Interplanetary will feel obliged to prosecute you for the hopper theft. You could be incarcerated for a very large part of your life."

"Yes," Jackie said, "I suppose I could. I imagine that Interplanetary doesn't want to be held responsible for customers lost in the Void any more than PanGalactic does. People can be so unreasonable when it comes to their loved ones. How do you suppose they will react when the truth about the return of the *Golden Arrow* becomes public knowledge?"

"The *Golden Arrow*'s escape was a lucky accident," Goodman snapped. "It doesn't justify endangering scarce personnel resources in a hopeless search for other Void survivors. Even if they exist it would be impossible to locate them."

"Maybe so. Maybe there's no way we can get to them. But given our experience, I'm betting I can convince the public that it's a worthwhile attempt."

Goodman's face darkened with anger. "I hardly think the word of a convicted felon will carry much weight."

"It might with the backing of crew members from the *Golden Arrow*," Dan said.

"Including its pilot," Jackie's father added.

Goodman rose from his chair and leaned on the table, glaring furiously at Dan and her father. "Two malcontents who PanGalactic fires for incompetence? How much credence will that buy?"

"You forget," Captain Paliki said quietly, "there are hundreds of passengers and crew members who view this young woman as little short of a saint. And should the press question me or my staff on the details of this incident, we would feel compelled to be factual in our statements."

And there, Jackie thought, went PanGalactic's last hope of keeping this under the table. With Captain Paliki backing her up there was no possibility of a cover-up. At that moment, she could have kissed him.

Goodman slowly sank back in his chair, a new wariness in his eyes. "But I can't turn Scarf loose," he said. "PanGalactic would never permit it—bad publicity or not."

"No one's asking you to." Jackie said. "I've talked this over with CAP. There are precedents for authorizing alternative forms of punishment."

"Such as what?"

"Such as community service."

Goodman snorted. "Surely not for hijacking."

"Scarf had no intention of hijacking the *Golden Arrow*. He wasn't even aware of his ability to do it. His only real crime was hiding out on the ship."

"A serious offense in itself."

"But one open to alternative forms of punishment. Instead of putting Scarf in jail, why not give him pilot training and let him serve his sentence trying to hunt down and rescue others who have been lost in the Void?"

Goodman and Kistna exchanged glances.

"Just think," Jackie continued, "of all the points PanGalactic would make for initiating such a search and rescue mission. You'd be heroes."

"You think he'd agree to such a deal?" Goodman asked.

Then he shook his head. "Even if he did, the kid's a delinquent—too much of a wild card. We couldn't trust him to head up such a mission."

"He won't," she said. "I will."

"Now just a minute," her father said, "if you think I'm going to let my daughter go back to risking her life running around—"

"I'm just as guilty as Scarf," Jackie insisted. "I won't let you shield me just because I'm your daughter. I'll share in whatever punishment Scarf is given, whether it be Void or jail."

Defeated, her father slumped back into his chair. Jackie turned to find Goodman looking at her with a puzzled expression, as if seeing her for the first time.

"You're really willing to go back into the Void?" he asked.

"I am."

He turned thoughtful. "With you involved, PanGalactic might just consider such a proposal. Why don't we contact Mr. Scarf and see what he has to say about it?"

Jackie flashed him a smile of appreciation. Things were working out just fine. "I'm sure he'll be as delighted as I am, once he sees the possibilities." She paused. "And one more favor," she added, "I'd like to be the one to tell him."

—ABOUT THE AUTHOR—

R. EDWARD MAIN views his Ph.D. in human behavior as a great asset in exploring the minds and motives of his fictional characters. One of his short science fiction stories won an award from the San Diego Writer's Center and was later published in the Canadian literary journal, *Writer's Block*. But his first love is the novel and he intends to keep them coming. He now resides with his wife, Jackie, in Salem, Oregon.